BLACKMOORE

A PROPER ROMANCE

JULIANNE DONALDSON

SHADOW
MOUNTAIN

Library of Congress Cataloging-in-Publication Data

Donaldson, Julianne, author.
  Blackmoore / Julianne Donaldson.
     pages cm
  Summary: Having decided she will never marry, Kate Worthington plans to escape her meddlesome family by travelling to India. Her mother agrees on the condition that she gets—and rejects—three marriage proposals. To fulfill her end of the bargain, Kate travels to the manor of Blackmoore in northern England, where her plans go awry.
  ISBN 978-1-60907-460-9 (paperbound)
1. Marriage proposals—Fiction. 2. Manors setting—England. 3. Eighteen twenties, setting. 4. England, Northern, setting. I. Title.
  PS3604.O5345B57 2013
  813'.6—dc23   2013022950

Printed in the United States of America
Edwards Brothers Malloy, Ann Arbor, MI

10 9 8 7 6 5 4 3 2 1

For dreamers everywhere

Kate Worthington

CHAPTER 1

A woodlark sings of heartache. A swallow calls in the two-tone rhythm of a race. And a blackbird's song is the whistle of homecoming.

Today it was the woodlark that called me to my window. I stopped pacing and rested my hands on the sill, leaning out to hear him better. For just a moment, my restlessness eased as I listened to this woodlark's tale of heartache, of sorrow; his falling notes never ended happily, no matter how many times I heard him sing.

I usually loved the woodlark's song better than any other. But today his sorrow made me nervous. I backed away from the window and turned compulsively to check the clock on the mantel again. It read only three. I cursed the slow crawl of time on this nothing-to-do-but-wait day. Several hours remained before night would fall and I could sleep and then wake and leave for Blackmoore. The waiting should have been comfortable for me—I had been waiting to visit Blackmoore all my life, after all. But on this last day, the waiting felt more than I could bear.

Opening my traveling trunk, I removed the Mozart piece I had packed away earlier that morning and left my bedchamber. The sound of crying reached me as soon as I opened my door. I hurried down the hall and took the stairs two at a time, stopping on the step above the one on which Maria lay sprawled.

"What is it? What's wrong?" I bent over her prostrate form, imagining all sorts of calamities that might have befallen my younger sister while I was pacing in my room.

She rolled over, her face toward the ceiling, her dark, wavy hair clinging to her damp cheeks, her chest heaving with the force of her sobs. I grasped her arm, shaking her lightly, and said, "Tell me, Maria! What has happened?"

"M-Mr. Wilkes has gone away and m-may n-never return!"

I leaned back and looked at her doubtfully. "Really? You are crying over Mr. Wilkes?"

She answered with a fresh sob.

Pulling my handkerchief from my pocket, I thrust it toward her. "Come, Maria. No man is worth this amount of grief."

"Mr. W-Wilkes is!"

I seriously doubted that. I tried to wipe her face with the handkerchief, but she pushed my hand away. I sighed. "You know, there are more comfortable places to cry than the stairway."

She clenched her hands into fists and yelled, "Mama! Kitty is being unkind again!"

"Kate," I reminded her. "And I am not being unkind. Only practical. And speaking of practical . . ." I reached toward her face with the handkerchief again. "How can you breathe with all that fluid on your face?"

She waved my handkerchief away with a sob. "Take your practicality elsewhere. I don't want it."

"Of course you don't," I said, my patience snapping. "You want to cry on the stairs for a man you have seen only five times."

She glared at me while screaming, "Mama! Kitty is being unbearable again!"

"Kate," I said, my own anger flaring. "My name is Kate. And Mama is not even here. She is out on calls. And if you refuse to see reason, then I refuse to comfort you. Now, please excuse me. I have a Mozart concerto to practice."

She locked her gaze with mine and refused to move so much as an inch, forcing me to hold onto the banister and jump over her to reach the bottom of the staircase. Shaking my head in disgust, I entered the drawing room and shut the door firmly behind me. A moment later another one of Maria's wails rose high and loud, and my cat, who sat perched on the pianoforte, arched her back and yowled in time. I shot her a look of disgust. "Oh, not you too."

There are many wrong ways to play Mozart and only one right way. Mozart was meant to be played as precisely as one would work a mathematical equation. The music was meant to be marched out in regular fashion, each note a little obedient soldier, taking up only its allotted space in time. There was no room in Mozart for the disturbing influence of passion. There was no room in Mozart for a cat named Cora that clawed at my shoulder while attempting to climb away from the noise. And there was certainly no room in Mozart for sisters who wailed outside the door of the drawing room at the precise moment that I was trying to practice.

After several minutes of trying to play over the noise of Maria's wailing, I was definitely playing Mozart the wrong way, pounding the keys with so much passion that I broke a fingernail. "Drat!" I muttered, and another sobbing wail came from the hall. I tipped my head back and yelled out over the noise, "Mozart is not meant to be played this way! It is an insult to his musical genius!"

I heard quick footsteps outside the door, and Maria's sobbing turned to nearly incomprehensible speech. "Kitty was so unbearable, Mama, and she has no compassion for my heartache and told me to cry elsewhere when anyone could see that I did not choose a place to cry, I simply *had* to cry and happened to be near the stairs when the impulse struck—"

"Oh, not now, Maria!"

At the sound of my mother's voice, Cora leapt from my shoulders to the floor. In a streak of grey fur, she dashed across the room and hid herself under a chair.

The next moment the door flew open, and Mama marched into the room. She had not stopped even to take off her bonnet, and her chest heaved in an almost violent fashion from her quickened breathing.

"Is it true?" She placed a hand on her heaving bosom. "Can it possibly be true, Kitty?"

"Kate," I reminded her, playing on. Mozart required concentration, and now that Maria's wails had quieted to whimpers, I intended to make good use of the comparative quiet.

In an instant, Mama stalked over to the pianoforte, her shoes making hard clicks on the wood floor, and snatched my music off the instrument.

"Mama!" I stood, reaching for my music, but she backed away and held it above her head. Only then did I manage a really good look at her face, and my heart quickened with dread.

"Is it true?" she asked again, her voice low and trembling. "Did you receive an offer of marriage from Mr. Cooper and reject him? Without even consulting me?"

I swallowed my nervousness and lifted one shoulder in a casual shrug. "What was there to consult about? I have told you how I feel about marriage." I reached for my music, but she held it higher, outstretching me with the two inches she had on me in height. "Besides, it was Mr. Cooper! He has one foot in the grave! He will probably not live to see another year, if that."

"All the better! Would that all of my daughters were so fortunate! How could you have thrown away this opportunity, Kitty?"

My upper lip curled in distaste. "I have told you over and over again, Mama. I have no intention of marrying anyone. Now please give me my music. Surely you want me to perform well at Blackmoore."

Her lips pinched together, her face turned red, and she threw my music onto the floor. It landed badly, with pages scattering, bent, like the wings of wounded birds. "Mama! Mozart!" I crouched down, hurrying to retrieve the pages.

"Oh, Mama!" Her voice was high and mocking. "Mozart!" She fluttered her hands around her face. "Mama, I do not want to do anything sensible like marry well. Mama, I want only to go to Blackmoore and play Mozart and waste every hard-earned opportunity."

I stood, my music gripped to my chest, my face hot. "I do not think my goals, although they may be different from yours, can qualify as a waste—"

"Your goals! Oh, my, that is rich." She paced in front of me, her shoes clicking hard with every step, as if she would stamp out my will and my voice too if she could. "What exactly are your goals?"

"You know my goals," I muttered.

She stopped in front of me, her hands on her hips. "What goals? To disappoint? To waste precious resources? To turn into an old spinster like your aunt Charlotte?" Her dark eyebrows flattened above her eyes. "Is this why I have invested in you? To gain *nothing* in return but a silly girl who cares only for Blackmoore and Mozart?"

I lifted my chin, willing it not to quiver. "That is not true. I care about more than that. I care about India, and I care about Oliver, and I—"

"Oh, do not mention India to me, girl. Not again!" She threw up her arms. I flinched involuntarily. "I cannot believe Charlotte would dare to invite you against my wishes. India! As if you already were not enough of a burden on me, with your stubbornness and your—" She whirled around and stalked back toward me. I told myself not to shrink. I hugged Mozart to my chest and commanded my chin to stay raised. I held her gaze.

"This is the end, Kitty," she said, raising a finger and shaking it in my face. "I have had enough of your willfulness. I will show you that I know what is best for you, and I will do it starting now. You will not go to India. I will write to your aunt Charlotte myself and tell her I have finally made a decision. And—" She grabbed my chin, forcing it up to close my mouth, which had opened in automatic protest. Leaning close, so close I could smell the stale tea on her breath, she whispered, "—and you will not go to Blackmoore. You will stay here and learn your proper place, and do not bother speaking to your father about it, or you will be in even worse trouble than you are right now."

She released me with a flourish, a triumphant light blazing in her dark eyes.

I shook my head, my heart pounding. "No, Mama. Please. Not Blackmoore. Please don't take Blackmoore from me—"

"No? No?" She held up one finger, silencing me with the hard stare of her eyes, and said in a low voice. "Go to your room and unpack, Kitty."

I stared at her eyes. They were the same color as an old, rusted trap I had found in the woods when I was seven. A rabbit had been gripped in its iron teeth. The little thing was no longer struggling when I found it, but it still breathed, and it saw me. Its eyes moved when I bent over it. I tried frantically to free the animal, but the rusted old metal would not yield to my prying fingers.

In desperation, I had finally run to Delafield Manor and dragged Henry back through the woods. He looked at the rabbit. He shook his head. He picked up a large rock and told me to turn away and cover my ears. I cried, but I did as he said.

A few moments later, his hand was on my shoulder, and I opened my eyes and lowered my hands. He said that the rabbit was no longer suffering. He said that was the best we could do for the poor thing. I supposed Henry got rid of the trap later. I never saw it again, even though I spent nearly every day in the woods. But I could not forget the look of it. I could not forget the large teeth and the rusted color and the tenacity of its grip.

In this moment, I saw the same cold tenacity in my mother's eyes. She would take Blackmoore from me and the hope of India, and there was nothing I could do to stop her. There was no prying at her, no freeing myself from her will. Despair beat at me with barnacled fists.

"My name," I said in a low voice, "is not Kitty. It is Kate!" I marched past her, reached under the chair for my cat, and left the room without crying. I tripped over Maria, forgetting that she was sprawled across the stairs, and fell hard on both elbows as I held on to Cora and Mozart.

I did not cry, even though pain shot up both arms and Cora scratched my cheek in an effort to wriggle away. I did not cry as I scrambled to my feet amid the yells of Maria to watch where I was stepping, and I did not cry as I ran up the remainder of the steps, down the hall, to the last bedroom on the right, and locked the door behind me.

I set Cora down and threw my music onto the bed. Pain throbbed in my elbows and shins, but the twisted, impotent pain of my helplessness screamed louder than any physical pain. I clutched my hair with both hands and paced the floor, fighting back the urge to cry. I should have anticipated something like this. It was so typical of Mama to swoop in and ruin everything, just when I thought I would finally have my heart's desire. But even more infuriating than Mama's interference was the fact that I was wholly powerless. At seventeen I was caged in this house of stone and glass and hardened feelings and expectations I would never meet.

A stifled scream rattled in my throat. An overwhelming urge to destroy something possessed me, shocking me and stilling my steps. The last time I had given in to such an urge, I had lived to regret it. My gaze dropped to the loose board under the window. I looked at the wooden chest at the end of my bed. It had been locked for so long. But I had nothing to lose by looking inside it now.

My hands shook as I pried at the loose board under the window until, with a protesting creak, it came free of its constraints. I plunged my hand into the hole, scraping my fingertips on the old, splintered wood, until my fingers closed around the smooth metal of the key. I knelt in front of the wooden chest and stared at the lock I had not turned in ages. Finally I took a deep breath, inserted the key, turned it, and raised the lid.

The scent of cedar wafted up. It smelled like my childhood, like secrets. I held my breath as I lifted the model from inside the chest. It was always heavier than I remembered it being. I set it down on the floor, then lowered the lid, and set the model gingerly on top of the chest.

Sitting back on my heels, I gazed with a mixture of admiration and regret at the wooden model. It was always thus. I loved it and regretted it at the same time. I loved it for what it was. I regretted what I had done to it. With one finger, I carefully traced the outline of the roof, stopping when I reached the spot where the roof was destroyed, the remains of the careful workmanship a splintered wreck. I lifted my finger, skirting the wreck, and set it down again where the model was whole. "This is Blackmoore," I whispered to myself. "It has thirty-five rooms, twelve chimneys, three stories, two wings . . ."

CHAPTER 2

FOUR YEARS BEFORE

"It is the hardest thing to bear that you visit Blackmoore every summer and I have not been once! I thought you were going to ask your mother if I might join you this year."

My best friend, Sylvia, watched me with a wrinkled brow from her seat by the window. "I know," she said, reaching out a comforting hand that I did not want. "I am sorry, Kitty! You know I have asked Mama dozens of times if you might go with us. She has refused. Again."

"But why? I know there are plenty of guest rooms at Blackmoore. I do not eat much. I would not be in the way. Why has she refused?" My pacing took me to one side of the room and back, but still Sylvia answered me nothing. "Does she have something against me? Is that why I have not been invited?"

Sylvia shrugged, shaking her head vaguely. "I cannot answer that."

I threw myself on the settee beside her, covered my face with my hands, and uttered a muffled scream. My hair settled around my shoulders in a dark cloud.

Footsteps sounded, then Henry's voice. "What is all the screaming about?"

"Kitty is longing to see Blackmoore. Again." Sylvia spoke with an air of forced patience, which made me sit up straight and drop my hands.

"You do not understand. Neither of you." I looked from her to Henry and back again. Both watched me as if I were slightly mad. "You have always been

able to go there, and I never have." They could not comprehend my feelings about being left behind every single summer for as long as I could remember. They could not imagine the strangling sense I felt when I imagined them exploring the coast and the moors and the great old house with its secret passageways while I stared at the same stone walls and the same old hedgerows I had known all my life.

"But it is just a house, Kitty," Sylvia said, looking at me as if I had lost my mind.

I shook my head. "It is not just a house." Because it wasn't. Not to me.

To Sylvia, Blackmoore was simply her grandfather's estate, a place for her family's annual summer holiday. But for me, it represented the opening of a lifelong cage. It stood in my imagination as an escape from everything that was the same and unendingly monotonous about my life at home.

"Then what is it?" Henry asked, his grey eyes more serious than I usually saw them. He watched me as if my answer meant something important.

"It is adventure," I stated, and the word tasted like freedom. "I have never even left the county I was born in. I've never seen the ocean or the moors. And every summer, you two leave me for this great house perched on a cliff overlooking the ocean with the moors at its back. And you tease me—" I gave Henry a pointed look, and he grinned back unapologetically. "You tease me with rumors of ghosts on the moors and secret passageways and smugglers and refuse to tell me if any of it is actually true." I sighed and muttered, "I would give anything to go to Blackmoore."

"Anything?" Henry asked with a doubtful look. "I think you are exaggerating."

"I am not exaggerating, Henry! I swear to you that I would give anything to go!"

"Such as . . . ?"

I tried to think of a suitable example, so they would understand the force of my feelings. I looked down. Not my fingers. One needed all one's fingers to excel at the pianoforte. A toe? Perhaps a little one?

"I would give a little toe to see Blackmoore," I declared.

Sylvia blanched. Henry's eyes lit up with interest.

"A little toe?" he asked. "Not a large one?"

I chewed on my lower lip. "No, I think large toes are crucial for balance. A little toe. Perhaps my smallest one."

Henry leaned forward, mischief lighting up his eyes. "And how would you go about severing a little toe?"

"Henry!" Sylvia interjected.

He held up a hand, quieting her, and challenged me with a look.

I swallowed. "I would . . . I would ask Cook to cut it off."

Sylvia looked horrified. "Blood? In the kitchen? No, Kitty. It would not do."

I tried to think bravely of the idea. "It would not be so bad. Surely there is an occasional bit of blood in the kitchen, now and then, from raw meat or . . ."

Sylvia cupped her hands over both ears, shaking her head. "Say no more, I beg of you."

Henry could hardly keep his grin in check, although he appeared to be try-ing. "And what would you do with that little toe, Kitty? Hmm? Is there some market for toes in exchange for trips to Blackmoore?"

My frustration quickly boiled over into anger. I picked up the pillow at my side and threw it at him. He batted it away with infuriating ease. "I do not know if there is such a market, Henry Delafield. Perhaps you could tell me, since you will one day own Blackmoore. Hmm?" I imitated his madden-ing half-smile. "Is there a market for little toes?" I bent over and started to unlace my boot. "Because I will cut it off right now, and pay you for my trip there, and I don't care if your cook does object to blood in the kitchen."

My trembling fingers could do nothing with the laces that had somehow become knots. I tugged at them without success, my face hot, my eyes clouded with the threat of tears. I blinked hard, squinting at the tangle of laces, when suddenly Henry was climbing over Sylvia, pushing her aside, and sitting be-side me. He grabbed my hands, pulling them away from my boots.

"Kitty," he said in a low voice. "Stop. Stop." I fought his grip but only

halfheartedly. "I am sorry," he whispered, leaning his head close to mine. "I should not have teased you about Blackmoore. I know how you feel about it."

His words had the same effect on me as water thrown on a fire. I pulled my hands away from his grip and covered my face with them, breathing in deeply. I had overreacted again. It was a great weakness of mine. It was a great weakness of all Worthington women. And now, pulled from the heat of my anger, I was embarrassed. But no less sad. No less bereft. No less frustrated. For a moment, I felt Henry rest a hand on the back of my bent head, lightly.

"Come, Kitty. Let us have no blood today," he said, his tone light and cajoling. "Instead, let us plan what you are going to do while we're away. You should plan some great adventure so that you will have something exciting to share with us upon our return."

I dropped my hands and glared at him. "You know as well as I do that there is no adventure to be had here. If there was, we would have already found it! At any rate, it is no fun to have an adventure by oneself." I crossed my arms over my chest, sullen and resentful. "But my question is, Why? Why has your mother never allowed me to go?"

Henry and Sylvia stayed silent, even though I looked at them pointedly, waiting for an answer. An ugly suspicion crept into my mind with the heavy, weighted steps of jealousy. It whispered to my mind—a question so abhorrent that my mouth turned down, as if I had bitten into something sour.

"Is Miss St. Claire going to be at Blackmoore again?"

The reluctance in Henry's expression answered my question. Sylvia shot me a look full of pity.

My suspicion—my jealousy—laughed with glee and wriggled itself into a more comfortable position, as if it planned to stay for a very long visit. My lip curled as I imagined Henry and Sylvia spending a month at Blackmoore with Miss St. Claire, of all people.

"So your mother has no objection to inviting guests. She simply objects to me."

"It is nothing personal, Kitty. You know she intends Miss St. Claire for Henry—"

"Sylvia!" Henry shot his sister a look of warning.

Sylvia's mouth fell open. "What? That is no secret! We have all known that for ages."

Nothing more was said for a long, awkward moment. I looked at the yellow fabric of the settee, thinking only of how much I resented this Miss St. Claire, whom I had never even met.

Henry turned to me, so suddenly that I started and looked at him with surprise. His grey eyes looked like steel, and in a flash I saw something in him I had never noticed before—an indomitable will. "One day I will take you to Blackmoore, Kitty. I promise." He grasped my hand again, squeezing it hard. "I give you my word."

I clamped my lips shut, keeping back my doubting words. Mrs. Delafield always had her way. Always. If she did not want me there, I would never go. But finally, because he would not stop squeezing my hand and because it was starting to hurt, I squeezed his hand in return. "Very well," I whispered, giving up the fight and smiling a little for his sake.

The next month passed so slowly I thought I would go mad. During that long summer month, lazy with idleness, with sameness, with incessant nothingness, whenever I thought of the Delafields at Blackmoore with Miss St. Claire, I gritted my teeth and cursed under my breath.

Finally, at long last, on a day just like any other, I heard from a servant that the Delafields had returned. I ran down the stairs, grabbing the banister to round the corner at the first floor, and jumped the final three steps before I noticed that the front door stood open.

Jameson, our butler, was bending over and blocking my view of the door. When I stopped still in surprise, a voice called out, "If that is you, Kitty, cover your eyes!"

My heart raced at the sound of Henry's voice. I bent down, trying to see around Jameson's back.

"I mean it! Cover your eyes, or I will turn around and go home right now, and you shall never see your surprise!"

I sighed and clapped a hand over my eyes. "Very well. They are covered."

I had to wait much too long while a shuffling sound passed me into the drawing room. Only my belief in Henry's threat made me keep my eyes covered, for I was not a patient person. "Can I look now?" I begged.

In reply, a hand grabbed mine. "No, keep them closed," Henry said, his voice close to my ear. My heart pumped with excitement. "Come this way." He pulled me along by my hand. I bumped into a wall, then a doorjamb, and then collided knee-first with a piece of furniture.

"Ow. Can you not lead me more carefully?"

"Hush. No complaining allowed."

Henry released my hand and stood behind me, squaring my shoulders and then saying, "Now. You may look now."

I opened my eyes as quickly as I could and stared uncomprehendingly at the table before me. Henry had led me into the dining room, and on the table was what looked like a model of a house.

I turned my head to give Henry a questioning glance and saw him for the first time. Only a month had passed, but he had changed. His hair was longer and darker instead of lighter. He always came home from Blackmoore with light hair that had been brightened by the sun. But this year it was darker—a dark, golden color that almost begged to be called brown. His freckles had faded across the tops of his cheeks. His grey eyes were the same, though, with their ring of charcoal along the outer edge. And at this moment, his grin was so broad I felt stunned by the sight of it.

He stepped around me, gestured grandly at the model, and said, "I present to you, Miss Katherine Worthington, Blackmoore."

My heart beat so hard it hurt. I looked from him to the model and back, and when he nodded, grinning, I dropped to my knees, bringing the house to my eye level. The windows, the wood painted to look like stone, the front doors, the chimneys. It was all here. "Where did you come by this?" I asked in awe.

"I built it."

I looked up at him uncomprehendingly. "You built this?"

He said in an offhand voice, "My grandfather helped with the design.

And Sylvia helped at the end with the painting. But most of the handiwork was mine."

I continued to stare at him. "This must have taken you every daylight hour of your holiday."

He lifted one shoulder, but I could tell by the half-suppressed smile he wore that I was right. And that explained his appearance. I knew the cost of this project. I knew that Henry lived for being outdoors at Blackmoore. I knew that he spent all day on the moors and on the beach, and I knew that he loved to go birding with the gardener, and I knew that only the greatest of incentives would have kept him inside all month long.

I was overwhelmed and found it suddenly difficult to speak. I cleared my throat. "You must not have had much time to spend with Miss St. Claire."

He knelt beside me and pressed down a smile, a line creasing his cheek. "No. Not much."

I nodded, chewing on my lip. The question that rested there, on the tip of my tongue, I did not dare to ask. But I wanted to know—needed to know—if he had built this for me. If it meant something. If I meant something.

"Now I suppose I shall be indebted to you and I shall have to find some way to pay you back." I drew in a breath, my face hot with awkwardness. "Since you gave up your holiday and Miss St. Claire . . ."

Henry cut a glance at me, then smirked and said, "I didn't build this for you, Kitty."

"You didn't?" Relief mixed with disappointment rushed through me.

He shook his head. "No, you ungrateful brat, I did not."

He leaned closer, tilting his head, examining the model. Then he grasped the tiny door handle on the front door.

"I did it," he murmured, swinging open the miniature front door, "for your toes."

I stifled a gasp of delight. Bending my head down, I peered through the open front door and saw a black-and-white checkerboard floor, a fireplace on one side, and an arch at the furthest end of the room, leading to a staircase.

I bit my lip to keep myself from grinning, and then I blinked hard to keep *myself from crying. It was simply too much. "My toes thank you," I finally whispered.*

I could feel the width of Henry's smile, even though I did not look at him. It was like a ray of sunshine on my face, and my cheeks grew warm. Then he pointed at the model and said, "It has thirty-five rooms, twelve chimneys, two wings, a conservatory, stables, and a top-notch view. There is, reportedly, a secret passageway that was once used by priests during the Reformation, although I will neither confirm nor deny it, as you will, no doubt, find it more intriguing and mysterious if you have something to wonder about."

I pulled my gaze from the model to his face. He was talking quickly, saying something about the library containing over three thousand books. But all I could see was Henry, with the light in his grey eyes and the smattering of faded freckles across the top of his tanned cheeks and his dark golden hair falling over his brow and the quirk of his lips when he smiled as he talked.

"It faces the ocean and is backed by the moors," he said. "And now you know." A note of accomplishment entered his voice. "Now you know exactly what Blackmoore looks like. Someday you will see it for yourself, as I have promised." He met my gaze with a warm smile. "Until then, you may keep this."

CHAPTER 3

PRESENT DAY

A knock sounded at the door—two raps, a pause, and then two more raps. It was Oliver's code. I looked up sharply, startled out of my reverie. Another four knocks. Still Oliver. I opened the door carefully, just a crack, so that he could not see into my room—so that he could not see the ruined model of Blackmoore.

Oliver stood close to the door, his brown hair hanging over his hazel eyes. He needed a haircut. I would have to mention it to Cook.

"What is it?" I asked, hoping he did not notice my distress. I lifted the corners of my lips for his sake, trying to smile, when I would have done it for no one else.

He beckoned me closer, crooking one dirty little finger. I bent my head, and he loudly whispered in my ear, "Mr. Cooper is coming to dinner."

I pulled back. "No."

He nodded. "I heard Mama say so to Cook."

That disgusting Mr. Cooper whom I had refused was coming back? Mama must have given him reason to come back. She must have led him to suppose that I had changed my mind. That was it, then. I would have to run away.

"Thank you, Ollie," I sighed.

He stuck out a hand. "Do you have a penny? For a treat? Please?" He gave me such a winning smile that I could not resist. I took two pennies from my reticule and put them in his hand. Before he could pull his hand back, I grabbed it and turned it over, then clucked my tongue with disapproval. "Go and clean your fingernails, little man. They are atrocious."

He laughed, his eyes lit up with a mischievous gleam. "I like them atrocious." He ran down the hall, clutching the two pennies, and I could not help but smile as I heard his loud footsteps clatter down the wooden steps. He was the one person I would miss when I left tomorrow for—

I stopped my thoughts. No. I was not leaving for Blackmoore tomorrow. The despair struck me again. No Blackmoore, *and* I would have to endure Mr. Cooper's company at dinner? It was too much.

Just then the sound of a whistle lifted through the air and filled the room. It was a blackbird's song. I hurried to the window, set my hands on the sill and leaned out, looking down. Henry stood below my window, his hands cupped around his mouth as he whistled.

"I have set up the target," he called out. "Come shoot with me."

I shushed him with a finger to my lips and turned back to the room. I hurried to put the model back inside the chest, locking it tight and returning the key to its hiding place before turning back to the window. I threw one leg over the windowsill.

"What are you doing?" Henry called from the ground below.

"Can you please lower your voice?" I whispered fiercely as I threw my other leg over the sill. "What does it look like I'm doing? Leaving the house."

"No, Kate. Not the window. Just use the door, like a normal person."

"I cannot. Mama will see me." I turned over, gripping the inner edge of the sill, so that my stomach rested against the wood. "It is only a little more difficult since the lattice broke last summer." I searched for a crack in the stones with the toe of my boot. At that moment, Cora decided to explore my predicament and jumped onto my head.

"Oh, no. Not now," I said. "Get down!"

But after peering over my head, she proceeded to walk slowly and elegantly down my back. Henry laughed.

"This is your fault," I muttered. "She is going to see you."

Just then, Cora seemed to decide that the slope was too steep for her comfort and dug her claws into my legs and back. I jerked with the sharp pain, and she lost her balance. She meowed pathetically, scrambling to catch hold of something but with no luck. I looked over my shoulder to watch her twist in the air as she fell. Henry caught her before she hit the ground.

"Well done," I said. He set her down, then reached up for me.

"Just drop and I will catch you," he said, as I continued to fumble for my customary foothold.

"No. I don't need that much help. Let me find that crack and then you may give me a hand . . ."

"Does it really matter exactly how much assistance I render here? I am going to help you anyway. Let me catch you."

"A hand will suffice."

He muttered something. I found the crack, shoved the toe of my boot into it, and slid my hands to the outer edge of the windowsill. "What are you muttering about?" I asked.

"Stubborn. Something about this stubborn young lady I know."

The sound of footsteps came through the window above me. Mama was coming to speak to me, and she was still angry, by the sound of her sharp steps. A loud knock sounded at my bedroom door. In that instant, I realized I had forgotten to lock the door again after opening it for Oliver. I pushed away from the wall and let go. I had no doubt that Henry would catch me. From the corner of my eye I saw him lunge forward. He grabbed me around the waist in time to slow my fall. I stumbled as I landed, but he pulled me to my feet and ran with me around the corner of the house. I pressed myself against the stone wall and tried to quiet my breathing.

"Kitty? Kitty!" Mama's voice reached us from the open window.

Henry looked down at me, and his amused expression turned suddenly sharp with concern.

"You are upset," he said.

I pressed my lips together, refusing to either confirm or deny his statement. His eyes narrowed. "Who has upset you?"

"Kitty!" Mama's yell came again, louder this time. "Katherine Worthington! Answer me this instant! If you have been climbing out of your window again—"

The next instant Henry left my side and walked around the corner of the house. Panicked, I reached out to grab him, to stop him, but he was already out of my reach. All I could do was stand still and wait, tense with nervousness. Cora twined herself around my ankles, meowing, and I picked her up to quiet her.

"Oh. Henry." Mama's voice held a note of pleasure. I could imagine her smoothing her hair and leaning further out the window. I could imagine her smiling at Henry as he lifted his face up to her. "I was just looking for Kitty. You have not seen her, have you?"

"Not today. Perhaps she has walked into town?"

"Hmm. You're probably right. I will send one of the servants directly. Thank you, Henry. You are a dear boy." A pause, and then her voice lowered and she laughed, a low, throaty sound. "Oh, dear, but you are not a boy anymore, are you? And you are certainly growing more handsome every day." I closed my eyes, sick with shame. "You must come to dinner tonight. I don't know how many times I have told Kitty to invite you since your mother and Sylvia left for London, but she has failed me time and time again. I do want you here, dear Henry." Her voice was sultry. "I want you very much."

Cora meowed, wriggling in my arms, and I realized that I was squeezing her—strangling her, almost. I loosened my hold but did not let her go, burying my face in her fur. I wished I could bury all of me, somewhere far, far away from my shameful mother.

"Thank you for the invitation, Mrs. Worthington, but I must decline.

George has invited the Farnsworths to dine tonight, and they are expecting me."

"Oh." Her voice took on a complaining tone. "I am sure your brother and his wife can get along fine without you for one evening."

"I am sorry. Perhaps another evening. If you will excuse me . . ."

"Very well. But I will hold you to it. One of these evenings, Henry, you will be at my side."

A moment later, Henry rounded the corner and stood before me. Full of dread, I threw a glance up at him. His cheeks had reddened and his lips were pressed together, as if he was trying very hard not to say something. But his eyes, when he looked at me, were only kind. The line of his mouth softened, and he gave me a quick, small smile.

"The target, as I was saying, is set up, and I believe I have thrown your mother off your scent. Will you come?"

I trembled with anger and shame and wished I could apologize for my mother. But to apologize for her would be to acknowledge her behavior, and I couldn't do that. I set Cora on the ground. "That is exactly what I need right now."

I made sure nobody was watching from the nearest windows as Henry and I darted for the woods, Cora at our heels. The clearing was almost perfectly halfway between our two houses. When we reached it, Henry took off his coat and hung it over a tree branch. The target was set up beside the large maple tree. Two bows and two quivers of arrows rested on a large tree stump. Everything looked just as it should—just as it always had every other day we had spent in this clearing practicing our archery. But I was so angry at Mama that I doubted I could hit anything.

I picked up a bow and a quiver of arrows. Henry stood beside me, watching me in silence. My hands shook with anger. I took a deep breath while I lifted the bow and looked at the target. I released the arrow. It flew wide. No surprise, but still I glared at the offending target.

Henry nocked an arrow, pulled it back, and narrowed his eyes as he looked at the target. The sun glinted off his hair. He released the arrow. It hit the target with a satisfying thunk. He never missed.

"Are you ready to talk yet?" he asked.

I picked up another arrow and nocked it while I considered his question. Staring at the target, I imagined my mother's cold eyes. "My mother," I said, releasing the arrow. It hit the outer edge of the target. Pathetic.

"Of course," Henry said. "But what has dear Mama done this time?"

His second arrow hit home just as soundly as his first had done.

"She is the most unfeeling mother in creation," I said, picking up another arrow. "She does not comprehend my dreams, nor does she value my desires. She only wants me to marry. And you know how I feel about *that*." I released the string. This time the arrow buried itself in the grass.

"Indeed."

"Indeed!" I grabbed another arrow, upset with the arrows for not flying true and at Henry for being so calm when I was so angry and at Mama for not understanding me at all. "In fact, how many times have you heard me vow that I will never marry?"

He smiled, a little half-smile. "How many times? I have not kept count, Kate."

"Estimate, then."

He sighed. "Very well. I would estimate two dozen times, at least, since last Christmas. Perhaps another fifty times last year. Maybe a hundred in total."

I felt accomplished. "And do you believe that I am serious in my intention?"

"Yes, I do." Henry's jaw was set as he stared down the arrow at the target.

"See? You understand me on this matter, and you are only my friend. But my own flesh and blood—!"

He flinched, his head jerking to the side to look at me, and his arrow fell off his bow. He lowered the bow and gave me a piercing look, his grey eyes glinting like steel. Then he raised it again and leveled his gaze at the target. "*Only* your friend?" He narrowed his eyes at the target, his pressed lips causing a line to crease in his cheek. "I think I deserve a better title than that."

"Like what?" I asked, looking at him askance.

"Oh, I don't know." He released his arrow. Another solid hit, right on target. "Perhaps The Giver of My Heart's Desire?"

An outraged laugh burst from me. "The Giver of My Heart's Desire?" A smile crept across his lips. "I will never call you that," I said, picking up another arrow.

"Why not? I earned it. I think you should call me by that title every time you see me."

"How do you believe you earned it?" I demanded.

"I gave you your cat, and that is the thing you love most in this world." He gestured at Cora lying in the grass nearby. "Therefore, I have given you your heart's desire."

I scoffed, then drew back the string and released the arrow. It hit the target. Finally. I smiled with satisfaction. "I am not going to call you The Giver of My Heart's Desire. That is ridiculous."

Henry looked at me with a satisfied smile. "There. Your eyebrows are back to normal now."

"You are not supposed to tease me about my eyebrows, remember? We made that pact five years ago."

"That was a one-time arrangement, after you tried to shave them off with your father's razor." He pulled back the string on his bow, leveling his gaze at the target. Henry's form was something I had always admired but never more so than now. At age twenty his back was broader, his shoulders stronger than ever before. The muscles in his arms stood out, cords of light and shadow. There was that line in his cheek again—that line that was more crease than dimple, and I had to look away. I heard Henry's arrow hit the target while I bent down and drew the last arrow for myself.

My last arrow flew true, and I breathed a sigh of relief. This was better. I had found my aim again. I set down my bow and walked over to the target with Henry. After prying my arrows loose and gathering the errant ones, I wandered over to the large maple tree that stood on one side of the clearing. It was so tall that its lowest branches began far above my head. I leaned against its familiar, mottled bark and sighed deeply. My temper was in check, but resentment and grief still burned within me.

Henry joined me, leaning against the tree as well. I held my arrows in my hand, studying their feathers and wishing, not for the first time, that I could fly away from this place. I felt Henry's gaze on my face.

"What is really bothering you, Kate?" he asked in a quiet voice. "This problem with your mother is nothing new. What has happened today to upset you?"

I ran the feathers of the arrows between my fingers, fighting back another round of angry tears. I drew in a deep breath, struggling for some control over my emotions.

"She has said I may not go to Blackmoore," I finally said.

"What?" Disbelief mingled with anger. "Why not?"

I tipped my head back and covered my eyes with my hand, hiding the fight against my tears. "She is angry with me for refusing Mr. Cooper's proposal."

"Mr. Cooper?" Henry's voice was appalled. "The man is diseased!"

I laughed a little, a tear leaking out of one eye. "I know!" My stomach turned as I recalled his most recent visit. "The last time I saw him, his ear was bandaged. Why is it always a different part of his body that is bandaged?"

"I cannot answer that," Henry said in a serious voice. I looked at him, and there was such a look of revulsion on his face that I burst out laughing.

"The bandage was stained, too," I said, wheezing with laughter. "A greenish color."

Henry shook his head. "Stop. Say no more."

I was laughing so hard that tears ran down my cheeks. But they reminded me of what I really had to cry about, and the thought sobered me.

"It is entirely unfair," I said, "that when we have finally convinced your mother to let me visit, my mother has put a stop to it."

Something flashed in his eyes—something that made him look away for a moment. "How right you are." He sighed. "So . . . I take it this means that your mother has not yet accepted how fundamentally stubborn you are. She thinks she can still convince you to marry? Turn you into a proper, obedient daughter, hmm? Will she be rearranging the order of the universe while she's at it?"

I smiled sadly. "Something like that."

"You know, you never have explained to me your decision never to marry."

I shook my head. No matter how many times he had asked me about that in the past year and a half, I refused to give an answer. "Not today, Henry. We have more important battles to fight." I looked over at him, meeting his gaze with my own. "I must go to Blackmoore. I *must*," I whispered. "I think I will resent her for the rest of my life if she keeps me here."

He nodded, his grey eyes serious, as if he understood perfectly the gravity of the situation. If anyone did understand, it was he. He had made me that model, after all. I wiped away another tear, and that time I was sure Henry saw.

Henry nudged me with his elbow. "Come, now. There is no need to despair. We are two very intelligent people capable of outsmarting one mother, I think." He stepped away from the tree and began pacing. "What does your mother want, more than anything?"

"For me to marry," I answered immediately.

"Yet you are determined not to."

"Precisely."

"Hmm." More pacing. Then he paused and turned to me. "Can you not pretend to *want* to marry? Tell her there will be many eligible gentle-men at Blackmoore, and you may make a match there."

I shot him a look of disbelief. "No. There is no point in winning the battle if it means jeopardizing the war." I tapped my arrows against the tree, willing myself to think of a solution. "But what else does my mother want in life?" I thought hard for a long moment, then shrugged. "Nothing. This is all my mother lives for—marrying off her daughters." *And flirting with as many men as she can,* I added silently.

Henry looked at me sharply. "Her daughters," he said slowly. "Plural."

"Yes. There are four of us. Three if you don't count Eleanor."

He smiled. "Maria."

I looked a question at him.

"Tell her that Maria may come as well and that she will have a chance to make a match at Blackmoore."

I considered his suggestion dubiously. "What will be her incentive, though?"

"To be rid of Maria. To give Maria a chance to make a match." He paused, and a wicked gleam lit up his eyes. "To enrage my mother."

I smiled crookedly. My mother and Mrs. Delafield had been polite enemies for the past four years, even though we continued to associate as families. I wondered if Henry knew the reason behind their dislike of each other. I had never broached the subject with him since I had found out what had caused their rift. And I certainly was not going to be the one to tell him.

"It could work," he insisted.

"I don't know if I can convince her," I said. "She seems so intent on punishing me . . ."

"And having Maria along is not a punishment?"

I laughed. "You are right. It is." I chewed on my lip while thinking of Henry's plan and had to admit to myself that I had no better plan to try. "Will your mother object, do you think? Or Sylvia?" Sylvia and Mrs.

Delafield had been in London the past four months enjoying Sylvia's first Season and were going to meet us at Blackmoore.

Henry shook his head. "Not a bit. There is plenty of room for one more."

I shrugged, finally saying, "It is worth a try, at any rate. She cannot take away anything more important than my dearest dream." I handed him the arrows. "I shall try at once, so that if this plan fails, we may still have time to try another."

I took a dozen steps toward the house before I stopped and turned around. "Henry." He had walked back to our shooting place but turned to look at me. "You are a good friend."

He shook his head, nocking an arrow and lifting the bow. "Try again, Kate. Say, 'You are The Giver . . . '" He pulled back on the string, then shot a look at me, as if waiting for me to continue.

I laughed. "Never. I shall never call you that."

His grin flashed, and he turned back to send his arrow flying straight and true, finding easily the center of the target. He never did miss.

I found Mama in her bedchamber, sitting at her dressing table. She was already dressed for dinner, and her makeup containers were spread over the top of the table. She darted a glance my way as I walked through the door and began to speak before I had a chance to begin.

"Where have you been?" she asked, leaning forward to peer at her reflection. "I sent John to town to look for you. If you have been climbing out of your window again, I will have no choice but to have it nailed shut. And why have you not invited Henry Delafield to dinner during his mother's absence? He should have been dining here at least twice a week, and now he is leaving tomorrow for Blackmoore, so we will have no further opportunity for his company. He has grown far too handsome not to have here, Kitty, and you must invite him for my sake, if you will not do it for your sisters'—"

"Mama, it is about my sisters that I have come to speak with you. In fact, I have come to offer you something you will want." I took a breath, waiting to see if I had successfully stopped her in her rant. She raised one eyebrow but said nothing, which I took as a good sign. I went on, choosing my words with care. "You will agree, I believe, that Maria has been unbearable since Mr. Wilkes left the area. Surely you cannot enjoy yourself with her constant crying, and as long as she is here crying, she is not out meeting other eligible gentlemen."

I paused. Mama leaned forward to look closely in the mirror while she rubbed rouge on her cheeks. I winced. She always wore too much rouge when company was coming for dinner. "Go on," she muttered.

"Well." I took a deep breath, then plunged in. "I am offering to take Maria off your hands and give her opportunities to meet new gentlemen . . . at Blackmoore."

Mama paused in her application, and I saw one eyebrow lift with interest. "Who gives you the authority to invite your sister to Blackmoore?"

"Henry. It was his idea."

"Hmm." I heard the note of interest in her voice. "So you have been with Henry."

"Yes," I admitted in a quiet voice, wishing I had not noticed the look on her face—wishing I had not seen the arch in her eyebrow, the twist of her mouth.

Quiet sat uncomfortably between us, and I shifted my weight from one foot to the other while she focused all of her attention on the application of a single beauty mark high on her cheek.

After leaning back to look at herself from a new angle, she said, "Now that you mention it, I am sure Mrs. Delafield will invite many of her acquaintances to see the new wing she has had remodeled. It would be a nice opportunity to meet new gentlemen."

More rouge, dabbed on her cheeks, and then, in an offhand voice, "I suppose I might allow you to go if you take Maria with you."

I held perfectly still. I could not believe I had won so easily. "Do you mean it?"

She laughed. "Of course I mean it, you silly girl! Why should I deprive you of this opportunity?"

And then, because she seemed to be in such a calm, reasonable mood, I decided to press my luck. "And may I also write Aunt Charlotte and accept her invitation to accompany her to India?"

She slapped her open hand on the dressing table. "No! You are supposed to marry. Not every woman has a chance to look like us, Kitty. It is a sin against nature to throw such beauty away."

My face flushed with anger. I hated it when she compared my appearance to hers. We did not look exactly alike. True, we did have the same coloring—the dark, wavy hair and the dark eyes. She had aged well. Her hair had not gone grey yet. Her eyebrows were still those dark, dramatic slashes that they had been when she was young. My eyebrows. The ones I had tried to shave off. It was what linked us together the most strongly. But in many ways I was not like her. In the most important ways, I was not like her at all.

"I am not going to marry, Mama. When are you going to believe me?"

She turned around on her stool to face me, her smile at odds with her steely gaze. "I will never believe such nonsense, Kitty. Because if I were to believe that, then I would have to admit that everything I have done for you has been a waste. A waste of my time and my attention and my resources. You would be a waste of a human being. Is that what you want to be?"

My face burned, my anger poised, like a wild animal coiled to spring. I gripped my hands together, fighting to keep my temper under control. After a deep breath, I spoke in a low voice. "Yes, Mama. I want to be a waste of a human being. I want you to give up hope of my ever marrying."

She laughed. "How droll you are, Kitty."

"Kate. I wish to be called Kate." I wanted to scream in frustration. My voice rose, despite my great effort to control it. "How many times have I told you that? And how many times have I told you that I have no desire to be like you? Or Eleanor? To make a brilliant match—or any match at all! Hmm, Mama? How many times? Because Henry swears it has been at least a hundred, and I have held fast in my decision for nearly two years now. I will refuse every man who is fool enough to propose to me. So how many proposals must I refuse before you accept the fact that I will never marry?"

She narrowed her eyes, tilted her head to one side, and considered me in silence for a long moment, while my hands shook with anger and my face flushed hot. Finally she said in an offhand voice, "Three." Then she turned back to her mirror.

My head jerked back with surprise. "What?"

"If you refuse three proposals while you are at Blackmoore, then I will accept the fact that you are a lost cause." She picked up a hairbrush and ran it through her dark hair.

I caught my breath. "Are you saying that you will let me go to India if I refuse three proposals?"

Her smile flashed. "Oh, yes. That is exactly what I am saying."

I stepped back, reeling, uncertain why, or how, I had suddenly won this allowance. "Thank you—" I started to say, but she held up one finger.

"And in return—"

My heart fell.

She laughed lightly at my expression. "Yes, darling, in *return*. For every bargain has two sides to it. Every interaction with another person is a potential transaction, an opportunity for gain. For everything you gain, you must pay. The wisest transaction is one in which you have the potential to gain far more than you pay."

I hated it when she talked of business transactions. I hated how cold and unfeeling she was in her interactions with me. I hated feeling like I was nothing but a potential gain for her.

"Now let us discuss this transaction. If you succeed, you will go away to that godforsaken country where you might die or be lost at sea or some other calamity, and I will have lost a daughter who otherwise might marry well and make our family proud and provide for me in my old age."

My mouth pulled tight with distaste.

"This is a great sacrifice I am willing to make for you, Kitty. And so you must be willing to make a sacrifice for me. If you fail to secure three proposals at Blackmoore, then you must agree to do whatever I ask of you." She raised one dark eyebrow. "*Whatever* I ask of you, Kitty, without question, without running away, without fighting."

My thoughts raced, balancing the allure of India against the very real consequence of being in my mother's power should I fail. "Doing whatever you ask of me—that sounds like a highly open-ended agreement."

"And?"

I hedged, trying to think of a valid reason to refuse her request. "And . . . what if you were to ask me to do something criminal? I could not agree."

She turned back to her mirror with a look of disgust. "You should know me better than that. I would not ask you to do something criminal. But if that concern would stop you, then perhaps you do not want to go to India as badly as you maintain."

"I do!" My hand shot forward, as if attempting to grasp the hope she was dangling before me. "I do wish to go to India. I will agree to your terms, Mama. I will agree—without argument."

A small smile tugged at the corners of her mouth, and a deep sense of foreboding filled me, causing my heart to fall. What had she to smile about? What trap had I just fallen into? I backed away from her, wishing away the unease I felt. I would prevail. I would win my proposals. I would go to India, far from my mother's reach. There was nothing to fear. I lifted my chin and said in a confident voice, "I will win three proposals at Blackmoore, and as soon I have them, I will leave. I will go directly to

31

Aunt Charlotte's. I shall not come home first." I was nearly to the door. I reached for the handle.

She lifted one shoulder in a careless shrug. "It makes no difference to me when you leave, child. I will have washed my hands of you by then." I opened the door. "Oh, Kitty?"

I paused, halfway through the doorway. She continued to brush her hair, gazing at her reflection with that small smile hovering around her lips. "No changing your mind, now. We have an agreement."

I lifted an eyebrow in scorn. "You should know me better than that, Mama. I never change my mind."

Watching her brush her hair, the hot anger I had been reining in gave a furious leap, breaking free of its restraints, and galloped through me. She had won, in some way. Even though I had gained what I had come here to ask of her, I still felt sure that she had somehow won. Some trap had closed over me, and the chill that sat deep in my heart testified of it. Now she did not even watch me as I left the room. I lingered by the door, while my anger grew hotter and hotter, until finally I said, "By the way, Mama, I will not be dining with the family tonight. You will have to give my excuses to Mr. Cooper." I paused, then delivered my final line with a lifted chin. "And Mama? You wear entirely too much rouge."

I closed the door quickly, just in time for it to block the hairbrush that flew across the room, aimed at my head. I heard it hit the wooden door with a loud thunk. I turned and sauntered away, a smile tugging at my lips. I was running before I reached the woods.

Henry was watching for my return. He turned to me as soon as I stepped into the clearing. "Well?"

"Well . . ." I had hidden my grin, hoping to tease him. "I am afraid to say . . ."

But I could not restrain myself. My grin slipped out from my control, and Henry's face broke into a broad smile.

"Success?" he asked.

"Success." I picked up my bow with a sigh of happiness, noting Cora still curled up on the grass next to Henry's feet. That cat had always been attached to Henry.

"I was right, then," he said, his smile broad and triumphant. "I am a genius, in other words."

I laughed. "Your humility is astonishing, Henry."

"I am a mother-manipulating genius who has, once again, granted you your heart's desire, thus earning the title of . . ." He grinned, his eyes all mischief.

I laughed again, shooting him a look meant to convey the fact that he was mad to think I would ever call him The Giver of My Heart's Desire. This time when I took aim, my arrow flew straight and true, hitting the target right next to Henry's arrow.

He glanced down at the cat sprawled in the grass. "What will you do with Cora while you're away?"

"I shall ask Oliver to take care of her."

He nodded. "It wouldn't do to take her to Blackmoore."

"I know. But I do hate to leave her behind."

He pulled back the string of his bow, squinting at the target in the late afternoon sun. "Just don't forget to take your heart with you to Blackmoore. I would hate for you to leave that behind."

CHAPTER 4

I stayed outside until dinnertime, then crept into the house via the French windows that separated the garden from the morning room. I paused outside the dining room door, which had been left open a crack, and peeked inside, observing the scene I had chosen not to be a part of.

Mama was leaning toward Mr. Cooper and smiling at him in a grotesque and desperate manner. Maria sat next to him. Judging by the forlorn expression on her face and the fact that she was not eating, I surmised that Mama had not yet told her of the invitation to Blackmoore. Then there was Lily, still innocent at twelve. Oliver would be eating in the kitchen with Cook, which made me happy.

My gaze stopped, finally, at the head of the table. Papa sat slouched in his chair, one hand gripping his wineglass, his gaze fixed on the spectacle Mama was making of herself. Even from this distance, the scorn in his expression struck me. It was weighty and sharp, violent in its strength, and I felt somehow battered after seeing it. I looked away quickly, remembering why I had stopped watching him years ago, and crept quietly down the hall and up the stairs to my bedchamber.

What Henry had said earlier about taking my heart with me reminded me of something even more important than my heart. I opened the locked chest at the foot of my bed once again, and this time I drew out the small box inlaid with ivory. Room could be made for this in my traveling trunk with a few adjustments. All I needed was my clothing, my Mozart, and this ivory-inlaid box. Even more than a heart, hope was a necessary traveling companion.

I hardly slept that night, and eagerness pulled me from my bed as soon as sunlight crept over my windowsill. After dressing, I checked my trunk once more, then made my way downstairs for breakfast. Mama rushed toward me with hurried feet and a worried expression.

"Oh, Kitty, you will never guess!"

I dropped my spoon, so frightened by her panicked demeanor that I jumped.

"Maria has come down with a fever in the night! She is too sick to travel."

I stared at the pinched skin between her eyes as dread pooled in my stomach. "You do not mean—you do not mean to keep me at home as well, do you?"

She waved her hands. "No, no. You must go. The Delafields will be expecting you."

I stared at her as surprise rendered me speechless. But before I could wonder any more at her agreeable mood, she hurried off to "see to Maria's comfort." Watching her go, I tried to remember if I had ever heard her utter such a phrase before.

Unease stirred within me, but I shook it off and focused on this one thought: Maria would not be coming to Blackmoore after all! My smile stretched wide before I had to time to recall it. Of course, I should have worried about Maria's health. But this fever was probably only a result of her refusing to eat and crying in odd places yesterday. Surely this was nothing serious.

Counting myself fortunate, I went forth to complete my last duties of the morning before I would be free to leave. I found Oliver in the kitchen, sitting on a stool next to Cook, who was rolling out pastry dough.

"Ollie, I have something to ask of you."

Cook turned to reach for the flour, and Oliver sneaked out a hand, quick as a flash, and grabbed a piece of the pastry dough.

"What is it?" Oliver asked, popping the dough quickly into his mouth. At seven, he was missing several teeth, and his cheeks and nose were dusted generously with freckles. I sometimes watched him, when he wasn't aware, and thanked my good fortune to have finally been granted a brother after so many sisters.

"I need you to take care of Cora while I am away."

"What will I have to do?"

"Not much. Just keep an eye out for her. Don't let the dogs terrorize her, and make sure Cook does not hurt her when she sneaks into the kitchen. Don't let Mama get rid of her, either."

Cook gave a loud *humph* when I mentioned her, but she went on rolling the dough, her beefy forearms covered in flour. Oliver stole a longing glance at the pastry dough again.

I cleared my throat to bring his attention back to me. "If you agree, I am prepared to offer you something very special as payment."

That brought his eyes to me. They were large and hazel, like mine. "What would you give me?"

"Something from Blackmoore. Something special that nobody else has."

His eyes widened. "What? What is it?"

I leaned forward, resting my hands on the table, and smiled at him. "A seashell."

He frowned. "That is not so special."

My smile fell.

Cook clucked her tongue. "Nay, Oliver, your sister is right. A seashell is a very special thing."

"Really?" Oliver lifted his gaze to Cook, who nodded and turned the dough, causing a puff of flour to lift into the air.

"Aye. Especially one that is found under the light of the moon. Some say it can bring the owner great luck."

Oliver's eyes grew wider, his mouth crooking up into a gap-toothed smile. "Great luck?"

Cook nodded, winking slyly at me when Oliver was not looking.

I grinned in return. "Would you like such a thing, Oliver? A lucky seashell?"

"Oh, yes, I would. Very much." He was watching the pastry dough again, which Cook was cutting into strips. He stretched out a small hand while Cook was deliberately looking away.

"So you will watch over Cora? And not let any harm come to her?"

Oliver nodded, pinched off a piece of dough, and shoved it quickly into his mouth. But even though Cook pretended not to notice, I saw the smile on her flour-dusted face. I reached across the table to grab his face with both hands. I planted a kiss on each of his freckled cheeks. He squirmed and protested halfheartedly.

"Good-bye, Ollie," I said, looking into his eyes. "I will miss you."

"Good-bye, Kate." He smiled at me before turning his gaze back to the dough.

I caught Cook's eye, grateful once again that she was kind and motherly and so very fond of my little brother. "He needs a haircut, and please do see to his fingernails. They're atrocious."

Ollie snickered and said, "I prefer them atrocious."

I threw an affectionate glance at his bent head, then whispered, "You will . . . take care of him . . . watch out for him . . ."

Cook shushed me with a frown that was a gentle rebuke. "Of course, Miss Katherine. Do not worry yourself about Master Oliver here. He and I shall have adventures together while you're away. Won't we?"

Oliver had eyes only for that pastry dough, but he nodded his head.

I left, if not with a light heart, at least without a heart troubled on his account.

There was only one more thing to do. I stopped before the door to the library and tapped on it softly, almost hoping he would not hear my quiet knock. But he did hear, and he called for me to enter. I opened the heavy door and leaned only my head and shoulders into the room. "Papa, I have come to say good-bye."

He sat in his chair by the fireplace, one leg crossed over the other. The sun lit the dust motes in the air, and the sweet smell of pipe tobacco mingled with the old leather of books. The smell was intoxicating to me, and one whiff of it brought a strong pang of nostalgia for things I was missing.

He lifted his head. "Hmm? Where are you off to?"

"To Blackmoore with the Delafields. And hopefully to Aunt Charlotte's afterward. She will take me to India with her."

"Is that so?" His gaze settled on me for a brief moment before he took his pipe from his mouth. The smoke drifted between us, disguising us from each other, making us strangers. "Well . . ." He looked back down at his book, turning his attention from me too soon. "Godspeed," he said, then clamped the pipe between his teeth.

I nodded, expecting nothing different, and quietly closed the door between us.

Then I turned to the front door and the carriage waiting to take me away, for the first time in my life, to someplace new.

Chapter 5

The Delafields' old nurse, Mrs. Pettigrew, sat across from me in the carriage, humming under her breath and knitting at a breathtaking speed, the needles clacking together in time with the clomping of the horses' hooves. I looked longingly out the window at Henry's back. He was riding, of course. I knew he would—I knew he always rode to Blackmoore. And a small, grudging part of me had to admit that I was grateful that his old nurse had agreed to come along to act as chaperone. But after two full days of this swaying carriage and that humming and those clicking needles, my head felt ready to split open.

We had taken advantage of the long summer daylight hours to travel a good distance yesterday. After twelve hours in the carriage with Mrs. Pettigrew's noise but no conversation to help pass the time, I had been looking forward to talking to Henry. But when we had stopped at the inn last night, Henry had not dismounted. He had only said that I would stay there, with the coachman and Mrs. Pettigrew, and he would go on to another inn down the road.

I had frowned at his retreating back and trudged inside the inn, where I did not enjoy my meal nor the room I shared with Mrs. Pettigrew. This morning, Henry was astride his horse and waiting for us outside the inn after breakfast. We were off with hardly a word spoken between us.

I had never truly appreciated either the restfulness of silence nor the entertainment of intelligent conversation as much as I did today. I sighed as I leaned my forehead against the window, wishing the rumble of the carriage wheels could drown out the clack and hum of Mrs. Pettigrew, wishing I had someone to talk to, wishing the long drive was already over. I shifted, trying to stretch my legs, without success. Mrs. Pettigrew glanced up from her knitting to smile briefly at me.

"It tries one's patience, doesn't it? The waiting. But it is well worth it."

With her smile, I was reminded that Mrs. Pettigrew had accompanied the Delafield family on their trips to Blackmoore every summer. She had been such a part of the family that when the children grew up and George had inherited Delafield Manor, he kept Mrs. Pettigrew on to be nurse to his own children. Henry must have been very persuasive to convince George to let her come with us. She leaned forward to peer out the window.

"Ah. It seems Master Henry has chosen the scenic route. This will be a treat for you."

"What is the scenic route?" I asked, eager to talk about anything after two days of humming.

"You'll see soon enough." She sat back and click-clack went her knitting needles, and the low drone of her humming filled my ears once again.

She could not know that "soon enough" had grown old years ago, that "at length" was sick and frail, that "finally" was a dying breath. Patience was not one of my virtues. Neither was endurance.

The humming took on a high, keening quality that reverberated inside the carriage and within the bones of my skull. I thought I would go mad with the sound. The horses slowed, and I looked out the window and saw that they were pulling us up an incline.

"You know, the horses are having a hard time with this hill," I said, moving toward the door, "so I shall just get out and stretch my legs a little."

Mrs. Pettigrew looked up, startled, as I opened the carriage door. "Oh, no! You will break a leg! Ask the driver to stop."

The carriage was traveling no faster than I would on foot. "I will not break a leg, I assure you." I jumped down lightly and swung the door shut behind me, breathing a sigh of relief to finally be free of that tuneless droning.

Henry had been riding ahead of us, but he looked back and turned his horse to me.

"Is something wrong?" he asked, drawing near.

I shot him a look of accusation. "Mrs. Pettigrew hums."

He laughed as he dismounted, his smile bright in the sunshine. "The humming! I had forgotten about the humming!"

"How could you forget about the humming? It is embedded in the very matter of my brain!" I imitated the high, droning, tuneless sound I had been enduring the past day and a half.

He just grinned, with a devious look in his eyes that made me wonder if he really had forgotten the humming after all. Realizing I was making my headache worse, I stopped humming and rubbed my forehead for a moment. Henry drew near me, leading his horse by the reins.

"So . . . you stayed at a different inn last night," I said.

He nodded.

I squinted up at him. "Was that really necessary?"

He shrugged and looked uncomfortable. "I didn't want to risk . . . your reputation."

"Ah." I looked away, my face hot. The memory of my sister Eleanor hung in the silence between us. I would not mention her name, though, and I breathed a sigh of relief when, after a moment, I realized that Henry was not going to mention her either.

Gesturing at the land before us, Henry said, "There is something you will want to see at the top of that hill."

"What is it?"

"The moors." He said it as if the word itself was a gift, just as he had always talked about the moors—as if they were as important to his inheritance as the house or the living.

Gripped with new excitement, I flashed him a grin and hurried to the top of the hill, Henry leading his horse and trailing behind me. A hearty wind blew my skirts, tangling them around my legs as I reached the top of the hill. I stopped at the crest and looked at a bleak valley of wasteland.

Dark heather covered the ground like a bruise. The laurel-green and gold of the grass and the occasional yellow flower did little to brighten the scene. Not a tree lived here—only some twisted, stunted cousin of a tree that grew no taller than the horses. In all, it was a muted, somber scene, and I could see no beauty in it.

"This is the moors," I said, my voice flat with disbelief.

Henry stood beside me, watching my face as I looked at the landscape before me. Not a blade of green grass soothed the eye here. There was nothing remotely close to civilization in this wilderness.

"Yes. This is the moors," Henry said.

"But . . . it is ugly," I said, my voice distraught even to my own ears. "It is so very ugly, Henry."

He laughed.

"No, truly, it is. You told me it was beautiful."

"It is beautiful. To me." I looked at him without comprehension. He gestured to the scene before us. "Can you not find even one spark of beauty here?"

I looked from him to the land, wondering for a moment if he had spent the last ten years lying to me or teasing me. But there was no deception in his eyes. There was only fondness and an excitement I could not understand. But I would try, for his sake. I walked a few steps away and bent down to feel the plants I was crunching beneath my boots. I wanted to know this land as beautiful, the way Henry did. The heather was an ugly, dark, brownish-purple color, like a ripe bruise. But these yellow flowers were bright as sunshine. Not bright like daffodils but deep yellow orange, like a drop of sun. I reached down to pluck a blossom and instead stabbed myself on a long, sharp thorn growing right beside its petals.

"Ow!" I sucked the drop of blood from my finger.

"I should have warned you. There is nothing soft here in the moors. Do not let the flowers deceive you. They are designed to withstand anything—even a flower-picking young lady."

My finger throbbed. "I suppose that's admirable—to be so hardy," I muttered, grasping for anything to admire in this land. A gust of wind suddenly tore across the moors, pulling my bonnet from my head and spinning it into the sky.

Henry plucked it from the air as if it had been thrown to him, and moving in front of me, he put the bonnet back on my head. Holding it by the ribbons, he leaned down, and there was a spark of something in his granite eyes that was new. Some life, some light, was new there. The moors had awakened in him something I had never seen before. He tied the ribbon under my chin, his fingers brushing my neck, my collarbones. Heat rushed to my cheeks, and I held myself perfectly still.

His gaze lifted from the ribbon to my face, and he said in a quiet voice, "I think the most profound beauty is found in what our hearts love. And I love this, Kate, more than I love anything else. It is beyond beautiful to me. It is home. It is . . ." He paused, and squinted a little, as if looking into the sun, but his gaze stayed steady on me. "It is the sight I want to see every day, for the rest of my life."

I was taken aback. I had known that Henry loved Blackmoore. I had known all along that he would inherit this land, this estate, this life. But seeing him here, seeing him own it, seeing him proclaim it his own home, struck me deeply.

In a flash of memory, I was hiding in a dim room in Delafield Manor with the smell of peonies so sharp and sweet I could taste it. And I felt once again, just as I had that night a year and a half ago, both deeply sorrowful and deeply lost.

I spun around, pulling the ribbon of my bonnet out of Henry's grasp, and pretended to study the view before me. But with my back to him, I reached up and rubbed my nose hard and breathed in sharply, telling myself to get control of my emotions. I felt Henry stand behind me, silent and waiting—waiting for me to love this place as he did.

"I think it may grow on me," I said, fighting hard to keep my voice steady. I breathed in again, willing my heart to slow. Clouds the color of granite streaked across the sky, pushed toward us by the unrelenting wind. I retied the bow of my bonnet ribbon taut, pulling it hard, making myself proper again. I would not give way to the pull of this wilderness. Looking toward the road, I saw the carriage stopped and waiting for us.

"Come," I said. "Let us go see your Blackmoore." I was happy to climb back inside the small, stuffy carriage. I was even happy to hear the mindless drone of Mrs. Pettigrew. This was proper. This was a place of rightness. Not that wild scene outside—not that wild land nor that dark-haired boy with the grey eyes who loved it more than he loved anything else.

CHAPTER 6

I sat back and watched the moors swallow us whole until there was no groomed green grass to break up the barrenness of this wasteland. And then, before I was prepared for it, the carriage turned south and the ocean suddenly became a part of the world.

Mrs. Pettigrew, with a glance out the window, remarked, "We're on the Whitby road. It won't be long now." I scooted over to the window on the left side of the carriage and watched the undulating coastline. The water looked grey-blue in the afternoon light and wide enough to swallow everything I knew about life. The sharp angles of birds in flight dropped and lifted and dropped again above the water. I knew nothing about birds that lived near the ocean. I would have something new to ask Henry about.

I looked back and forth between the two windows, with the sea on one side and the moors on the other, both prospects overwhelming me with their vastness and their strangeness. The sun was beginning its slide over the horizon, the light fading when we came upon a town—the famed Robin Hood's Bay, which I had heard about for as long as I had heard about Blackmoore.

I looked with greater interest at the steep, cobbled streets and the red-roofed houses that flowed down the hill toward the ocean. "Did Robin Hood really live here, once?"

"Legend says he did," came Mrs. Pettigrew's response. But legend and truth were two different things.

"Don't you know? For certain?"

She glanced up briefly from her knitting. "Nobody knows for certain, my dear."

I remembered what Henry had hinted at—something about smuggling. "But are there still clandestine activities taking place here? Like smuggling?"

She clucked her tongue in disapproval. "Of course not! What a fanciful imagination you have!"

I sighed with disappointment. Leaning forward, I lowered the window and caught my breath as the salty cool air rushed over me. If I were an outlaw, this would be a place I would choose for a stronghold. The streets were narrow, the houses crowded together like a band of ragtag rebels, shoulders crammed together, elbows locked. The angled red roofs met and blended and tumbled down the hill to the water's edge.

A moment later, the carriage stopped, the door opened, and Henry climbed inside. His shoulders seemed to fill the small space, and he smelled like the salty wind and the moors. He grinned at my look of surprise and sat beside me. "I don't want to miss this," he said, then rapped on the carriage roof. It rolled on.

The anticipation in his eyes made my heart quicken. Blackmoore must be near. I wished for speed, for flight, for "finally" to come.

Henry leaned forward, looking out the window, and pointed, saying, "There. On the top of the cliff."

I leaned forward eagerly, and he moved back to allow me the full window's view to see Blackmoore for the first time. I stared, then stared again. The light of day was fading, the sky painted navy. The building that stood between ocean and sky looked dead black. The house was misshapen, just as Henry had made it in the model, with one wing stretching much longer than the other. It hunched on the edge of the cliff like a deformed creature, and the candles that lit the windows from within made it look as if it had a dozen eyes, all turned toward the sea. As the daylight faded, I blinked while the image before me shifted and blurred. Whether it was my imagination or a trick of the light, I knew not, but for a moment the house looked to me like a hulking bird of prey, with wings unfolded, ready to drop from the precipice into the empty sky.

I blinked again, shaking my head to fix the strange twist in my eyesight, and my heart pumped. But it was closer to excitement than fear—this energy that coursed through me. I had wanted this my whole life. Now I had it. I had my visit to Blackmoore, and come what may, it felt as if everything in my life had led me to this place at this time.

I sat back, feeling breathless, and found Henry's gaze on my face. "Well?"

Shaking my head, I found myself speechless and could only smile. It seemed good enough for him, for he settled back with a contented smile on his face and watched me watch out the window as we approached his future home.

Daylight had vanished completely when the carriage wheels struck the gravel of the courtyard. Blazing torches illuminated the area as a footman stepped forward and opened the carriage door, holding out a gloved hand for me to take. I took it and stepped down onto the gravel. Walking away from the carriage, I tipped my head back to take in the extent of the house. It was a great hulking thing, perched here on the edge of the world between ocean and moors, an anchor of dark stone and towering walls.

Before this day, I had imagined the building—the dark stones, the peaked roof, the staggering line of chimneys—but I had imagined it in vacancy. Now I saw the bulk of it loom between a dark sky and a barren cliff that bore the brunt of endless crashes of ocean waves. The chill that ran down my spine reached beyond the cold wind and the fine salt spray. This building was born of an austere atmosphere made real. It was a haunting in stone.

The ocean wet the air, flavoring each breath with salt and freedom and foreignness. The towering building loomed overhead, darker than the darkening sky. The moors stood like a stretch of barrier—an impenetrable wilderness hemming and shielding and pushing this building toward the ocean. It was wild and dark and grand and tall and fierce and haunting all at once. And it thrilled me to the core. It thrilled me and it frightened me, for it whipped at my carefully closeted heart, much as the wind had whipped at my hair and skirts and sent my bonnet tumbling.

Such unfettering was possible within this sphere that I felt to shrink back with the power of what I felt here. I smelled the ocean and the peat. I tasted the salt in the air, and I heard the haunting cries of birds. The wind whipped at me still, with a cold blast from the ocean. This was a place where things came undone. This cliff would come undone by the crashing of waves. These stones would come undone by the wind. What power would it have in me? What in me might come undone here? So many things could be unfettered, could be loosed, could be thrown to the wind and the waves in this primal place of wilderness and natural power.

Henry flashed me a look of excitement as he walked quickly toward the open doors. I followed him just as quickly, eager to breathe my "finally" when I crossed the threshold of Blackmoore for the first time.

Henry waited for me at the door and watched as I walked into the great hall that I had first seen in miniature through a tiny wooden door. Here the details were the same as in the model—the white-and-black checkered floor, the ornately carved fireplace to the left, the arched opening at the opposite end—but the scale made everything feel new and foreign. I felt rather than saw the loftiness of its ceiling, which was swallowed up in darkness, despite the roaring fire in the fireplace and the candles lit all around. The cold ocean wind followed us through the door, chasing at our backs, causing the flames of the candles to flicker and cast strange shadows about the stone walls and floor. Despite the fire and candlelight, the room was losing the fight against darkness.

An older servant with the regal bearing of a butler approached Henry, bowing and saying, "Welcome home, Mr. Delafield. I trust your travel was uneventful?"

It was the word *home* that caught my attention. I looked at Henry's face and recognized it in an instant. That excitement to be here—those hurried steps—the look of happiness and contentment and deep peace filling his features: this was home to Henry.

"Thank you, Dawson. Yes, the journey was fine. And it is always good to be back." Dawson helped Henry out of his cloak, taking his gloves and hat, while I handed my bonnet and coat to a waiting footman.

Footsteps sounded, sharp on the tile, and then a familiar voice came from behind us. "Is that you, Henry? Have you finally arrived?" I turned around, forming my mouth into a polite smile for Mrs. Delafield, who looked more elegant than she had ever looked before. She must have benefited from the dressmakers in London, I assumed. But before I could greet her—before I could thank her for finally inviting me to Blackmoore, she froze mid-step and stared at me. Even in the flickering, dim light, I could see the surprise and dislike in her eyes.

"Katherine." Mrs. Delafield's voice was as chilly as the ocean wind. "What are you doing here?"

I looked in confusion from her to Henry, who stood close by my side.

"Yes, Mother, we have come sooner than expected. I thought Kate would enjoy a day here with Sylvia before the rest of our guests arrived."

Her expression was set in a look of distaste, and before she could answer, more footsteps sounded, and Sylvia and a young lady I had never met appeared at her side, almost seeming to materialize out of the darkness. At the same instant, a gust of wind shook the doors and the candles flickered and threw their erratic shadows again. My heart jumped.

"Kitty?" Sylvia asked, peering at me as if she did not recognize me. I smoothed down my hair, feeling self-conscious under the weight of Sylvia's stare. But after a heartbeat's awkward pause, she stepped forward and pulled me into an embrace. "I am so happy you're here!" She squeezed me tightly.

I relaxed with a sigh of relief. There was nothing amiss here. Mrs. Delafield had never favored me. That was nothing new. I had nothing to worry about.

"And are you surprised to see me, Mr. Delafield?" A laugh followed the words.

I pulled out of Sylvia's embrace, shooting a quick glance from Henry to the young lady who had entered the room with Sylvia. The young lady was not looking at me. Her hands were clasped together, and her gaze was steadfastly, affectionately, settled on Henry's face.

"Miss St. Claire," Henry said with warmth in his voice. "I did not know you had arrived already."

"Your mother was kind enough to bring me here herself. From London."

My eyes narrowed. So this was Miss St. Claire. The one Henry intended to marry.

Mrs. Delafield moved into my line of sight, and when I glanced at her, she smiled at me. If there was one thing she and Mama had in common, it was their arsenal of weapons. They both used smiles to hurt, to deceive, to injure. The smile she used on me at this moment was sharp and cruel, cutting at me like a quick knife.

"Miss St. Claire, this is Miss Katherine Worthington. An old friend of the family. Katherine, this is Miss Juliet St. Claire."

Miss St. Claire turned her gaze to me for the first time. That was when I saw the full measure of her beauty, with her deep auburn hair, her eyes, large and green, set apart just a bit wider than average. Her face narrowed in a heart shape, her mouth small, her nose straight and long. I felt my chest constrict. Taken altogether, the combination of her features was breathtaking. Otherworldly, even. As if she had been whisked to this place from some elfin realm. I shook myself, wondering where such a fantastical idea had come from. It must have been the shadows and the moors and the wild ocean wind that were making nonsense of my thoughts.

"Miss Worthington. Welcome to Blackmoore," the elfin queen said, her voice clear and confident. "We are so happy to have you here."

I stared at her for a shocked moment before shutting my mouth and swallowing my surprise. *She* was happy to have me? *She* welcomed me to Blackmoore? That was the duty of a hostess. I looked quickly from her to Mrs. Delafield, who was watching with approval, to Henry, who wore a completely guarded expression, keeping me from guessing his thoughts. Was something settled between them, then? Had Henry already proposed to Miss St. Claire? Was it decided that she was going to be mistress of Blackmoore?

I finally managed to nod and smile faintly. "Thank you. I am happy to finally be here." I could not keep myself from faintly stressing the word *finally.* I wanted Miss St. Claire to know that she might have visited here first, but my heart had belonged here longer than hers. I was ten when Henry and she had met for the first time. I knew him long before she did, and better, too. I had loved Blackmoore long before she had even heard of it.

"Dawson, please have Miss Worthington's things taken to her room," Mrs. Delafield said, taking charge. She glanced around the room. "Mrs. Pettigrew! What do you do here?"

The old nurse had finally put her knitting away and was standing a few paces away from our group. "Master Henry invited me to come along. As a chaperone."

Mrs. Delafield cast a sharp glance at Henry. "It seems Henry is full of surprises this evening."

Henry's jaw was tight, his eyes steely as they met his mother's. They looked as if they were at silent war with each other, and I had to guess that Henry won when Mrs. Delafield looked away with a sigh, glancing around the room as if looking for something she had misplaced.

"Katherine." She sighed again. "Where is your maid?"

"I—I didn't bring one." My mother had a lady's maid, but my sisters and I shared a maid among us, and Mama had not wanted to lose a servant to this trip.

Mrs. Delafield raised one haughty eyebrow and examined me as if I were a strange insect she did not remember stepping on. I had seen her look at me like that before. But this time I was all too aware of Miss St. Claire's watchful gaze and Henry standing close behind me. My face burned.

With another heavy sigh, she said in a bored voice, "Dawson, find someone from town to come here first thing in the morning to be Miss Worthington's maid. We must not allow her to run around like a wild thing here. Not with our guests coming."

"Yes, Mrs. Delafield," Dawson said, bowing.

"Sylvia, a word." Mrs. Delafield walked a few steps away, pulling Sylvia with her. They spoke with lowered voices, but I heard their words anyway. I was very good at eavesdropping. "No extra rooms in the east wing. She will have to be in the west wing."

"Can't someone share a room—"

"No. I won't inconvenience one of my guests for her sake. I told you so when you . . ." Her voice dropped to a murmur, and I strained to catch the stream of their conversation again without looking as if I was listening.

Another moment passed, and then Sylvia returned to my side and looped her arm through mine.

"Come. Let me show you to your room." She took a candle from a side table and tugged me toward the arched opening at the other end of the room. It appeared Henry had forgotten all about me. He was completely engrossed in whatever Miss St. Claire was saying to him in soft tones as they stood before the fire.

Before we passed through the archway, I could not keep myself from glancing back. Miss St. Claire had moved closer to Henry, and the firelight flickered over her hair, casting it copper. She laid a graceful hand on his arm and looked up into his face. The last thing I saw before turning away was Henry smiling down at her.

CHAPTER 7

"Mama told me to put you in the west wing," Sylvia said, looking at me with a flash of nervousness in her eyes. "The other guests will be in the east wing. You know Mama has spent the past year decorating it, and she has invited all of her friends here to show off her work. But Mama was not counting on you, and we have no extra bedrooms over there. So you will be alone in the west wing. You will not mind, will you?"

"But . . ." I stumbled over the top stair and caught myself on the banister. "But what do you mean? Surely your mother was expecting me."

"Hmm?" Sylvia cast me a quick glance, then looked back at the hall-way in front of us.

The hall was dark, the candle doing little to illuminate the vast cor-ridor stretching before us. A chill settled between my shoulders. I was sud-denly grateful for Sylvia's arm looped through mine. "What did you mean when you said, just now, 'Mama was not counting on you'? Your mother did invite me, did she not? Henry told me she did. He was holding a let-ter from her, from London. She did invite me, Sylvia."

My heart sick with dread, I watched her profile as she walked next to me, with the candlelight highlighting her golden hair. She looked very much like her mother. Tall, like all the Delafields. Golden hair that would turn ashy brown before it turned grey. And those cold blue eyes, like a frosted sky.

"Oh, I didn't mean *that*. I only meant that she had not counted properly—she had not counted all of her guests. She didn't count you. So when she made her plans for this party . . ." She waved a hand dismissively. "You will have to be in the west wing. That is all I meant."

Unease joined the chill that had settled over me, but I tried to shake it off with the thought that Sylvia would not lie to me, nor would Henry. If they said I was invited, I would accept their words as truth. I smiled a little. I was here, at Blackmoore. That was all that mattered. I had finally been invited. I had finally been included, and I would finally see where Henry would spend the rest of his life. I stopped my thoughts there, before they could add "with Miss Juliet St. Claire." My smile grew broader as I thought that I was fortunate to stay in the old west wing, which Sylvia had always told me was haunted. This was perfect. This was exactly how I would have chosen to experience Blackmoore. We climbed two flights of stairs and turned right.

Sylvia shivered next to me. It was colder here, in this wing. I could feel the wind leaking through the stone walls. I could hear it, too—a high, fickle moaning that came and went in sporadic gusts. A groan sounded from the wood floor where I stepped. Sylvia clutched my arm even more tightly and quickened her steps. I looked at her, smiling.

"Don't tell me you're still afraid of the west wing."

"Nonsense. I am eighteen. Of course I am not afraid," she scoffed. Then she swerved abruptly, nearly knocking me over in her rush to reach a door to my right. "Here. Here is your room."

The door was made of heavy, carved wood, and it creaked when she pushed it open. "I shall send a maid up right away to start a fire," she said, moving into the room and lighting the candles left on the bedside table and the mantel. She tugged on a rope by the bed, which would ring a bell downstairs to call a servant.

She looked around nervously and shuddered. "I do hate the west wing. I admit it. You will no doubt love it, though. You were always so fascinated by the hauntings of this place."

Looking around the room, I decided that I did love it. It was dark and chilly and matched perfectly the mood of the house.

"This is perfect," I said, sitting on the bed. After lighting the other candles, Sylvia set hers down on the bedside table. Now that we were here, I realized how much I had missed her these past four months while she had been in Town. "Now, tell me everything about London that you have not already told me in your letters."

She dropped onto the bed and said with a tortured sigh, "It was exhausting. Every day. So exhausting."

I snorted. "Adventures are wasted on you, Sylvia. You would rather curl up in front of a fire than go anywhere or see anything."

She smiled good-naturedly. "It is true. In fact, from now on, suitors will have to come to me. London is too tiring to do again."

"Speaking of suitors . . ." I raised my eyebrows. "Were there any promising men in Town?"

She sighed again, but this time a blissful smile slipped out, and stayed on her face, and her eyes took on a dreamy quality. Slipping her hand into the pocket of her gown, she drew out a small scrap of paper and handed it to me. In an elegant scrawl were the words, *What is light, if Sylvia be not seen? What is joy, if Sylvia be not by?*

She watched me with her eyes brimming with excitement. "Well?" she asked, her voice rich with enthusiasm. "Isn't he wonderfully poetic?"

"Shakespeare? Yes. He was." I handed her the paper.

Her brows furrowed. "No. Not Shakespeare." She leaned toward me, and even though the door was shut and no one was around to hear, she whispered, "Mr. Brandon gave me that. He wrote it. Just for me."

"Oh." I cleared my throat and, pointing to the paper, said, "But this is a line from Shakespeare, Sylvia." I did not speak the thought that followed—that if she had studied half as much as she had played with my cat, she might have known that herself.

Her crestfallen expression shot an arrow of regret through me. She stroked the paper with one finger. "I thought he had composed it himself."

"But it is very romantic of him," I hurried to say. "He must admire you very much. And it is the thought that counts, after all, and not necessarily the originality of the thought."

Her face brightened a little. "Yes. That is true. It is the thought that counts."

I felt wicked for having crushed her hope. "So tell me more about this thoughtful and romantic Mr. Brandon."

Her smile widened to a grin. "You will meet him for yourself. He is due to arrive tomorrow."

"Then I am doubly happy to be here."

"Yes. I am happy too, no matter what Mama may say—" She bit off her words with a look of consternation.

I looked at her pointedly. "No matter what Mama may say?"

Her cheeks turned pink, and she shook her head, as if advising me not to press the matter. But I did not let things go easily.

"What would your mother have to say about my visit? Did she truly not know I was coming?"

Sylvia looked down and traced lines in the quilt. After a long pause, she spoke hesitantly, carefully. "She is concerned that with you here, Henry might be . . . distracted. From his goal."

My brows drew together in confusion. "What goal?"

She took a breath and let it out on a sigh. "He *intends* to make things . . . final. With Miss St. Claire."

My heart pumped loudly. I fixed my gaze on her golden hair. "You mean he intends to propose to her."

She lifted her gaze, an apology written all over her face. "You knew this was coming," she whispered. "You've known it as long as we have. You've had years to come to terms with this, Kitty. And so has Henry.

And you saw him, tonight. Downstairs. You must have seen that he now welcomes this match."

My pride bristled. I set my expression in a look of derision. "I have no issue with Henry's match with Miss St. Claire. You needn't look at me as if you pity me, Sylvia."

"I didn't mean to——"

"And let us be clear. Did I not, for the past year and a half, make it very clear to everyone around me that I have no intention of marrying?" I glared at her until she nodded.

"Yes. You have made that very clear."

"So if you believe me, then there is no need to look at me like that or to apologize or to feel sorry for me. In fact, you should be happy for me, because I have finally convinced Mama to let me go with my aunt Charlotte to India."

Her eyes opened wide. "Have you really?"

"Indeed I have." I lifted my chin. "I will leave straight from Blackmoore. It is quite an accomplishment, you know."

"I know. I can hardly believe it. I thought she would never agree to your scheme."

"She has. She has agreed to it. And soon I will be accomplishing my own goals and fulfilling my own dreams. So there is no need to worry about me, Sylvia. Indeed, I have never been happier."

Relief softened the worry lines that had creased her face. She put her hand on mine and squeezed it gently. "I am so happy to hear it, my dear. So happy. And I am glad we could talk about this, because I have to ask something of you, and I did not know how to."

"What is it?"

"Mama has asked me to . . . see if you might be willing . . . to keep to your room tonight." She bit her lip.

I stared at her.

"You are probably tired from your journey at any rate," she hurried to say. "And it would be easier, for all of us, if Henry and Juliet had this evening to be together, without any other distractions. It was why we brought her here with us from London, earlier than the other guests."

My smile felt very stiff, but I tried to lift it anyway. "I see."

"Of course I will have dinner sent up to you. You need not go hungry." She laughed, an awkward, forced sound.

My face was hot with embarrassment, and when my eyes started to sting with tears, I knew I needed to get rid of Sylvia quickly. "I am happy to stay here. I am quite tired, as you say, and it will be nice to relax. So this is exactly what I would have wished for myself." I stood, walked to the door, and opened it. A footman was bringing my trunk down the hall. "Oh, look. Here is my trunk already. I will unpack, and you can go downstairs."

Sylvia stood beside me, looking ill at ease, as if she was searching for something to say. But I quickly hugged her, before she could say more, and said, "I am so happy to see you again." Then I gently shoved her out the door as the footman approached.

"Thank you, yes, that is mine. In here, please. Just set it by the end of the bed." I hurried him out of the room, grabbing the door to close it behind him.

"I will have some dinner sent up," Sylvia said in a quiet voice, lingering in the doorway. But my embarrassment threatened to overwhelm my control, and I did not want her to see that.

I nodded and, smiling bravely, closed the door between us.

CHAPTER 8

The servants at Blackmoore seemed quite efficient. Not ten minutes had passed since Sylvia's departure before a maid was in my room, getting a fire blazing in the hearth. With more light now, I saw that all of the walls had dark wood paneling, that the color of the drapes reminded me greatly of the color of the grass and the stunted trees on the moors, that the deep plum of the bedclothes mimicked the heather. I walked around the room, touching the velvet, running my hand over the smooth wood paneling of the walls, and pulling aside the drapes to look out the window.

The window was crisscrossed with metal casings that made diamond shapes of the glass. I wrestled with the latch on the window until I was able to push it open. It opened quite unwillingly, offering up a pathetic creak as metal screeched against metal. Leaning out the window, I looked to my right and left. To my right, around the corner of the house, shone the ocean, a dark, changing light under the luminance of the moon. To my left, beyond the house, stretched rough darkness: the moors. And below my window, two stories down, was a stretch of smoothness that might have been grass.

The night wind brought a chill into the room and made the candles sputter in their holders. I drew my head and shoulders back inside and closed the window, making sure I latched it properly. Then I closed the velvet drapes and turned back to the small space I had been assigned within this great house. I had distracted myself as much as I could, but now Sylvia's message ate at me from the inside. I rebelled against feeling caged.

I had become accustomed to Mrs. Delafield's dislike of me. I had become accustomed to being excluded. But to sentence me to my room, on my first night here, simply because they did not want me to distract Henry from Miss St. Claire . . . It was the worst kind of insult—the unexpected kind. I rubbed my nose hard and choked down the emotion that rose within me. I could not give way to it. It would make me a lesser person if I did. I could not care about being unwanted.

My dinner had not arrived yet, so I set about unpacking my trunk. My Mozart, my clothes, and the ivory-inlaid box with the letter from my aunt inside. All that I owned of any value. I traced the shape of the elephant on the top of the box before opening it and rereading the letter I had first read six months before:

Dear Katherine,

I found this box sitting on a shelf in a shop in London. It called to me from across the shop space, beckoning me to come nearer and discover its secrets. I did, and discovered a secret of my own: a dream I did not know lived within me until I held this box in my hands.

Katherine, I know that you, and perhaps only you, will be able to appreciate what this box represents: adventure! I invite you to take a journey with me for a moment—a journey of imagination.

Imagine standing on board a sailing ship, with nothing but ocean and sky around you. Imagine being pushed by the wind for months at a time. Pushed by a force both primal and controllable. A force of nature working to whisk you from one life to another. Imagine sailing along the African coast! Imagine the jungles, the beaches, the desert. Imagine dipping far south, to round the Cape of Good Hope, and then turning north and east. Toward India! Imagine a territory where all is new and unknown, where every day can be a discovery. Imagine a life where one may be whatever one desires to be. Imagine a country of endless beginnings, where the old you can be thrown off like a snake shedding its skin. Imagine a hot wind, and deep, vibrant colors, and strange new scents. Imagine with me, Katherine, a chance to be reborn and remade. Imagine the power of having your future in your own hands, far from the limitations of our culture's expectations.

Would this not be the trip of a lifetime? Would this not change you forever?

Now, Katherine, if this journey of imagination has enticed you to the least degree, pay close heed! I have been saving the inheritance I received from my Uncle Stafford. I have saved it for many years and invested it as well. Now I have quite a nice sum, and I have finally decided what I wish to do with it. I want to embark on an adventure of a lifetime. I want to go to India. And I want you to go with me!

I await your response with much eagerness and, as always, my most sincere affection.

Love,

Aunt Charlotte

I folded the letter and let hope enter my heart once more. Aunt Charlotte wanted me. She included me. And she was someone I could model my life after. She was unmarried and independent and happy to be so. I would fulfill my bargain with Mama and go on adventures with my aunt and learn how to be happy alone. Yes. That was my plan. And I was here, in this place, to achieve my future dreams. Slipping the letter back inside the ivory-inlaid box, I sat and looked around me, trying to buoy up my spirits.

But as I looked around me, I realized that I had done this same thing just three days earlier at my own house. I had sat in a room that I was trapped in and dreamed of escape. Blackmoore was supposed to be that escape. But I was just as trapped in this room of stone and glass as I had been in my room at my own home.

After I had waited half an hour with growing impatience, my dinner was brought by the same housemaid who had started the fire. I ate my meal in silence, the clock on the mantel ticking away the long, heavy minutes of my isolation. I tried not to think of Miss St. Claire with her wide-set eyes and auburn hair. I tried not to think of Henry smiling at her and hearing her whispers. And then, abruptly, I could take no more. I pushed the food away, stood, and grabbed a candle. I might not have been invited to the drawing room, but I certainly did not have to stay in this room all evening, no matter what Mrs. Delafield or Sylvia said.

Slipping from the room, I closed the door softly behind me and waited for my eyes to adjust to the dim light of the hallway. Looking left to the way we had come, I chose to go right instead. The candle did little against the dark here, providing only a small space of light in which to explore and examine. The floor creaked under my feet, and a rogue breeze slipped through the wall and made the flame flicker, causing shadows to dance and loom. I shivered and turned to my right and the unknown things that awaited me.

The hall stood thick with silence. I walked slowly, placing my feet carefully on the uncarpeted floor, which was warped and sloped. I hugged the right-hand side of the corridor, lifting my candle to see the wall. The problem was that I did not know what I was looking for. I stopped at a portrait and lifted the frame away from the wall, peering into the space behind it while trying not to singe my eyebrows with the flame of the candle. Reaching my hand behind the frame, I felt the wall behind the painting. But it felt as smooth as the other sections of the wall I had touched.

I moved on, pausing before a closed door. Setting my hand to the door handle, I considered entering the empty room. But I could not. The hall was dark and chill, but at least it was an open space. I could not summon the courage to put myself into a dark, closed room.

I continued down the hall, checking behind every painting I came across, until I reached the end of the hall where a window stretched from floor to ceiling. I peered through it but could see nothing in the darkness beyond the glass. Turning, I moved to the other side of the corridor and followed the same pattern, my hand trailing along the wall, stopping at anything that might possibly hide an entrance to a secret passageway. I moved beyond my room, and kept going, passing another window. Directly past the window, I reached a large tapestry covering the wall. This would be the perfect spot for hiding a secret door.

I held the candle aloft. My heart quickened its speed, pounding in my chest as I thought that I had finally found what I had dreamed of for so many years. I touched the edge of the tapestry, then slipped my fingers behind it, reaching for the opening, the latch, the crack that would signal that I had indeed found what I'd been looking for. I stretched farther, reaching, running my palm over the surface of the wall, my heart pounding. The tapestry was large. I slipped behind it, holding my candle next to the stone of the wall, away from the tapestry at my back, looking for anything that might hint at an opening.

I paused at a sound. At first I thought it was the wind—the sound that came to me. Then I realized it was weaker than wind. It came in spurts and sputters, and as I cocked my head, puzzling, and concentrated on the sound, I realized I recognized it. It was voices, coming to me on the wind of whispers, raising the hairs of my neck.

I pinched my candle out, the smoke rising to sting my nose, and held as still as I could while my heart raced. But though I strained to make out the whispered words, I could not discern what was being said or from whence the whispers came—from the hallway, beyond the tapestry I hid behind, or from some secret passageway on the other side of this wall.

Footsteps sounded, soft and scraping, and the whispers teased me, just out of reach of my comprehension. Sylvia's stories of ghosts haunting this wing floated through my mind, and I shivered with a sudden chill.

Without warning, I was gripped in terror so complete it seized every thought, every impulse. The tapestry hung heavy around me, trapping me. I dropped the candle and scrambled, pushing against the heavy tapestry, frantic to break free. When I stumbled from my hiding place, I collapsed against the wall, breathing hard and trembling. The corridor was dark, just as it had been before. I could no longer hear the whispers that had started my terror. In fact, I wondered if I had heard them at all, or if it had only been the wind or my active imagination.

I pressed my hand to my chest and willed myself to breathe slowly, to calm myself, to refuse to allow my imagination to rule my reason. Turning to the window, I looked at the scene below me. The moon was three-quarters full, and from this window I could see the full stretch of ocean. The silver-white light of the moon on the water calmed my soul, and after a few minutes I could breathe and think clearly again.

I had merely frightened myself by looking for the secret passageway. I had imagined the whispers and the footsteps. There were no ghosts. There was no such thing as a haunting. But just as I had finished telling myself this, I heard them again: the footsteps. I spun around, pressing my back to the wall.

This time there was light—a single candle held aloft, highlighting a familiar face. Henry. The terror drained from me, and a smile eased the firm line of my lips. He stopped at the door across the hall from where I stood and knocked on it. He waited, then called softly, "Kate? Are you awake?" and knocked again.

I breathed in, my throat constricted with sudden emotion, and he turned his head and looked directly at me.

"There you are." The moonlight bathed me in its silver-white glow, and the flame of Henry's candle shone golden around him. He stepped toward me, bringing his golden light with him until it merged with the moonlight.

"What are you doing standing here in the dark?" he asked.

"I did have a candle," I said, as if that would explain it all. My nervousness still coursed through me, causing my hands to tremble. "And what are you doing here? Why are you not downstairs enjoying Miss St. Claire's company?"

My voice held a sting, which I regretted as soon as I heard it.

He leaned one shoulder against the wall, turned toward me, and set his candle between us on the windowsill.

"I came to check on you. All alone, here, in the west wing? Sylvia would have already talked herself into seeing ghosts if she were in your place."

"I am not like Sylvia."

"I know." A note of affection—a smile—sounded in his voice.

"But, Henry, in truth there is something about this house . . . this wing. I thought I heard whispers just moments ago, when I was behind the tapestry."

His voice sharpened. "Whispers? Behind the tapestry?"

"Yes. I was looking for the secret passageway—you needn't grin like that. You must have known I would look for it first thing—and as I looked behind the tapestry I thought I heard soft footsteps and whispers. Is that madness?"

His eyes betrayed nothing, his face a mask of secrets. "Perhaps it was only the wind."

"Yes. Perhaps."

"You know, it will be much easier to discover a secret passageway in the daylight."

"I know." I smiled faintly. "I was just . . . passing the time."

His brow furrowed. "Passing the time? Why did you not come downstairs?"

I bit my lip as I debated how to answer him, then finally I asked him a question instead of answering his. "Why am I here? At Blackmoore? And do not tell me that your mother invited me, because it was obvious she does not want me here. I want the truth. Please."

He looked at me for a long moment while my heart pounded. In my mind, I silently begged him to tell me the truth.

"You are here," he finally said, "because I had a promise to keep."

"And this is your last opportunity to fulfill it."

His gaze turned sharp. "Why do you say that?"

"Sylvia told me. She told me that you intend to propose to Miss St. Claire during this visit."

Henry said nothing.

I cleared my throat, shifting from one foot to the other. "Is it true, then? You are going to propose?"

He studied my face for a long moment before answering. "It's a possibility."

I breathed. And breathed again. "I see."

"Now it is your turn. Tell me, why did you not come downstairs this evening? Why did you not join us?"

I took a deep breath. "Your mother did not want me downstairs. Sylvia told me I should stay in my room, so that I would not distract you from Miss St. Claire. Of course, you know how I feel about such things . . . about staying in my room." My voice shook at the end, despite my attempts to keep it steady.

Henry moved his head, just enough for the moonlight to show me the anger in his eyes.

I rubbed my nose and looked away. "I am not crying about it. Indeed, I appreciate the solitude, and as I said, I have been exploring . . ."

"Kate." His voice was gentle and tugged at the fragile strings that were holding my emotions together.

I rubbed my nose harder and turned away from him. My foot struck something hard, and bending down, I found my candle lying at my feet. I cleared my throat. "I should leave you to your guests," I murmured as I moved away from him. I crossed the hall and opened the door to my room, its glow of firelight and candlelight spilling into the dark corridor. I turned to thank Henry for checking on me and found him standing very close.

"Listen," he said, his voice intent and hushed. "You are my guest here, just as certainly as Miss St. Claire or any of the other visitors who will be arriving. You are *my* guest, Katherine Worthington. Blackmoore will be mine, not my mother's. In fact, my mother has no power here."

I loved the sound of those words: *my mother has no power here.* But Henry was wrong. His mother had power here in spades.

"Now. You may come downstairs whenever you wish," Henry said. "You may look for secret passageways as much as your heart desires." He lifted a hand and gently brushed his thumb over my cheek, wiping off a stray tear that had slipped past without my notice. I caught my breath in surprise. "But I would hate for you to spend any part of your visit here sitting in your room and crying because of something my mother has said or done. Just . . . ignore her. As much as possible."

I smiled a little. "Thank you. But to be fair, I was not sitting in my room and crying. I was exploring the west wing and decidedly *not* crying."

His eyes lit up with gentle affection. "Of course you were. I would never accuse you of anything else."

My heart reached out for him, and I had to pull it back under my control with a swift yank. I looked down, trying to hide my feelings. I was very good at hiding my gentler feelings from Henry, on a normal basis. But this night, in this darkened house on the edge of the world, I felt miles away from normal.

"So, Miss Kate, will you come downstairs this evening? Join us for a game of whist?"

I shook my head. "No. All of this exploring and not crying has worn me out."

"Not to mention the past two days of humming."

"Exactly!" I chuckled. "I swear you knew about the humming all along. Didn't you?"

He grinned. "I refuse to answer that question." He looked into the room behind me. "You will be alone in the west wing. Are you sure you want to stay here? I could find another room for you . . ."

"No. I love this room." And, truly, I did. I loved the dark wood paneling and the velvet drapes and the colors of the moors. In fact, in this room I was beginning to think differently of the moors. I could already see how they might grow on me. "I will be fine here. Don't worry about me."

He shook his head. "I think I will always worry about you," he murmured. He took a breath and looked at me as if he meant to say something more. But instead he abruptly turned to leave. I watched him cross the dark hall and pick up his candle where he had left it by the window.

"Henry."

He looked back but didn't come closer.

"I just wanted to thank you for keeping your promise. Thank you for bringing me here."

He smiled, but he continued to back away as he said, "I will always keep my promises to you." Then he turned and left as fast as his long legs could carry him, until he almost looked as if he was running. The flame of his candle flickered, and then he was gone.

I closed the door to my bedchamber, changed into my nightclothes, and slipped into bed, bringing the covers up to my chin, snuggling down against the chill of the room. A low moaning sound crept through the stones, and the drapes moved, just a little—a wave, a wrinkle of velvet. I wondered if the wind blew off the moors or the sea. Which wind made the moaning sounds and which made the howls? When something creaked outside the door, I wondered if someone was there, or if it was only the old house being moved by the fierce wind.

The fire threw shadows against the walls, and the drapes continued to move, idly, as if a small hand were twitching them. I closed my eyes tight while the wind moaned and the old house creaked around me. And finally, after a long time, I slipped into sleep.

CHAPTER 9

The wind woke me with its howls and moans throughout the night. I cracked my eyes open to a blackened room, then closed them again and slipped into strange dreams of howling birds and dark corridors and a boy who ran away from me and would not turn back no matter how I called for him. When I finally pulled myself from my dark dreams, it was to the sound of knocking on my bedroom door. I rolled over, blinking in confusion at my surroundings. The knock came again.

"Miss Worthington?" a voice called through the door.

"Yes?" I answered groggily, trying to shake off the remnant shadows of my dreams.

The door cracked open, and a young face framed by a maid's white cap appeared. "I am your maid. May I come in?"

"Oh." I sat up and pushed back my dark hair. "Yes, please do."

She entered the room and dropped a curtsy. Her cheeks were rosy and covered with freckles. Her hands fidgeted with her white apron.

I smiled to try to ease her obvious nervousness. "What is your name?"

"Alice, miss." She dropped another curtsy.

"And do you come from Robin Hood's Bay, Alice?" I asked, remembering Mrs. Delafield's instructions to Dawson the night before.

"Yes, miss."

"Well, I am very happy to have you."

She smiled bashfully and, gesturing to my trunk, asked if she should finish unpacking my things for me. I nodded, but when she moved to open the drapes first, I groaned with disappointment to discover how late I had slept. Moving to the window, I saw that the sun had risen during my dreams, and the moors were already brightly lit but shrouded by fog. How could I have slept past dawn on my first morning here? I had gone to bed with every intention of being outside before sunrise in order to hear the birds.

I shivered standing near the window with nothing but the cold floor beneath my feet. Tomorrow morning I would not oversleep. I would not let the nightly hauntings of this place steal my morning birds from me.

With Alice's help I dressed and then made my way downstairs for breakfast, finding only Sylvia and Miss St. Claire in the dining room. I paused in the doorway, trying to collect my composure and my good intentions. I had been tired last night after my days of travel. That was the only reason I thought Miss St. Claire a tad irritating and a bit presumptuous. Perhaps she was perfectly acceptable as a human being. Perhaps she would make Henry a good wife.

"Good morning, Miss Worthington," Miss St. Claire called as I made my way to the sideboard, where breakfast was laid out for the guests to choose from. "I hope you slept well."

"Yes, I slept well, thank you." I had to bite back other, less polite words, about how I was Henry's guest, not hers, and that she was not supposed to be here on my first and only visit to Blackmoore. It was supposed to be just me and Henry and Sylvia, like we had been growing up. If anyone asked about my sleep, it should have been Sylvia. I bit back the uncharitable words that rose to my tongue and struggled to think something kind about this interloper, this young woman who had come here to rob me of the visit I was supposed to have. I thought hard while I piled food on my plate, and by the time I turned to the table and the empty seat across from the two of them, I had thought of one thing: Miss St. Claire was a thoughtful interloper. I could grant her that.

"You are very interested in India, I understand," Miss St. Claire said to me. She looked pretty in the morning light. Her hair really was a deep, glorious auburn that glinted with a hint of copper when the sunlight shone on it the right way. And those wide-set, green eyes were a force to be reckoned with.

"Oh? Who told you that?"

Sylvia spoke up. "I did. Juliet and I spent a great deal of time together in London."

I tried not to resent that fact. I knew that Sylvia would have made new friends in London. But I did not like this stranger knowing things about me. Miss St. Claire was watching me, both eyebrows up, and I realized she was waiting for an answer.

"Yes, I am quite interested in India. In fact, I hope soon to travel there myself, with my aunt."

The elfin queen shook her head, making a gentle tsking sound. "I cannot conceive of why one would ever desire to go so far from England's shores. It seems so dangerous!"

"It can be."

"How long is the voyage?"

"Depending on the season, between four and six months."

Her green eyes opened wide. She carefully set down her cup. "Then one could not travel there and back in less than . . . a year. Conceivably."

I nodded.

She shook her head, her eyes large with compassion. "You poor thing." She reached her hand across the table and touched my own, stopping me when I would have lifted my fork to my mouth. "I understand that your situation at home is not as . . . ideal as some of us are blessed with. And I feel for you, I truly do, that things could be so uncomfortable that you would choose to put such a distance between yourself and your loved ones." She lowered her voice to a whisper. "I understand your parents are not as caring as mine are. You poor, poor thing." Her mouth pulled down into the prettiest frown I had ever seen.

I dropped my fork and darted a glance at Sylvia, who looked as if she would like to sink into the ground. How could she tell Miss St. Claire such personal things about me?

She tried to smile at me, but her eyes were full of dread. "You mustn't be angry with me, Kitty. You know that Juliet is like one of the family."

I wiped my mouth with my napkin, using the movement as an excuse to pull my hand out from under Miss St. Claire's unwelcome touch.

"Kate," I said quietly. "I wish to be called Kate."

"Oh, dear me, surely you are not upset that I know such details of your life!" Miss St. Claire put both hands to her chest. "I assure you, I am the soul of discretion! And I do not judge you in the least! My dear Miss Worthington, indeed, I feel as if you and I are old friends, so much have I heard of you over the years from the Delafields. No, no, you must not be upset. You must thank Sylvia for being such a good friend to you that she has enlisted my aid."

I sat very still and looked from her to Sylvia, who was squirming in her chair. "Your aid?" I cleared my throat. "What aid would that be, pray tell?"

Miss St. Claire looked to Sylvia, as if for permission, but Sylvia only shrugged, as if she had already given up control.

"Why, my aid in bringing you here, of course," the elfin queen said, with a beatific smile in my direction.

I was suddenly very aware of my heartbeat and the heat flooding my cheeks. "Oh?" I tried to smile. "Exactly what aid did you render, Miss St. Claire?"

She smiled on, completely oblivious to my feelings. "I assured Mrs. Delafield that I would not object to your company, knowing how *desperately* you need some positive influences in your life."

I looked with disbelief from her to Sylvia, who was staring at her plate with a steadfastness I had never seen in her before.

"Well . . ." I was at a loss as to how to respond to such condescending compassion. "I thank you for your generosity, Miss St. Claire," I finally said, my smile tight as I tried to keep back the astonishing number of impolite thoughts that entered my mind.

"I was happy to help," she said, picking up her fork and daintily proceeding with her breakfast.

I had completely lost my appetite, and I did not think I could stay much longer in Miss St. Claire's company without losing my temper. I took a deep breath, then tried to steer the conversation onto safer ground. "Sylvia, I hope you will introduce me to your grandfather this morning."

"I'm afraid Grandpapa is not well, Kitty," she said with a look of regret. "I doubt you shall have any opportunity to meet him while you are here."

My disappointment was great at this news. I had looked forward to meeting the man who had played such a significant role in Henry's life. "I am sorry to hear it."

Miss St. Claire tsked, shaking her head. "Indeed, it will be a great sadness to all of our family to lose Grandfather."

I cast a disbelieving glance in Miss St. Claire's direction. She was going too far, claiming this family as her own, and I could not tolerate one more minute of her company. Pushing my plate away, I stood. "Sylvia. Come show me the house."

She looked at me as if I had just asked her to grow a second head. "Kitty. The house is enormous."

"Yes, and I want to see all of it." I smiled encouragingly.

She groaned and leaned back in her chair. "The thought is too exhausting to contemplate."

"Come. A little movement will be good for you. It will help you to wake up."

She waved me away. "I have no desire to go traipsing all over. Go find Henry and ask him for a tour."

At that, Miss St. Claire dropped her fork and stood abruptly, bumping the table and making everything rattle. "I will give you a tour, Miss Worthington. It will be good practice for me."

I looked from her to Sylvia, letting Sylvia see the extent of my displeasure. "How kind. But I insist on Sylvia coming along."

"No, Juliet knows the house as well as—"

I shot her a dark look. If I was going to suffer in Miss St. Claire's company, then Sylvia was going to suffer along with me. After a moment of competing stares, she said, with great reluctance, "Of course I would like to come as well."

"We will start in the great hall," Miss St. Claire said, leading the way from the dining room and down the corridor to the entrance. She stopped in the middle of the room, right under the domed ceiling. I looked around curiously, glad for the daylight to illuminate what was hidden from me the night before.

"This is the original portion of the house," she said, gesturing to the circular room we stood in. "It was completed in 1504. Other parts of the house were added later. The most important feature here is, of course, the domed ceiling, painted to depict the story of Icarus."

I tipped my head back and studied the painting on the dome that stood two floors above us. "That is not Icarus."

"Yes. It is." Her voice was more forceful and disbelieving—as if she could not believe I would question her. "Of course it is."

She looked at Sylvia, who held up both hands with a "don't ask me" gesture.

I pointed up at the dome. "That is Phaeton, not Icarus. Phaeton drove the chariot sun across the sky, lost control of the horses, and was killed by a thunderbolt from Zeus after burning the earth. Icarus also suffered death after trying to fly," I went on, "but he flew with wings made by his father, Daedalus, so they could escape Crete. He plunged to his death when he flew too close to the sun and the wax of his wings melted."

Miss St. Claire's brow puckered as she looked at the dome above us.

"Hmm. I suppose you may be correct, but you do sound like quite a Bluestocking, Miss Worthington, and if you want my opinion . . ." She moved closer to me, bent her head to mine, and said, "I would not want to be considered a Bluestocking, myself. It will hurt your chances, you know."

It was all I could do to keep my mouth curved up into a smile. "My chances of what?"

"Marriage, of course," she said with a laugh. "How droll you are. Sylvia told me you were quite studious, but I did not believe her. Isn't that right, Sylvia? I did not believe you when you told me how very well read your friend was." Sylvia had sagged into a chair by the fireplace, as if standing was too much exertion for her. "But now I see she was quite right! But how dull your youth must have been, to sit for so long in a stuffy library reading old books! I declare, the more I hear of your life, the more I pity you, Miss Worthington. Indeed, I do."

I could not believe her. I had never met someone so thoughtful and yet so offensive at the same time. But I had one secret that she did not seem to know, and for that reason I had to bite back a smile. What she did not know was that my days spent in the old library at Delafield Manor were anything but dull. What she did not know was that Henry was my study companion for years.

"What shall we see next, Miss St. Claire?" I asked.

She turned on her heel. "This way."

I dragged Sylvia up from her chair and urged her on, linking my arm through hers. She groaned. "My legs are already tired, Kitty. You can explore the house yourself, on your own, you know."

"Don't worry. I will act on that offer as soon as I can," I murmured.

My opportunity came several rooms later. Miss St. Claire had shown me the dining room, the drawing room, the library, the music room, and the long gallery, and was about to turn around to take me upstairs via the great entry hall again. But I noticed, at the end of a hall, tucked into an alcove, a door. It looked forgotten. And, as a sympathizer of forgotten things, I asked, "Where does that door lead?"

Miss St. Claire waved a hand in dismissal. "That is just a small, second music room."

I walked toward the door, ignoring Sylvia's protests about her aching feet. The door was intricately carved, unlike the other interior doors I had seen. I ran my hand over its surface, finding vines and leaves and a scattering of small birds carved into the wood. I turned the handle and swung open the heavy door, walking into a room held in darkness by heavy drapes. But something stirred in there, and a matching something stirred in my heart. With quickened steps, I crossed the room and threw open the drapes across three tall windows that rose from floor to ceiling. Sunlight poured in, and I turned. It was a small room with a high ceiling. My gaze darted around the room, skimming over the pianoforte in the center, the stuffed armchairs, the tapestries covering the walls, the paintings, looking for that thing I had sensed—that stirring thing. And then my eyes landed on an ornate, gilded birdcage tucked into a corner, nearly hidden by the drapes.

And then I understood why I had thought something stirred in this room. A dark bird fluttered wildly around the cage, its feathers hitting against the iron bars. But besides the sounds of its wings, the bird made no noise. I held my breath as I watched it and felt a connection with this dark, wild bird that I could not explain.

"I told you this was a waste of time," Sylvia said from behind me.

Miss St. Claire stood on the threshold, a look of distaste wrinkling her perfect nose. "I hate the smell of birds," she declared, eyeing it with distrust. "This will be the first room to be changed when I—"

She stopped herself just shy of finishing her statement, but it was clear to me what she had left off: when she became the mistress of this house. Resentment and a burning dislike rose within me, swift and fierce, and I had an overwhelming urge to push her from this room—to lock the door behind her and to stand guard over this space, protecting it from her destroying touch.

This is my room.

The thought appeared in my mind without any planning on my part. It was simply a recognition of truth. This *was* my room. I felt it deep in my bones. This room should never cease to exist. These tapestries, these paintings, these tall windows and especially—oh, especially—this dark bird, should be preserved, should be treasured, should be esteemed.

"I hope this room never changes," I said, looking at her directly. "I love it. I hope it stays this way always."

Her smile was nothing but soft and innocent. "Everything will change, Miss Worthington. That is what happens when a house passes to new owners."

I stood there and felt helpless and furious all at once.

"Are you ready to finish the tour?" she asked, gesturing at the door.

"No." The word was torn from me. I could not abide her company for one more moment. "No. I want to stay here. I'll continue on my own in a little while."

Sylvia looked from me to Miss St. Claire, as if trying to choose between us. But only an instant passed before she made her choice. She took Miss St. Claire's arm, saying, "Let us go sit by the fire in the drawing room. We can watch out the window for the guests."

As they left me, I knelt in front of the birdcage, looking at the dark bird up close. Its feathers were a shiny, rich black that almost looked blue in the sunlight. Its tail was forked and twitched, over and over. This was a bird I had never seen before—not in books nor in the real world. And even though I watched it for a long time, not once did it sing.

CHAPTER 10

Alice did not disappoint. As she helped me dress for dinner that evening, she arranged my dark, wavy hair with a skill our maid at home did not possess. But she did not say a word, leaving me to my own thoughts.

It was time to think through my plan. To strategize. After a few hours of wandering on my own, I had spent the afternoon with Sylvia and Miss St. Claire watching through the window as carriages drove up to the courtyard. A stream of guests came all throughout the day. They were young and old, handsome and not. Tonight we would all dine together. Tonight I would have to set in motion my plan for earning my trip to India.

The thought made my heart quicken with nervousness. My bargain with Mama seemed, in a flash, like the most foolish thing I had ever agreed to. I was supposed to convince three gentlemen to propose to me? What madness had possessed me to make me think that was an attainable goal? I had only ever had one man propose to me, and that was Mr. Cooper, a decaying old man who only wanted a warm body to watch over his deathbed. He would have proposed to anyone with a pulse. But these friends of the Delafields—these were not people like Mr. Cooper. These were elegant, wealthy people who were not desperate like he was. And I was supposed to convince *three* of them to want me?

I felt sick. I would never win this bargain. I did not know the first thing about entrapping a man. And if I failed, I would pay far too high a price. Whatever Mama had in mind for me, I would not like it. I gripped my courage tighter, telling myself that I would prevail. I would succeed at this. Failure was not an option to me. Not with what I knew of my mother's goals and dreams and designs. She took what was not hers and swindled futures away from unsuspecting fools. Why had I been such a fool as to agree to this scheme? Why had I not limited what I would owe her if I failed?

My thoughts raced as panic took hold of me. I watched Alice in the mirror, arranging my hair, and I suddenly remembered looking into a different mirror, years ago, and watching Eleanor get ready for a ball.

"You are quite pretty," I told her, watching from the bed as our maid Mary pinned her hair into place. I was lying on my stomach, my chin propped on my hand. Eleanor and I looked much like each other and quite like our mother—the same dark hair, the same hazel eyes. In noticing Eleanor's beauty, I was also hoping for my own, at some future day. I was fourteen, and she was sixteen. I was not old enough to go to the ball, but I hoped to be at least as beautiful as she was in two years' time.

"With whom do you think you will dance tonight?"

She turned her head, watching Mary's work in the mirror. "I think I will dance with whomever I choose, of course."

I frowned at her. "You cannot choose. You must be chosen."

She laughed, and her gaze cut into me. "You are too young to understand." I frowned harder, hating the condescension in her voice. But before I could make a retort, Mary stood back and asked, "How is that, Miss Eleanor?"

Eleanor looked at her hair, turning this way and that, for what seemed like a long time, before nodding and thanking Mary, who left the room. And only then did I say, "I am not much younger than you, you know. You could be nice and train me so that I will know what I'm doing when I am your age."

Eleanor faced me, a kind smile lifting her lips. "Of course I will train you, Kitty. But I don't have time tonight. I will only tell you this: you are always in control. A man may think he has chosen you as his interest, but you will be the one to turn his head."

"What do you think, miss?" Alice's voice brought me back from my reverie. I turned my head this way and that, just as I had seen Eleanor do, and then I smiled faintly and said, "It is very nice. Thank you."

Alice let out what sounded like a sigh of relief as she stepped back. It was time, then. As I made my way downstairs, I thought of Eleanor's words. She had never taught me any more than that, for I had stopped asking her by the time I was old enough, in her opinion, to know such things. But if there was anyone in the world who could accomplish this goal, it was Eleanor. So if I could simply behave the way I had seen her behave, I would be on the right road to success. I breathed deeply, telling myself it would all work out, but my heart would not slow down, and my hands would not stop their trembling.

The drawing room was already crowded when I made my way to its grand doors after winding through the west wing and down two flights of stairs. Sylvia saw me as soon as I entered and took hold of my arm.

"Come. Let me introduce you," she said, pulling me into the room.

The fire was too hot, the room too crowded, and the stuffiness of the air weighed on me. Heat prickled through my long gloves, and I wished for a fan. There were so many gowns and so many shoulders and so many feathered headdresses. I was not prepared for the new London styles here. I had heard of them, but I had not seen them before. The effect was disconcerting. I felt like a bird who had wandered into some strange flock, surrounded by a different species.

And there were so many gentlemen here to choose from. How could I select three? And how would I know which three would be the most likely to propose to me? The realities of my bargain struck me again, and I regretted ever making that deal with Mama. This was overwhelming.

Regret made my steps falter, and I turned this way and that, looking for something besides shoulders and backs and feathers and struggling to breathe in this hot, stifling room. Then my gaze, in my panic, rested on a familiar sight. The dark hair caught my eye, then the grey eyes, and the crease next to his mouth, his face tilted down, a smile beginning to form. And I saw the person he was smiling at: Miss St. Claire, who was standing too close to him and speaking to him, her body leaning toward his. Her eyes seeming to twinkle in this light.

The sight burned through my regret and indecision and doubt; it strengthened my resolve. I would win my three proposals, and I would leave for India, and the sooner, the better. If I had known she would be here—if I had known that I would have to watch them together, and be a witness to their courtship—I would not have come.

Sylvia stopped leading me and turned my attention to the two gentlemen standing before her. "Mr. Brandon and his son, Mr. Thomas Brandon."

Ah. Sylvia's Mr. Brandon. My interest piqued, I pushed aside my own concerns and turned my full attention to the handsome young man in front of me. He had brown hair, nice eyes, and a wide, infectious smile. I cast a sideways glance at Sylvia, thinking, *Well done, my friend.* A happy-looking gentleman with an appreciation for Shakespeare and a fondness for my best friend? I could not be more pleased. For Sylvia's sake, I tried not to grin.

His father, the elder Mr. Brandon, was not half so enthusiastic about being there. He looked as if he would be much more comfortable in a study, like my father. This was clearly a man of quiet habits.

His son, however, was not. He rubbed his hands together and eagerly said, "I cannot wait to explore the coast tomorrow. And was that a ruined abbey we passed, just south of here a mile or so?"

Sylvia nodded, and his face lit up even more.

"We should take a picnic there! Tomorrow!" He looked from Sylvia to me and back. "What say you?"

I liked his enthusiasm. "I would like nothing better."

The younger Mr. Brandon turned to his father. "And you, Father? Will you join us?"

The elder Mr. Brandon hesitated, then said in a quiet voice, "The air is so chilly here, right by the ocean."

"But we shall not let that stop us, Father. Not when there is adventure to be had!"

I grinned at this younger Mr. Brandon. Here was a man I could relate to. Here was a kindred spirit. I glanced at Sylvia and beamed when I saw the besotted smile on her face. I was flattered, really. She had chosen a man very much like me in temperament. It was meant to be a successful match, without a doubt. Sylvia and I had grown up together, and we were the dearest of friends. We balanced each other, complemented each other. So undoubtedly this Mr. Brandon would be perfect for her.

"It is settled, then," said the son. "A picnic tomorrow! Let us hope for clear skies."

"Indeed," Sylvia said, pulling on my arm. "Excuse us. I have more guests to greet."

The men nodded and bowed, and I noticed as we walked away that the elder Mr. Brandon's gaze lingered on us, following us. A thought came to me—an idea. "Where is Mrs. Brandon?" I asked Sylvia quietly.

"Mr. Brandon is a widower," she replied.

I smiled to myself. A widower was always on the hunt for a wife. And older gentlemen were much quicker to propose than younger gentlemen, or so I had heard. The elder Mr. Brandon might be a very good possibility for my bargain. And I would be helping Sylvia in the process, by keeping him occupied so that she could claim the full attention of his son, her admirer. Perhaps my situation was not quite so dire as I had thought.

By the time Sylvia had introduced me to all the guests, I had two more possibilities to consider for my bargain. Besides the elder Mr. Brandon, I had chosen a younger, nervous-looking gentleman named Mr. Dyer, and a Mr. Pritchard, who had recently returned from India. My thoughts turned from my goal only when Sylvia introduced me to Herr and Frau Spohr, musicians from Germany.

"Herr Spohr is a composer," she said, after the introduction. "And we heard the most lovely duet performed by him and his wife in London on the clarinet and harp. They were very generous to prolong their stay in our country to come here and grace us with their music."

Herr Spohr was a middle-aged man with hair that looked untamed. His wife was younger than he, with rich brown hair and a quiet but elegant air.

"A pleasure to meet you, Herr Spohr, Frau Spohr," I said. "I look forward to hearing you perform."

"Miss Worthington is a musician herself," Sylvia said, which caused me to blush.

Herr Spohr looked interested at that. "Oh? What do you play?"

"Just the pianoforte."

His gaze turned into a gentle rebuke. "Never say *just* the pianoforte. Never slight the instrument, Miss Worthington."

"It was not the instrument I meant to slight, Herr Spohr, but rather my own skill," I explained. "I think very highly of the pianoforte. In fact, I am a great admirer of Mozart."

I would have said more about the great musician who had won my loyalty, but dinner was announced and it was time to make our way, with the crowd of guests, into the dining room. I saw Henry and Miss St. Claire again. Her copper hair made her difficult to miss in a crowd.

But to my gratification, I was not completely invisible either, for Henry saw me and looked twice. I thought of Alice's work on my hair and had to keep myself from touching it self-consciously. He threw me a questioning look, as if to ask if I was well, and I smiled back in response. I was quite well, now that I had a plan.

CHAPTER 11

My plan was not advanced one bit at dinner, as I was seated between two married men. So I took advantage of the first opportunity I could find when the gentlemen joined us in the drawing room. The man who had recently returned from India took a seat first, on one of the settees arranged in front of the fire. I hurried to join him before anyone else could claim the seat next to him.

"Mr. Pritchard," I said. "I am very interested in talking to you about India."

He was probably twenty years older than I, but Sylvia had confirmed that he was not married. He had sandy blond hair and was very tan. I had chosen him knowing that we would have common interests.

He took his time taking a snuff case out of his pocket, tapping it with a fingernail and then flicking it open. Looking at me, he took a pinch of snuff and said, "Yes? What about?" He held the snuff to a nostril, sniffed, then did the same to the other nostril. He dusted off his fingers and pocketed his snuff case before looking at me again.

Now that I had set the plan in motion, my nervousness had returned in full force. What was I doing? And how would I actually go about encouraging this man to like me?

Eleanor. The thought came to me again, and I thought of all the times

I had watched her flirt. I thought of her smile, and the tilt of her head, and how she would stand and sit and what her hands did.

I slid closer to him on the settee, aware suddenly of the people around us. Tilting my head to one side, as I had seen Eleanor do, I smiled at him. "I would love to hear what India is like."

He stared at me without blinking. "Hot."

I blinked enough for both of us. "Hot?"

"Yes. Hot."

My smile faltered, especially as I saw the amusement on the faces of the people listening to us.

"Yes, I understand that it is a warmer climate, Mr. Pritchard. But I was hoping you could tell me something more. You see, I plan to travel there myself, very soon." I remembered how Eleanor would lean toward a man she was interested in. So I leaned toward Mr. Pritchard.

A movement at the corner of my eye caught my attention. Henry was standing there, watching us with an unsmiling expression. In fact, his expression went beyond unsmiling. His jaw was set, his eyes like steel.

"You plan to go to India?" Mr. Pritchard surprised me by actually showing some expression on his face. "With whom?"

"With my aunt."

"Just the two of you? Alone?"

I nodded.

He looked from me to the people who were watching and listening to us, then chuckled, as if it was all a great joke. They smiled in return. Miss St. Claire smiled, and so did Sylvia, and an older couple whose names I could not remember. My face was hot. I felt sure I was the cause of those smiles and that laugh, but I could not guess why. The nervous-looking Mr. Dyer smiled the broadest of them all. I did not look at Henry to see his reaction.

"Why is that amusing to you, sir?" I forgot to smile and lean toward him.

"Two reasons." He held up his fingers and ticked them off one at a time. "Two single ladies. Going to India alone." He shook his head. "I have never heard of anything more foolish in my life." He shifted in his seat, as if dismissing me, and turned from me. But my pride would not let me lose.

"I do not think it foolish," I said, loud enough for everyone in the group to hear. "I think it is adventurous."

Mr. Pritchard turned back to me, with one eyebrow raised, and looked me over with disdain. He shifted again, but this time he leaned closer to me. Looking straight into my eyes, he said in a blunt voice, "India is no place for girls looking for adventure. It is a hostile country. The journey alone has a good chance of killing you. And if you are not lost at sea, you will probably die of some disease once you are there." His eyes drifted over my figure lazily. "You are not ugly. It would be better for you to get married and save the adventures for those suited to them."

He stood, straightened his jacket, and walked away from me. My face burned. I did not dare look at anyone, but I felt their gazes. I felt Henry's gaze, and I was so humiliated I did not think I would ever be able to meet it again. After sitting awkwardly for a long moment, I stood and walked away with as casual an air as I could force myself to adopt.

I did not know where to look or go. I knew only that I had to leave the group that had witnessed my humiliation at the hands of Mr. Pritchard. Crossing the room, I did not have a safe harbor in mind. But then, like a ray of sunshine, I saw the gaze of the elder Mr. Brandon. He was watching me from where he sat in a corner, far enough removed from the group that he could not have overheard my conversation.

Grasping my courage with desperate hands, I turned my steps to him. I would try once more. Mr. Pritchard had been cruel, and the nervous Mr. Dyer had clearly agreed with him. But Mr. Brandon was kind. I could see it in his eyes.

He stood as I approached, bowing to me, and offered with an outstretched arm the chair next to his. I smiled with relief. I had not erred in my judgment here. He was a kind man.

"Miss Worthington, you look rather flushed. Perhaps the fire was too warm for you?"

I pressed a hand to my hot cheek, thinking of how my face burned from embarrassment, not heat.

"Perhaps." I thought bravely of my bargain with Mama and my escape to India and the example of Eleanor. I would try again. I had to try again. I could not give it all up because of one man's rudeness. Sitting next to him, I smiled in the way Eleanor had smiled, and I leaned toward him, and I asked him to tell me about himself.

"I need to speak with you, Kitty." Sylvia stood before me. Her gloved hands were clenched into fists, and a warning blazed from her cool blue eyes.

I had just left speaking with the elder Mr. Brandon for the past hour. Acting like Eleanor had exhausted me, and the room was much too warm. Seeking the coolness of the hall, I had walked toward the doors when Sylvia intercepted me.

"Of course," I said, a little surprised by her demeanor.

I followed her out of the room, down the hall, and into the dining room, which had been cleaned after dinner and now sat empty. She closed the doors carefully behind us before whirling around to face me.

"How *could* you, Kitty?"

I fell back a step, startled. "How could I what?"

"How could you do this to me? After everything I have done for you?" Her face was a splotchy red, and tears made her eyes glisten.

Completely dumbfounded, I shook my head. "What have I done to you?"

She stepped toward me, pointed a finger at my chest, and said with a sob, "You have just spent the past hour trying to steal Mr. Brandon from me! After I told you I liked him! After I showed you the . . . the quote

. . . that he gave me." Her lips trembled. "The quote about me. Maybe you did not think it was significant, because he didn't write it himself, but I loved it! It was the sweetest thing any man has ever done for me, and I could easily fall in love with him, and you knew that, and you just sat there and—and—*flirted* with him, in the most obvious and disgusting manner!"

My mouth had dropped open at her first sentence and I stared at her, stunned. "You mean that paper was from the *elder* Mr. Brandon?"

"Of course it was!" She wiped at her cheeks. "Who else could it have been from?"

"The son, of course!" I was yelling now. I was horrified at what I had done, but I was appalled, too, that Sylvia had not imagined that there could have been some confusion on my part. "The man who is closer to your age! The handsome one!"

Her eyes opened wide with incredulity. "He is a *younger* son, Kitty. My children would never have a chance at inheriting anything. The father at least has a title, even if he is only a baron. Besides, I would never be interested in the son. He would drag me all over the countryside, talking about adventures and making me go places that I did not want to go. It would . . . it would be like being married to you! I would hate it!"

I reared back, feeling as if I had been struck. "I . . . I thought it was a compliment to me that you liked the son. I thought we . . ." I took a breath, and let it out with a feeling of great loss. "I thought we were the dearest of friends."

She was quiet for a long moment. "I think we were good childhood friends, Kitty. But we have been different now for quite some time."

I sighed and rubbed my forehead, feeling suddenly much too tired for this. "Kate. Please. Please, just once, call me Kate."

Her expression hardened again, and she looked at me with tightly closed lips.

"You never liked who I grew into, did you?" I asked, suddenly realizing the truth. "That is why you refuse to call me Kate."

She lifted one shoulder in a halfhearted shrug. She did not need to confirm it. I knew it was true. And with the knowledge came a heavy sense of loss.

"Never mind," I said. "It doesn't matter what you call me. I am so sorry I flirted with your Mr. Brandon. I had no idea. If it makes you feel any better, I don't think there is any chance of my having stolen him away from you. He kept looking your way."

"Really?" A small smile appeared.

"Yes. Really. Hopefully no permanent harm has been done."

I pulled out a chair and sat down heavily, feeling defeated. There went two of my prospects. Mr. Pritchard and Mr. Brandon both had to be crossed off my list. That left only the nervous Mr. Dyer, and I had no hope in him. I rested my chin on my hand. Sylvia pulled out the chair next to me and sat down, turning toward me. I could feel her gaze on my face, but I was too embarrassed to meet it.

"I have never seen you behave like that," she said in a quiet voice. "I have never seen you flirt with any man, much less two in one night. But watching you reminded me very much of someone else."

I covered my eyes with my hand, dreading her next words. I shook my head. "Don't say it."

"You looked very much like Eleanor in there. First, with Mr. Pritchard. And then with Mr. Brandon."

I closed my eyes tight and fought back tears.

"I need to know why you acted that way, Kitty. If you want to stay here, I need to understand."

Her words sounded like a threat. If I wanted to stay here? I dropped my hand and looked at her with disbelief. Would she really make me leave Blackmoore simply because I had flirted with two gentlemen? She met my gaze directly and did not look as if she was teasing.

"Very well. I will tell you why I flirted this evening, even though flirting is no great crime." I drew in a deep breath. "I made a bargain with

Mama. She will give me my freedom—my independence—to go to India if I receive and reject three marriage proposals."

Sylvia stared at me, then laughed, one short, mirthless laugh. "So you thought you could flirt with some gentlemen and then they would *propose* to you?"

My face burned again. "It has happened to other young ladies."

She was shaking her head, and her disbelief turned to something I hated even more: pity.

"I have to tell you something, Kit—Kate. And I am not telling you this because I'm upset with you. I am telling you this because I am your friend and you deserve to hear the truth."

Dread pooled within me. My heart picked up speed with nervousness. I was quite certain I did not want to hear whatever she had to say.

Leaning toward me, she looked into my eyes and said, "No man here will propose to you."

I flinched. My pride reared up. "You sound so sure of yourself, Sylvia." My voice sounded bitter. "How can you say that?"

"Because all of the people here are friends of my mother. And all of them know about Eleanor."

I blanched. "But that is old news. She is married now. She cannot hurt me anymore."

Sylvia shook her head, and her cool blue eyes were full of pity. "There are new rumors in London. I didn't want to tell you, but everyone in our set, the entire Ton, is whispering about her."

"But she is married," I said again, unable to think past that idea.

"Married women can cause as much scandal as unmarried ones," Sylvia said with a jaded look.

I dropped my head into my hands, feeling all hope leaving me.

"In fact, when Mama heard the rumors, she wrote to Henry and told him you could no longer come to Blackmoore. But Henry fought her, and I stood up for you, too, Kitty. I told her that you had never behaved like Eleanor, and you never would. I told her that our guests would have nothing to fear from your company . . . that they would not be tainted by any scandal while you were with us."

I breathed in and out, trying not to cry. "I only want to go to India. It's the only reason I did what I did."

She was silent for so long that I raised my head and looked at her. Condemnation was written all over her face—judgment and reproach and dismissal. "Even if there was a chance that you might succeed, I cannot believe you would use some unsuspecting man to get what you want. Did you not think of the moral implications of your plan? To use these men— to toy with their hearts—to lead them to fall in love with you, all the while knowing you would reject them! It's heartless. Absolutely heartless. And selfish and . . . and . . ." She sucked in a breath. "It sounds like your mother, to be honest. It sounds exactly like something she would do."

I flinched at the words she threw at me. "It does not," I said, my voice sounding savage. I pushed back my chair and stood, hands clenched into fists. "I am not my mother. I am never going to be like her. I can't believe you would say that. After all these years of knowing how I feel about her and knowing how loath I am to become like her! How could you say such a thing?"

She stared at me, her eyes filled with pain but her lips pressed tight. An apology would not escape, she seemed to say. She was separate from me. She looked at me as someone she pitied but not someone she cared for.

The truth of her words pounded at my soul, but I would not let them in, just as she would not let an apology out. We were beyond each other's reach, and after a long stretch of tension and silence and stubbornness from both of us, she looked over her shoulder at the door. At the way back to the world she belonged in.

"I should return to the guests. Mama will be wondering where I am."

She waited, shifting from one foot to another, and I felt a crack in my defenses—a weak place where truth knifed and twisted and pried for an opening. I could not bear to have her witness my vulnerability. I brushed past her and opened the door myself. I left her with a strong stride and a lifted chin and the injured pride of someone who would not admit her own mistakes.

But as soon as I opened the door to the second music room—the room I had claimed as my own, and the room with the stirring, silent bird in it—I lost everything that had been protecting me. I pressed the heels of my hands to my eyes as the truth found my weakness and expanded it and then poured in, blinding me with the pain of illumination. I had spent the last few years running away from becoming like my mother. But in my effort to escape my fate, I had become her. I had been willing to use others for my own gain. I had been willing to target the weakness of others—their hopes and dreams and the most tender feelings of their hearts—and manipulate them and trap them and then gut them. All for my own dream of India. And in that moment of illumination, I hated myself.

CHAPTER 12

Only one thing could soothe a soul as wretched as my own. I sneaked out of the second music room—the bird room, as I now thought of it—and found the back stairway I had discovered during my exploring earlier. I could not risk having any of the guests see me like this. I was not crying, but I was very, very close. Too close to allow my heart to remain in this vulnerable state.

I hurried up the two flights of stairs and down the maze of corridors until I reached the west wing, shivering with the chill of the wind seeping through the old stone walls. I stayed there only long enough to grab my Mozart from my room and then fled back down the stairs, hurrying faster and faster, feeling my heart crack open with the weight of all of my discoveries this evening.

When I ran back inside the bird room without being seen, I took only a moment to light the extra candles in the room, carrying one close to the pianoforte. I glanced over at the bird in his cage. He regarded me with solemn, bright eyes, turned his head, and flapped his wings. But he did not sing.

Then I spread my music across the top of the instrument and sat down. Closing my eyes, I told myself that I would silence my aching heart. I would banish the humiliation that burned within me. I would stop my frantic thoughts at what I had lost when I entered into a bargain with Mama. I would not think of how I had become like her. I would not feel despair at the truth. Mozart would fix all of this. Opening my eyes and taking a deep breath, I set my hands on the keys and began to play.

The notes of Mozart's Concerto No. 21 were designed to march. I always made them march, and in controlling those notes, I controlled my heart. This was how a heart was schooled. Discipline. Order. Reason. This was the essence of classicism.

But the little soldiers would not march tonight. As soon as I sat down to play, Sylvia's words flooded back to me. The humiliation doled out to me by Mr. Pritchard stung anew. And the realization that I had never had a chance to win my bargain with Mama—the realization that I would now have to give myself up to her will—darkened my soul with despair of the deepest kind.

I yearned for Mozart to fix all of this. I yearned for detachment and clarity. I played my concerto all the way through once and started over again. But my heart was heaving within my chest with despair and humiliation and the futility of everything I had attempted to make happen for myself. My heart shouted at me that no music could fix this—that no philosophy could make amends for losing this bargain with Mama. Nothing could undo the work I had done when I set out to become like her.

I struggled with the music, even as tears poured down my cheeks. I struggled with those little note soldiers, and with my heart, but the soldiers came loping out, or crashing into each other, or they fell sideways and would not stand in place.

"Stop!"

I jerked back from the keyboard, startled. My gaze flew to the man who strode across the room, waving his arms. "Stop! Stop this at once."

It was Herr Spohr, with his untamed hair and his thick German accent. He walked quickly, urgently, and came to me. "You must stop this, what you are doing. It is not right."

I stared at him, dumbfounded. He rubbed a hand over his head, breathing hard, as if he had just run all the way from the drawing room. Then he asked, in a gentle voice, "What are you doing, Fräulein?"

"I . . . am . . . playing. I am playing Mozart."

"No. This is not playing." He shook his head and waved his hands, as if trying to wipe away what he had just heard. "This is fighting. You are fighting this music."

He leaned over me, peering into my face. He had clear blue eyes, and for a moment I felt a thrill of fear. Here was someone who could see into my soul, I felt. And there was so much I did not want anyone to see.

"There is some war—some inner struggle—here." He tapped my chest just below the collarbone with two fingers. "The demon you fight is keeping you from making excellent music. You must find the right music for your struggle—for your demon." I could only look at him in confusion. I understood his English, but his words made no sense to my classically trained mind.

He tapped my chest again. "Find the music that sets this beast free. This beast that fights and struggles within you. You cannot subdue it. The music will suffer. You will suffer. Do you understand?"

I understood nothing. Perhaps he could see that bewilderment in my face, because he sighed and ran his hand over his hair, back and forth. "Mozart is not the answer for you. Mozart is hurting you." He leaned over and grabbed my music, pulling it to his chest. Then he bowed his head to me and said, "I am sorry, but I must take this away."

Without another word, he walked hurriedly across the room and out the door, leaving me bereft. I stared at the door, stunned, waiting for him to return and tell me it had all been a joke. But he did not reappear. I slid off the piano bench and walked numbly to the birdcage. Kneeling before the cage, I gazed at the dark, silent bird. I touched the gilded iron bars, softly, then ran my fingers up and down their length. My heart was breaking. There was no mending of this crack. It ran too deep.

My fingers curled around the iron bars of the cage, and I felt how this cage was as strong as it was decorative. And suddenly I hated it. I hated everything about the cage and everything about the cage of my own life. My rage rising within me, I rattled the bars without thinking. The bird flew madly in response, its wings a blur, beating against the bars. I reared back, startled, my heart racing. Feathers fell to the bottom of the cage.

"I'm sorry," I whispered to the frantic little thing. I leaned my forehead against the bars as tears rained down my face. "I'm sorry. I'm sorry. I'm sorry."

The floor was hard and cold under my knees, but I did not leave my vigil in front of the birdcage. It was both a tomb and a shrine to me—a symbol of what my life had become as well as an altar at which I prayed for deliverance. And I did not know how to leave this spot until I had regained some hope for my future.

I did not turn when I heard the door creak open. I did not turn when I heard my name, with a question in the voice. I did not turn as the footsteps came soft and measured and stopped right next to me. I kept my gaze trained on the bird, who had settled back onto its perch, but out of the corner of my eye I saw Henry lower himself to sit on the floor next to me.

"What did Sylvia tell you?" My voice was rough, my nose still stuffy from all the crying I had done.

"Sylvia? Nothing."

I glanced at him then. "Then why are you here?"

I should not have looked at him. His gaze was too gentle—too worried. It made my eyes well up with fresh tears. I could hardly breathe as it was. More tears would suffocate me.

"I overheard what Mr. Pritchard said to you. When you left and didn't return, I thought he might have upset you. So I looked for you." He glanced at the bird in its cage. "I should have known you would be here. I don't know why I didn't think to come here first."

I traced a gilded iron bar, from bottom to top, watching the dark bird inside as it solemnly watched me. "It doesn't sing," I said, almost to myself.

"I know." I heard the sadness—the compassion—in Henry's voice. "That's why I suggested my grandfather keep it in here, where it could at least hear music, even if it could make none of its own."

My gaze moved to his face. He was watching me, not the bird. His eyes were dark in the dim light, and his gaze held pain and worry and something else—some pull or temptation or battle that I could not name.

"He should not have spoken to you like that," he said in a voice threaded with anger. "I don't agree with your dream of going to India, but nobody should ever treat you with such derision, such . . . dismissal."

My face burned in remembered embarrassment.

"Should I call him out?" he asked.

I chuckled and blinked at unshed tears.

"I am in earnest." He rubbed his chin and narrowed his eyes. "We'll have a duel in the morning on the moors. Plenty of fog. It will be quite dramatic, I daresay. And I will shoot him to avenge your honor."

I laughed again and a little half-smile twisted his lips.

"No?" he asked, raising an eyebrow.

"No. But thank you." I drew in a rattled breath. "Besides, it was not Mr. Pritchard who upset me. Not really."

His eyes narrowed. "Then who?"

I immediately wished I could recall my last sentence. I was not prepared to admit to Henry my own shameful realization of what I had become. Nor was I willing to share with him the humiliation of my conversation with Sylvia. I wished he had never discovered me here. My nose ran, and I wiped it on my sleeve, for lack of a handkerchief.

Good heavens! I was behaving exactly like Maria! I was sitting in a strange place, crying, and letting my nose run and tears stream down my face. I shook my head, disgusted with myself. How had I sunk this low in just a few short days?

Pushing my hair back from my face, I said, "It was nobody. It was nothing."

"Kate, I have never seen you cry like this. Surely it was not *nothing*."

I shook my head. "I can't . . . I can't tell you, Henry." I watched the little dark bird, but all I was aware of was the weight of Henry's focused gaze on my face.

After a long moment of silence, he said, still in that low, quiet voice, "Do you remember that day in the woods? The day my father died?"

My gaze flew to his face. I caught my breath. I could not believe he was bringing that up, after all of these years of silence on the subject. We had never mentioned it since that day—not to each other. I had not spoken of it to anyone else, either, and I seriously doubted Henry had. And now, after all of this time . . .

"Of course," I whispered.

His gaze caught mine, and something built between us—some charge of emotion that made the distance between us measurable in movements: a shift, a leaning, an outstretched arm, a bent head. But we sat perfectly still, with only this memory connecting us.

Until he leaned forward and reached out a hand and touched my wrist. His hand moved up my arm, gently, until it rounded the curve of my shoulder. And only when he had anchored me there did he say, "I could never find the words to tell you what that meant to me." His voice was so soft and husky, like a caress. Something shivered within me. "Even now, after all of these years, I am at a loss. But on that day I promised myself that if I ever found you drowning—if I ever found you in need of saving—that I would do anything in my power to help you."

A tear slipped down my cheek and hung on the edge of my jaw. Henry moved his hand from my shoulder and brushed the tear away. Then he leaned back, away from me, and sighed. "But you do not confide in me." He lifted one eyebrow. "Perhaps I have not earned your confidence?"

My lips trembled, and with a shaky breath I said, "No. You have."

He sat there, waiting, as if he would wait all night long if he had to.

And suddenly, I had to tell him. Not what had happened with Sylvia, but what I was doing here, in front of this cage, crying. I wrapped my fingers around the bars of the cage again, but this time I did not shake it. I did not want to scare the bird again. But the bird took flight anyway, and suddenly words were forcing themselves up my throat and pouring out of my mouth.

"I feel caged. Always. I feel like I am this bird, trapped and stifled and caged, and I keep looking for a way to escape, but I am barred at every turn." I drew in a breath, and looking at the confusion on Henry's face, I said, "Perhaps you cannot comprehend—you are a man. Your life is different in so many ways. But have you ever . . ." I drew in a deep breath, feeling my heart aching. "Have you ever wanted something so much it hurt? That the wanting actually caused you physical pain?"

He was perfectly still, watching me with those dark eyes. "Yes," he said in a quiet, solemn voice.

"That is how I feel about India. I want to go so badly the wanting hurts. But I am afraid that I won't ever go, and I'm afraid that I will never realize this dream, and if I don't realize *this* dream, then it's possible I won't realize any dream. And I'll just live a bleak, dreamless life without adventure or joy or choice or—or—*living*." My breath caught. "When I think about it—when I think about how *stuck* I am, and what is expected of me, and what I am allowed and not allowed to do, and how little power I have or will ever have, simply because I was born a girl—I feel a million wings inside of me, beating so hard it hurts."

Now my voice wavered as fresh tears spilled out. "And I cannot even play Mozart without Herr Spohr telling me it is wrong for me, and if I cannot have India or Mozart, then what am I left with? How am I going to live inside this cage that is my life?" I shook my head, feeling wild and undone, as tears streamed down my face. "All I can think is that I will end up like this poor bird. I will beat myself against the bars of my cage until I am too exhausted, and then I will give up and live the rest of my life without a song and inside a forgotten room."

My voice cracked, and I pressed my lips together, sealing off any more words that wanted to be set free. I could not look Henry in the eye as I struggled to control my emotions. It was silly—comparing my sorrow at losing my dream of India to Henry's sorrow at losing his father. It was silly of me to feel so deeply about this. That was what I supposed Henry thought. He had never understood my desire to go to India. And I was suddenly, achingly afraid that he would dismiss my words or fail to understand their sentiment or dismiss my dream as something trivial.

Instead, he said, in a careful voice, "So you are this bird. In this cage."

I nodded.

"And you see only one option for yourself: to beat yourself against the bars until you are exhausted and give up all your dreams."

I nodded again, and then dared to look at him. He was watching me with an expression of compassion mixed with affection. After a long moment of looking at me, he looked back at the dark bird in its cage. Then he did something with the cage—some small movement that made the door swing open. He reached inside, and I held my breath as I watched him catch the bird. He was so careful, and so gentle, as he cupped it in his hands and pulled it free of its cage.

Henry turned to me, holding out his hands.

I stared at him and then at the bird, which was fluttering and struggling to be free.

"Here. Take it." He held the bird toward me, cupped in his fine, gentle hands.

I hesitantly reached out. I slipped my hands inside of Henry's, until my fingers curved around the small bird. The glossy black feathers felt like silk beneath my fingers, and I felt the fragile bones underneath and the stirring of wings wanting to fly.

"Do you have it?" Henry asked.

I nodded, my breath coming fast with nervousness. Then Henry pulled his hands away, and I held it alone. I felt its eagerness to fly, its quick movements, the swift, thrumming beat of its heart. I opened my hands. And it flew.

The bird took flight with a flurry of wings and an almost frantic speed. As I watched it wheel overhead I felt suddenly, sharply alive. I laughed for a reason I couldn't explain. I looked at Henry, who was watching me with a smile.

"There has to be more than one option in life, Kate," he said. "There just has to be."

I leaned against the wall and tipped my head back and watched the dark bird soar while Henry's words turned over and over in my mind.

He leaned against the wall, next to me, arms touching.

"We will have to catch it," I said. "And return it to its cage." I looked at the high ceiling and wondered how catching that bird would be done. "Not an easy task, I think."

"No. But worth it."

After a long stretch of quiet between us, I whispered, "Thank you. For the bird."

I found myself leaning against Henry, the late night leeching my energy from me, until my head rested against his shoulder. Neither of us moved, and our silence was deep and comfortable as we watched our little dark bird fly and fly and fly.

When the clock chimed twelve, I forced myself to move. I straightened and yawned. "How are we going to catch him? I assume your grandfather cares about him."

"Let him have a night of freedom. I'll come take care of him in the morning."

I watched sleepily as Henry went around the room and blew out all the candles but one, which he picked up and took with us as we left the room. He closed the door carefully behind us. The house was dark and completely silent except for the creaking of the stairs beneath our feet.

We walked in silence to the west wing, and when we reached my room I felt a nagging sensation—as if there was a solution to my problem right in front of me, which I could not see. But the harder I tried to peer at it, the fuzzier it became. Henry stopped before my door and opened it quietly. "Good night, my little bird," he murmured, so softly I wondered if I imagined the little bird part, or the tender note in his voice.

I stood in the open doorway of my room and watched him walk down the hall. He did not hurry this time. And I did not move until the light he carried with him slipped around the corner, leaving me in darkness. Only then did I face my quiet room and the fears I was left with.

It was one thing to set a bird free. But how on earth was I supposed to set myself free? I lay awake, listening to the moans and creaks and the wind blowing off the ocean and across the moors. I thought of my bargain with Mama, and hopelessness overwhelmed me again. Over and over I vacillated between images of the rabbit caught in the trap and the dark bird flying free, feeling despair, then a glimmer of hope, until I could no longer sort through my own thoughts or feelings. And finally, exhausted and spent, I fell into a troubled sleep.

CHAPTER 13

I awoke to birdsong. My room was shrouded in darkness, and in my restless sleep the bedcovers had wrapped around my legs, cocooning me in dark plum. I kicked myself free of them, then shivered as I hurried across the cold wood floor to pull aside the drapes and throw open the window.

Fog blanketed my view to the right and the left, covering the ground like another cocoon. The sun had not yet risen, but there were signs that it was on its way—the brightening of the sky in the east and the calls of the birds. Resting my elbows on the windowsill, I leaned out and breathed in the wet, cold air. I closed my eyes and listened for the songs I knew— the blackbird and the swallow and the woodlark, the sparrow and the thrush and the goldfinch. But I had traveled far from home, and the birds here on the edge of the land sang songs that were new to me.

Pulling my head in, I shut the window and hurried to dress. I had to be quick, before the sun rose and quieted some of these birds. Throwing on my warmest clothes, I did not bother with my hair and put my boots on while I ran down the hall, hopping one-footed as I bent over and tugged. Then I ran down the stairs, and did not bother to look for a back door. I ran straight through the great entry hall and out the tall front doors.

The fog folded me into itself, its chill, wet fingers creeping around me. I walked straight west, which I knew would lead me toward the moors, as the ocean bordered the east side of the house. The land was obscured in white, but when I felt the dry crunch of heather beneath my feet, I knew I was in the right place.

A large outcropping of rock rose out of the mist, and I turned my steps toward it. The navy sky lightened to a clear, light blue as I walked. The bracken and heather, wet with dew and fog, brushed my skirts. Horses neighed from pastures far away. It was the birds I was really listening to, though.

When I reached the rock, I paused only long enough to look for a way to climb it. It was larger than I had thought at first from a distance. It rose like a jagged, wind-carved castle, and I had to tip my head back to see the top of it. I slipped twice on its wet surface, but grabbing hold with my hands, I pulled myself to its top. Sitting on my perch, I folded my hands in my lap and breathed in the chilly air and watched the fog grow thin while birdsong sounded all around me. There were chirps and squeaks, cluckings and whirrings and sweet, high, piercing whistles. I knew none of them.

Sitting atop that rock in the middle of the moors, surrounded by an unfamiliar land and unfamiliar birds, I felt small. Or rather, I felt the vastness of what I did not know, had not experienced, had never seen. It frightened me to realize how little I actually knew of the world. It frightened me because I had no idea how to fulfill my bargain with Mama. I had no plan for earning my freedom. And if I could not earn my freedom, then my world would always be precisely this small.

The sky had a pink and peach cast to it now, and I knew the sun would show itself soon. Soon the fog would burn off the land and leave everything clear. But I could not fathom how the uncertainties of my future could be burned away—how I could see my way clearly from here to a new life in India with Aunt Charlotte.

Henry had said there had to be more than one option in life. But the fact was I had bound myself to Mama. I had entered into a bargain that I could not win. I could not win it either practically, nor could I win it ethically. I could not come up with three gentlemen here who would propose to me. That left me in my mother's power, and regret at my hasty bargain threatened to turn me inside out. I closed my eyes and wished I could go back in time and undo the pact I had made. Why had I given her such an open option with the outcome? Because I could not anticipate failing. Now, though, I shrank inside at the thought of what she might do once she learned of my failure.

A few obvious ideas came to mind. She could force me to marry Mr. Cooper. She could send me to live with Eleanor in London and take care of her children. She could even come up with some scheme, as she had for Eleanor in Brighton. I shuddered at the thought of what she might dream up. There were no bounds to her opportunism and no moral limits either.

A familiar whistle caught my ears. I tilted my head, listening hard, and heard it again. It was a blackbird, with its call of homecoming. A smile crept across my face. I cupped my hands around my mouth and whistled back. A moment later the call came again. We called back and forth, and I peered through the fog for Henry's figure. He never came, though, and after a long stretch of waiting I realized, to my chagrin, that it must have been a real blackbird I had been hearing.

I sighed, leaned back on my hands, and tipped my face up to the lightening sky. A thought nudged at my conscious. A hint of a thought, even. Some sense that there was a solution to my problem and that I would find it if I just thought about it long enough and hard enough.

I replayed in my mind the conversation I had had with Mama in her bedroom. She had wanted me to commit to marrying—I had insisted I never would. I had shouted at her, I remembered. I had asked her how many proposals I would have to refuse before she believed that I was serious about never marrying. *Three.* I sat up straight. Was I sure those were our words? I thought carefully. The conversation felt burned into my memory. It was too significant—I would not remember it wrong. Yes. I was certain. I had asked about proposals. She had given me the number three. I did not have to convince three gentlemen to propose to me; I had only to receive three *proposals.*

Hope and relief surged through me, as light and free as the dark bird soaring outside its cage. I needed only one man who would be willing to propose to me three times, one man who was friend enough to grant me this favor. A smile flashed across my face.

But almost immediately, the flying of my hope faltered. My heart sickened. Could I do such a thing? Could I really ask Henry to propose to me? And if he agreed to this scheme, could I endure the agony of hearing him say the words I had craved for so long, knowing that I would have to refuse him?

Dread roiled around within me, tugging at the parts of my heart that I had shut tight. I gripped my wind-blown hair in one hand and rested my forehead in the other. Danger lived in this scheme. Not for Henry—he had his path set out ahead of him. He had his Miss St. Claire and his Blackmoore and the living of this estate to provide him with lifelong comfort and respectability. He would not suffer from granting me this favor. But, oh, it was very possible that I would suffer.

I lifted my head and shoved the thought away, quickly, before it had time to take root. Nothing bad would happen. This was my escape! This was the answer to all my problems, and my heart was in no danger. I had locked it up tight a year and a half before. It was secure. It would do exactly what I demanded of it. After all, I had seen Henry practically every day of these past eighteen months, and never had I faltered in my resolve. Not once had I questioned my decisions or done anything to weaken them—not by touch or word or deed. I could ask Henry for three proposals. He would do that for me. And then I would have my dream of India.

Excitement surged so fast and furious within me that I felt in danger of breaking into flight. I stood up from my perch and clambered down the outcropping of stone. My feet slipped on the slick rock. My hands scraped. I skidded and slid, and the ground rushed up much too fast.

A quick thudding reached my ears as I scrabbled for a handhold and caught myself, legs swinging free. Looking over my shoulder, I checked the ground below, and finding it within reach, dropped to my feet, brushed off my hands, and turned with a smile.

Mr. Brandon—the younger Mr. Brandon—stood not more than a yard away, a look of great surprise on his face.

"Oh!" I was startled and couldn't think of anything more to say.

"That was brilliant!" A slow smile curved his lips, and admiration gleamed in his eyes. "I was running to save you, but apparently I could have spared myself the effort."

His footsteps must have been the thudding sound I had heard as I started slipping down the rock.

"Yes. Well . . ." I rubbed my forehead, feeling awkward, and wondered how rude it would seem if I were to just walk away. But he looked as if he was waiting for some sort of explanation. So I shrugged. "I climb out of windows a lot."

His full smile was beyond infectious—it was stunning, especially with the sunlight that finally shone through the fog, highlighting his brown hair with gold.

"Do you really?" he asked, moving closer to me.

I pushed my tangled hair back, thinking of how I had come to the moors straight from bed, how the wind had been whipping my hair, and how I must have looked at least bedraggled, if not worse.

But the admiring gleam did not leave the younger Mr. Brandon's eyes, which were, I noticed, almost exactly the same laurel green as the vegetation surrounding us. His smile felt like an extra dose of sunshine directed at me.

"And why do you climb out of windows *a lot,* Miss Worthington?"

I felt my face grow warm. I suddenly remembered what Sylvia had told me the night before—about how everyone thought so little of me because of my family's reputation. I remembered how she had laughed at the idea that any man here would ever propose to me. And while I had never acted scandalous, I had certainly not tried very hard to act proper this morning.

But just as I squirmed inside with the embarrassment of all of these realizations, one clear, redeeming thought came to mind. I had discovered my other option. I would escape here with Henry's help and go to India and I would never have to see this Mr. Brandon or his father again. I would never have to be ashamed to be a Worthington. My sister's scandals would not touch me there, and my aunt Charlotte would understand me. I would never have to try for a man's attention again.

I smiled with relief—with pure, unfettered happiness at the thought of the freedom and independence that lay within my grasp. And I decided I did not care one jot what this Mr. Brandon thought of me. I answered him honestly.

"I frequently feel the need to escape."

Both eyebrows lifted. "And the window is your chosen avenue of escape? A door does not suffice?"

A wistful smile twisted my lips. "Sometimes a window is the only adventure to be had for a young lady, Mr. Brandon."

He stepped even closer, and now I could see the faint stubble along his jaw line, and I had to admit that he was handsome. He was very handsome, in fact.

"You become more interesting by the moment, Miss Worthington." His eyes were saying the same thing, as he studied me with such intensity that I blushed and worried once again about my disheveled appearance. "Are you a great adventurer, then? Is that what has drawn you out of the house at this early hour?"

"Nothing so interesting, I am afraid." I smiled. "I only came out to listen to the birds. They are different from our birds in Lancashire. Obviously." He was staring at me as if I was some strange creature he had never before encountered. What *did* my hair look like? I pushed it out of my face, but the wind blew it back around, whipping at my hair and my skirts and causing the heather to sway and the long grass to undulate like waves in the sea. Backing away from Mr. Brandon, gesturing over my shoulder in the direction I thought the house was in, I said, "I should return to the house. If you will excuse me—"

"No, I will not."

I stopped and stared at him. "Pardon me?"

He shook his head. "No. You cannot tell me you came out here to listen to birds and then leave me with nothing but curiosity."

I laughed uncertainly. "It is not such an unusual thing, I am sure, to like birds."

"Oh no, I am sure it is not. Who does not like birds?" His voice lowered and grew more intimate as he said, "But you came out onto the moors before sunrise to listen to birds. And that, Miss Worthington, makes you fascinating."

His words, his smile, and the look in his eyes, all combined, surprised me and robbed me of speech. I could only stare at him, while he smiled at me, and a blush crept up my face.

"You look surprised," he said in a soft voice.

I laughed. I did not know what else to do. "I am sorry. I am not accustomed to people finding my interest in birds *fascinating*."

His smile stretched wide. "All the better for me, then."

"And what do you do out here, Mr. Brandon, so early in the morning?"

He breathed in deeply and lifted his face to the sky, where the sun had just sprung over the horizon in all its golden glory. "I came outside to explore. It's my first time on the moors, you see. And to be in such a location—to have both the ocean and the moors at once—it's rather . . ." His gaze settled on me. "It's rather ideal, is it not?"

I nodded, agreeing with his sentiment. The sunlight grew stronger, the light changed, and I changed my mind about his eye color. They were not the green of the moors. They were the green of the trees at home. He was golden in the dawn light—golden hair and skin and light stubble across his jaw and chin. He was tall, I realized—probably as tall as Henry.

And I suddenly wondered how Sylvia could overlook the son and like the father instead.

He gestured to his left. "Shall we walk back together? I am quite famished after all of my exploring, and I imagine you must be as well, after your own adventure."

I walked beside him. After a moment I cleared my throat. "Speaking of my adventure, do you mind not telling the others about that? I'm afraid some would not approve."

He looked quickly at me, his brow furrowed, but only smiled. "I am happy to share a secret with you, Miss Worthington." I hardly had time to think of his words before he said, "Now. Tell me about your birds."

I looked at him, the wind blowing my hair around my face. "What about them?"

"Everything. Something. What interests you?"

"Their songs. Their natures." I glanced at him, wondering if he was really as interested as he sounded. But his gaze hardly strayed from my face, and the expression on his face was no less than fascinated. Very few people actually gave me an invitation to talk about my interest in birds, and I found myself suddenly eager to talk. "They are deceptive, as a group. One might think that all birds are similar, but they are quite unique from one species to another."

He nodded, so I went on.

"Each bird's song is identifiable. Their calls are so much more complex than tweets or chirps. The blackbird, for example, sounds like this." I produced the whistle that Henry and I had spent hours perfecting one rainy day a few years ago.

His eyebrows lifted. "That was you, earlier. Wasn't it? I heard that whistle out on the moors."

I nodded. "Well, one of the whistles was mine. One was . . . an actual bird. I suppose." I thought again of how disappointed I had been when Henry had not walked out of the fog.

"What is your favorite bird?" Mr. Brandon asked.

I waved his question away. "That is impossible to answer."

His smile flashed. "Very well. Tell me about *one* of your favorites."

I thought for a moment before answering. I would have told him about the woodlark. But I felt that I would be somehow betraying Henry to talk about the woodlark.

The dry heather gave way to the green grass surrounding Blackmoore. The sun was fully up now, the golden light and heat burning off the fog, little by little. Mr. Brandon stopped walking and faced me, waiting.

I stopped too and thought of the birds I loved. Finally I answered. "The mistle thrush."

"What about it?"

I looked a question at him.

He waved a hand, as if urging me to continue. "What makes that bird one of your favorites?

He asked it as if he was genuinely interested in my thoughts about birds. It seemed so strange to me.

"Er . . . well . . . If you really want to know . . ."

"I do."

"For one thing, if one sees it from above, it looks like it's wearing a smooth grey coat. But its chest and belly are speckled. White with dark grey speckles that look quite festive. As if it is going to a party. You might think it a proper and boring creature, until you see those jaunty speckles, and then you know that you misunderstood it initially. You underestimated it." I drew a breath. "But I think what I like most about the mistle thrush is how . . . audacious it is. It perches at the top of very large trees and sings into the face of a storm. As if daring the storm to frighten it. As if trying to prove that it can outsing a gale. It is so very brave." I smiled and shrugged. "I admire it."

He was studying me with a look I could not interpret. He almost seemed to look at me in the same way I looked at my birds. I suddenly felt transparent and crossed my arms over my chest. "Do you think it strange? That I admire a bird?"

"Not at all," he said briskly. "In fact, I have suddenly become very interested in birds myself."

The wind blew off the ocean, throwing my hair across my face in a tangled mess. I pushed it back and held it with one hand, turning so the wind blew my hair behind me. "Speaking of gales . . ." I said.

"Yes. Let's go inside," Mr. Brandon said and walked beside me across the green and the courtyard and through the front doors of Blackmoore. I crossed the great entry hall, eager to get upstairs and make myself look decent before anyone else saw me in this state. At the curve of the staircase, I could look up and see the painting of Phaeton on the domed ceiling. Or I could look down into the entry hall below me. I looked down. And standing there still, looking up at me, stood Mr. Brandon, with that infectious smile on his face. And I could not help but smile in return.

It was clear he saw my answering smile. My face burned for a reason I could not name, and I hurried to turn away and hide my blush from him. I saw only a blur before I bumped into someone standing right behind me.

"Oh! Pardon me!" I said, gripping the banister to regain my balance.

Mrs. Delafield reared back. "Do watch where you're going, Kitty."

"I'm so sorry. I didn't see you."

Mrs. Delafield turned her chilly blue eyes to my face, then her gaze traveled upward and settled on my hair. "Have you been *outdoors,* Kitty?"

"Kate," I reminded her, resisting the urge to smooth my hair. "And yes, I have been."

She sighed and looked upward, as if seeking divine help. "I must speak with you about acceptable behavior while you are here."

I could not stop myself from glancing over my shoulder. I felt a lecture coming, and I did not want Mr. Brandon to overhear it. But he stood below, still looking up, and Mrs. Delafield's voice carried clearly across the domed space between us.

Mrs. Delafield stepped forward, looked over the railing, and her hand gripped the wooden banister, the veins on the back of her hands bulging.

"Mr. Brandon." Her voice was the epitome of strained politeness. "Good morning. I trust you slept well."

"Indeed." His smile changed from the infectious width I had just admired, becoming more controlled, more strictly polite.

I edged away from the banister. "If you will excuse me, Mrs. Delafield . . ."

"Kitty, I would like to have a word with you."

I paused and watched with a growing sense of dread as she drew close to me. Leaning toward me, she whispered, "Were you outside with Mr. Brandon? Alone? Did you two have some sort of . . . *assignation*?"

"Of course not," I whispered back, appalled. "We ran into each other outside, but I did not plan to meet him there."

Her eyes narrowed, a warning in their blue depths. "There will be no scandal here, Kitty. Not like at Brighton."

I burned with the shame of her implication. "I am not Eleanor, Mrs. Delafield. I never have been."

I turned my back on her and climbed the stairs with an air of calm I did not feel. As I turned the corner, the temptation to look down overcame me. Against my better judgment, I looked over the railing. Mrs. Delafield had descended the stairs and was crossing the foyer to Mr. Brandon. She was nearly to him now. He glanced up at me with a frown and then turned to her, as she took his arm and spoke quietly in his ear.

My face was on fire, imagining what she was telling him about me. But I shoved from my thoughts the lingering shame I felt and turned my steps to the west wing. It did not matter to me what Mr. Brandon thought of me. I was going to find Henry and get my three proposals and leave at once for India. Nobody would be able to look down on me there. Nobody would exclude me or try to control me. India would solve everything.

CHAPTER 14

I needed to speak with Henry. The hope of my escape—the open door to my cage—worked such nervous energy within me that I could not be still. I had to speak with him. I had to ask him if he would grant me this favor, if he would release me from my cage. But when I found him in the dining room at breakfast, I could not speak to him alone. And I was certainly not going to ask him to propose to me while others were around to hear.

At least half the company was assembled in the dining room. The room was loud with chatter and the clanking of silverware. I stood inside the doorway and scanned the company, trying to decide where to sit. He threw me a questioning glance, and I remembered how he had left me last night, when I had sunk into the depths of despair. I smiled to let him know that I was no longer despairing. He looked content and turned away before I could signal to him that although I was not on the verge of tears, I desperately needed to speak with him alone.

Frustrated, I picked at my breakfast and watched Henry's conversation with Herr Spohr with growing impatience. Sylvia entered the room, and I caught her eye as she sat across the table from me.

My cheeks grew warm as I remembered how we had spoken to each other the night before. Her glance at me was fleeting and hesitant. I wasn't sure how to behave. She had been blunt to the point of cruelty the night before, and I was half surprised she had not come to apologize to me before breakfast. Miss St. Claire sat beside her and leaned over Herr Spohr to tell Henry good morning.

Henry smiled at her and I looked away, disgusted.

And then Mr. Brandon entered the room. His gaze fell on me. I met it briefly, struggled to hold it, and then glanced away. I was sure that he intended to snub me—sure that Mrs. Delafield had poisoned him against me. But when I glanced up again he was crossing the room with long, easy strides that reminded me of how he had looked walking across the moors. He stopped beside my chair and gestured at the empty seat next to mine.

"May I join you, Miss Worthington?"

I sat up in my chair and looked at him with surprise. "Of course you may."

He sat next to me, pulling his chair closer to mine than it had been, and turned toward me, ignoring everyone else in the room.

"You have put your hair up," he said, in such a quiet voice it was almost a whisper. I touched my neck self-consciously, remembering how wild I had looked on the moors this morning. His gaze roamed over my face, and then he said, still quietly, but matter-of-factly, "You are quite beautiful. But never more than you were this morning on the moors."

My face burned. I looked fleetingly across the table. Henry was staring at me, and so was Sylvia.

I cleared my throat and looked back at Mr. Brandon, at his clear green eyes looking directly into mine. "You have robbed me of speech, Mr. Brandon."

"That would be a shame if it were true, Miss Worthington." He flashed me his wide smile and then turned his attention to the other side of the table. "Good morning, Miss Delafield, Mr. Delafield, Miss St. Claire."

Murmured responses and surprised looks met his greetings.

"I believe we had planned last night on a picnic to the ruined abbey today, and it looks like a perfect day for it." Mr. Brandon looked from the others to me, and his eyes were lit up with excitement. "We should all go."

So. Whatever Mrs. Delafield had told him, it had not resulted in the snubbing I expected. A smile tugged at my lips, and I lowered my gaze so that Mr. Brandon would not see how happy his invitation made me.

"It looks like rain," Henry said, his voice curt.

I turned around in my seat and looked out the window. The sky was clear blue and the fog had burned off with the morning sun.

"Does it?" I said, turning back around and frowning at him.

He frowned back at me and then looked down at his plate, stabbing his fork into a piece of ham before attacking it with his knife.

"I think a picnic sounds lovely," Miss St. Claire said, smiling at Henry and trying to angle her face so as to catch his eye. But he was glowering at his plate and would not look at her.

"Will your father be joining us?" Sylvia asked.

"Of course! The more the merrier, I say." There seemed to be no limit to Mr. Brandon's enthusiasm for his plan. "What about it, Henry? Can you have your excellent kitchen staff put together a picnic for us?"

Henry pushed his plate away. "Of course I can, Mr. Brandon." He looked at me, and his eyes were hard like flecks of granite, something like accusation in his expression. "If you all are eager to go along with this plan."

I lifted an eyebrow. "Why would we not be? It sounds like a fun adventure."

He shrugged, shoved his chair back from the table, and stood. "Then we shall meet in the foyer at noon." He nodded briefly to us before walking away without another word.

I watched his retreating back and wondered what he had against Mr. Brandon's plan. I tried to remember if Henry had ever mentioned a ruined abbey to me. He had spent hours telling me stories of Blackmoore. Or rather, he had spent hours answering my questions about Blackmoore.

But I could not remember ever hearing him tell of a ruined abbey. I wondered why.

The walk across the moors to the ruined abbey was fraught with awkwardness. Sylvia still had not spoken to me since our conversation the night before. She stayed apart the entire walk, placing herself close to the elder Mr. Brandon. Miss St. Claire had a very firm grip on Henry's arm and seemed intent on never leaving his side. Henry did not smile or laugh—he did not look at all like he was enjoying himself, and he had not spoken to me either. The only person, in fact, who seemed at all inclined to talk to me was the younger Mr. Brandon, who was full of enthusiasm for everything about the day, the weather, the walk, the food we would be eating, the sky, the ocean, and anything else that caught his attention.

We walked in the middle of the group, with Henry and Miss St. Claire at the front and Sylvia and the elder Mr. Brandon bringing up the rear. Servants led two ponies that carried the materials for our picnic. The sun shone down on us in a clear blue sky, but the wind whipped at our bonnets and hats and skirts. We followed a rough trail through the heather and bracken, and it suddenly struck me that neither of my two best friends was speaking to me.

This was not the way this visit was supposed to go. We were supposed to be here together at Blackmoore, at last, and we were supposed to enjoy every moment, and there was not supposed to be any awkward silence or strangers coming between us. Anger and frustration rose up within me until I hated the sight of Henry's back and Miss St. Claire's arm tucked through his. I hated Sylvia's silence.

We topped a rise in the moors, and I could see the ruined abbey stretched below us. I caught my breath and my feet slowed, then stopped, as I took in the sight. The scattered towers and crumbled walls and arched, blackened window openings rose in a sea of green grass. It was so very lovely, in a wild and ruined way.

When I pulled my gaze away, I found Henry watching me, a look of expectation in his eyes.

"There it is!" Mr. Brandon called next to me. "The ruined abbey! Come, Miss Worthington! Let us be the first to explore it!" He grabbed hold of my hand and pulled me along, grinning back at me with his wide smile. His hand felt strong and warm wrapped around mine. And I did not mind the feeling at all.

Rooks wheeled about in the sky, claiming the highest tower as their own. Their calls were harsh and vulnerable at the same time, their black shapes foreboding above me. The abbey was magnificent. The building itself was magnificent, but its ruin was magnificent also. I was drawn to the crumbling stone, the roofless walls, and the blank, blackened windows.

After exploring for half an hour, we sat in the shade of one of the towers. Our picnic was placed before us on the blanket we sat on. The sun slipped behind a cloud, and the wind cast a chill over us. It was not just the wind that chilled the outing, though. It was Henry's silence and his accusing looks whenever I met his gaze. I wanted nothing more than to pull him aside and ask him what he had to accuse me of. And then I wanted Henry my friend back so that I could ask him to grant me my wish and make it possible for me to go to India.

I nibbled on a cucumber sandwich while listening with only half my attention to Mr. Brandon's exclamations about the glory of the ruins. He had not left my side during the entire outing. Miss St. Claire had done the same with Henry. Now she sat beside him, and I watched how thoughtfully she treated him. I watched how she noticed the food on his plate and offered him more strawberries and poured his lemonade before the servant had a chance to wait on him. I watched her gaze settle affectionately on his face when he spoke. I watched the elegance of her actions and heard the lilt of her laugh and noted that even the dirt did not seem to want to spoil her white gown.

She was too good. I wanted to hate her, yet to hate her would be a greater condemnation of my own faults than of hers.

I did not want to watch Miss St. Claire and Henry any longer. Brushing off my hands, I sat up and said, "Henry, tell us about the smugglers here."

He looked at me. "What about them?"

"Aha! You admit there *are* smugglers! I have finally caught you!"

He smiled at me. It was the first smile he had given me all day, and the force of it made me catch my breath. "You infer too much," he said.

"Are there truly smugglers in these parts?" the younger Mr. Brandon asked.

A look of irritation flashed over Henry's face, and his smile vanished completely. He looked ready to say something curt to Mr. Brandon, but Sylvia spoke up before he could.

"We always hear rumors of smuggling, especially in Robin Hood's Bay. But there is nothing to worry about now. Mother would never stand for anything inappropriate happening at Blackmoore."

"I surely hope so," Miss St. Claire said, her large green eyes opened even wider than usual.

The elder Mr. Brandon nodded his head and offered another sandwich to Sylvia, which she accepted with a bashful smile. Henry said nothing. He only continued to frown at the younger Mr. Brandon, who had just asked me if I would like to explore the ruins some more.

I watched Henry from the corner of my eye as his jaw clenched and he scowled at the rooks wheeling above us. I wondered what about this lovely day had put him in such a foul temper. I stood and brushed the grass from my skirt. "I would like that very much, Mr. Brandon," I said.

But it was a lie. What I would really have liked was for all of these strangers to go away and leave me here alone with Henry and the ruins and the birds.

The walk to the ruined abbey, the exploration of its crumbling form, the picnic, and the return to Blackmoore took the greater part of the afternoon. As pleasant as Mr. Brandon's company was, I wished the whole time for the company of only Henry and Sylvia. But not Henry and Sylvia as they were behaving today: angry and cold, respectively. I wanted the Henry and Sylvia who had been my dearest friends all my life. What had happened to us? And how had it happened in such a short time?

And then there was the need to speak to Henry alone. I had to ask him for my proposals. This day, just as much as last night, solidified the rightness of my decision to leave. There was no happy life for me here. Sylvia would marry and move away. Henry would marry Miss St. Claire, and they would live together at Blackmoore, and I would most likely never see him again. And I would be left home, alone, with no prospects and no independence. No. It was India or a caged life.

But Henry was impossible to speak to alone. At every opportunity when I might have had a quiet word with him, Miss St. Claire was at his side, finding a reason to touch his arm, or smile at him, or find an errant streak of sunlight to illuminate the copper in her hair. She was altogether too pretty, and worse than that, she seemed to know it.

By the time we returned to Blackmoore, it was time to dress for dinner. And dinner was a grand affair with all forty guests in the grand dining room. I was seated next to Herr Spohr, far down the table from Henry and Sylvia. I did not mind, though, as I had something important to ask of him.

"Herr Spohr, I believe we had some sort of misunderstanding last night. When you took my music away from me."

I watched him chew a piece of roasted duck. He chewed it for what seemed a long time while I awaited his response. I had to have misunderstood his intentions last night. Gentlemen did not walk around confiscating the belongings of young ladies. His behavior was so highly irregular. Surely there was some explanation for it.

He finally swallowed, looked at me briefly, and shook his head. "No. Mozart is not good for you."

"But it belongs to me. You cannot just take something that belongs to someone else."

He speared another piece of duck. "It is for your own good, meine kleine Vogel. Trust me."

At a loss, I shook my head and would have felt inclined to resent his heavy-handed attitude, were it not for the rather charming combination of his wild hair and his German accent and the term he called me. Little bird. And I did feel rather in awe of him—a real composer. A professional musician. I respected him, despite his unorthodox methods of separating young musicians from their musical geniuses.

"Do you know Faust, Miss Worthington?"

I sat up straight. "What?"

"Faust." He regarded me steadily, his eyes a deep blue.

My heart lurched in my chest. My gaze darted across the room, to where Henry sat at the head of the table with Miss St. Claire at his right hand. His gaze was down, his dark hair shone in the candlelight, and he occupied that seat of authority with a casual grace that could not be taught, only earned. I looked away and tried not to think of the morning I had first heard of Faust. I nodded. "Yes. A little."

"What do you know?" Herr Spohr had set down his fork and was regarding me with the unwavering attention of a tutor for his pupil.

"Faust was a brilliant man who yearned for more than he already had. He struck a bargain with the devil—with Mephistopheles. He bargained away his soul in exchange for greater wisdom, greater favors, greater accomplishments."

"And in the end?" Herr Spohr prompted.

I swallowed. "In the end, he lost his soul."

Herr Spohr nodded, his hair flopping with the movement. "Yes, Fräulein. That is good. You know the important things. The ambition. The restlessness. The greed. The great struggle for more." He rubbed a hand over the top of his head. "I wrote an opera about him, you know. About Faust." He picked up his fork and speared another piece of meat. I watched him, waiting for more, as he chewed thoroughly, then picked up his drink and took a long swallow.

"But what does Faust have to do with Mozart?" I finally asked, impatient.

He shook his head. "No, no. Faust has nothing to do with Mozart." His gaze settled on me, weighted with significance. "Just as you have nothing to do with Mozart."

He turned back to his dinner, clearly dismissing me, and I was left with nothing but confusion.

The crowd of guests was infuriating. I doubted I would ever have a chance to find Henry alone with all of these guests around. After dinner we all sat in the drawing room and enjoyed a short recital by Herr and Frau Spohr, who played a violin and harp duet—an original composition by Herr Spohr. After the music, Mr. Brandon found me and asked me to be his partner for a game of whist with Sylvia and his father. My mind was not on the game, though. I was only thinking of how I needed to make my escape to India, and how I needed to speak to Henry, and how every time I looked for him he was occupied with one guest or another. Half the time Miss St. Claire was at his side. And more than once I caught Mrs. Delafield staring at me in a warning way. As if I was going to repeat my mistakes of the night before, when I had tried to flirt. I felt scrutinized, and unhappy, and frustrated. And then I could not find Henry at all, and my plan to get his help seemed doomed to fail before it even began, and I could not bear to stay in that drawing room one minute longer.

Disappointment accompanied me up the stairs when all the guests dispersed for the night. I had spent the whole day trying for one simple thing—a chance to speak with Henry alone. Now it was nighttime, and another day here had passed without advancing my plot of earning my trip to India.

Alice was waiting for me in my room, but I was not ready to go to bed. I had to accomplish something this day. I asked her, "If one wished to go outside at night, without being seen, how might one accomplish that?"

A startled look passed over her face. "You are not thinking of going outside, miss. Not at night."

She said it like a statement rather than a question. "Perhaps I am thinking of it. Why should I not?"

A hint of fear shadowed her eyes. "Ah, no, miss, you mustn't. Not a soul ventures out at night in these parts. Everyone knows to beware of Linger's Ghost." She looked at me more closely. "You must have heard of Linger's Ghost, miss."

I shook my head. I did not believe in ghost stories, and I thought Alice would have grown out of them by now as well.

"He travels the moors on horseback at night, miss, especially on the nights of a full moon. If you see him, you must hurry and hide yourself, and if you're out on the moors, with nowhere to hide . . ." She shook her head, her hand creeping to her throat. She squeezed it, as if trying to strangle the idea of a supernatural meeting on the moors at night.

A shiver ran through me, and I took a step away from her. "I do not believe in ghosts."

Shaking a finger at me, she said in a low voice, "You needn't believe in something for it to be real, miss."

We stared at each other for a long moment, neither of us giving an inch. I sighed. "I only want to go down to the beach. I promised my brother a seashell that I find under the light of the moon. I have no plans to go to the moors at all."

Her eyes widened. "The beach? At night?" Her voice cracked. She pressed her lips tightly closed and shook her head. "No. It is unwise. You shouldn't go, miss. You should never go to the beach at night."

I clenched my fists, feeling my frustration burn into anger. "But I want to go to the beach and find a seashell for my brother. That does not seem like too much to ask."

"I cannot help you, miss. I am sorry." She bent her head and stood before me in an attitude of such humility that I could not be angry with her.

I sat on my bed with a sigh of defeat. "You may go, Alice."

"Do you not want my help undressing?"

I shook my head. "No. Thank you."

She opened the door and slipped out of the room before I could say another word. I looked from the closed door to the closed window, feeling the stir of restlessness grow greater within me. I had to leave this room.

CHAPTER 15

I waited and watched the clock hands turn until ten minutes had passed since Alice left me. Then I picked up a candle, opened my door, and ventured out into the halls of Blackmoore.

It turned out that I did not need Alice's help to slip out of the house unnoticed, although I would have appreciated it. I found a back stairway used by the servants. I was wearing a cloak and nobody saw me. Then it was just a matter of finding a window that I could open, because the doors would not do. A window was necessary for this kind of escape. The only thing I did not bargain for was the rose bushes planted directly underneath the window. A thorn scratched my hand when I jumped from the windowsill.

I shook off the sting of the scratch and crept around the corner of the house until I was facing the ocean. Drawing in a deep breath, I closed my eyes and let the sound of the waves and the chill of the air wash over me. After several moments, I felt free of the restlessness that plagued me inside and set about finding a way down to the beach.

The house was perched on a cliff overlooking the sea. But surely there would be some way to access the beach from the estate. I was grateful for the bright moon—just a few days from being full—for lighting my way. When I found the steep stone steps leading down the face of the cliff, I did not pause. This was what adventures were about—the rush of the leap, the elation of the landing. This was what my soul needed on this night of frustration and caged dreams.

I counted two hundred seventy-six stone steps until my feet touched sand. By then my legs shook from the effort of the climb down the cliff, and I waited a moment to catch my breath and really take in the scene before me.

The moon shone a silver ribbon across the water. A cold wind blew, and I wrapped my cloak more tightly around myself. I looked to the right and the left, seeing the lights of Robin Hood's Bay probably a mile away. I wondered what Alice had against going to the beach at night and why she thought it was something she had to warn me against. I walked toward the water and leaned down to touch it. It was frigid and foaming and curling up on the sand. I dragged my fingers through the wet sand until I had a handful of small shells. Closing my fingers, I dipped my hand in the water, shaking it back and forth to try to rinse off the sand. My hand was almost numb after a moment of that, and I stood and thrust the shells into the pocket of my cloak, wiping my hand off at the same time.

Then I stood with my head tipped back and regarded the moon and the stars and the ocean stretching out into forever. This very water could carry me away to India. It could carry me away from all of my troubles here. If it weren't for that bargain with my mother, I could . . .

A splashing sound caught my attention. I stepped forward, then back in alarm. Something was in the water. Right in front of me. Coming toward me, in fact. Something large enough to make those splashes. Too large to be a fish. I racked my brain for another explanation. A dolphin? A shark? What else might be coming toward me?

I thought of Alice's fear, and I wondered for a brief moment if I had misjudged her. Perhaps there really was something dangerous in these waters. Perhaps there was something here to be truly frightened of. Perhaps . . .

The *something* stopped splashing, and emerged directly in the path of moonlight.

Linger's Ghost.

My heart pounded against my ribs. The pale figure moved toward me. I backed up a step, then two, and a scream filled my throat, when suddenly a strange idea occurred to me.

I stopped, peering at the figure in the moonlight, and with a nervous voice called out, "Good evening!" I felt infinitely stupid, not knowing how else to address what surely was a man in the water.

The ghost—the man—stopped moving and peered in my direction. "Kate? Is that you?"

My mouth fell open. "Henry?"

"Yes."

He started moving again, and I stammered, "Er . . . are you . . . uh . . . clothed?"

A pause met my question. "No," he said with a laugh.

My face was hot. I turned my back to the water and called out, "I need to speak with you. Can you . . . come out? And put some clothes on?"

I waited, my face on fire, as another low chuckle reached my ears. Then I heard soft splashing, and I imagined him walking onto the sand. Or, rather, I tried *not* to imagine him walking onto the sand without a stitch of clothing on. The seconds stretched on for so long I thought I would die of embarrassment. I was losing my nerve and starting to question the wisdom of my idea.

Then soft footsteps approached me from behind, and Henry's voice said, "You can turn around now."

I turned around, but I was not fully prepared for the sight before me. My jaw fell open before I could catch it. Henry had put on his breeches— slung low around his hips—but nothing else. The moonlight glimmered off his bare chest and shoulders, drops of water clinging to his skin. His skin was smooth and more muscled than I had ever dared to imagine. His muscles went on and on, lean and defined, and yet he stood there without any self-consciousness, as if looking like a Greek god was something that came easily to him.

"What did you need?" he asked, rubbing his hand over his wet hair.

I forced my mouth to close, and then I tried to swallow. All rational thoughts had flown from my mind, and I could not pull my eyes away from his shoulders, his chest, his . . .

"Kate?"

I pulled my gaze up to his face, but that was no better, with his eyes dark as night and his lips . . .

"Do you . . . have a shirt?" I spied a white bundle in his hand. "Is that it? You should put it on." I was speaking much too fast, and my voice cracked.

Henry chuckled, a low, sultry sound. "Why? Does this bother you?" He wore a wicked grin. My face flamed hotter.

"No. I only thought you looked cold. Isn't the water cold?" I was still speaking too fast, but I couldn't stop myself.

"Don't worry," he said and did not move to put his shirt on. He did, however, rest his hands on his hips, which only drew my attention to how low his breeches were sitting. "What are you doing out here?" he asked.

I pulled my attention back to his face, cursing myself silently for becoming so distracted. "I was looking for a seashell. For Oliver. But I am glad to find you here. I was hoping to speak to you. Alone."

His brow furrowed. "Why?"

"I need you."

The words struck me as sounding much too forward and leaving too much open to interpretation. I saw that Henry thought the same thing by the way his head reared back.

I hurried to fill in the space I had opened. "I need your help, rather."

He folded his arms across his chest, but that made things worse for me, watching how the muscles in his arms bulged. I really needed to stop thinking about his muscles.

"Does anyone know you're out here?" he asked.

I shook my head. "I sneaked out." I expected him to smile. But he didn't. If anything, he looked more severe than before.

He shook his head, blew out an exasperated breath. He raked a hand through his wet hair, releasing drops of water. I expected a lecture about my habit of sneaking out, but it didn't come. Instead he said, "And what about Mr. Brandon?"

I looked at him, puzzled. I could not understand this severity, this sternness about him. No, it was more than sternness. It was anger.

"What about him?"

"What does he know?"

I was more confused than before and shook my head. "I don't know what you mean."

He stepped closer—so close I could smell the salt of the ocean on him. My heart quickened. The moonlight was doing all sorts of favors for Henry, casting him midnight and silver and dark and strong.

"Have you told him what you've told me a hundred times?" His voice was low, a thread of something running through it—anger? Or some other emotion? "Have you told him that you have no intention of marrying? Ever?"

I blinked in surprise, struggled for words, and found myself completely dumbstruck. Some strong emotion was coming off Henry in waves, and I felt struck by the impact. I stepped back from him.

"I don't think that's something I need to tell him." In fact, the very thought of it struck me as completely presumptuous.

"Why not?"

I lifted my hands, at a loss. "I have done nothing to encourage his affection."

His jaw clenched, and he shook his head, a look of reprimand in his dark eyes. "A man does not need encouragement to lose his heart."

My heart thumped hard. I drew in a shaky breath. This was going all wrong. "I did not come out here to talk about Mr. Brandon. Let us agree to disagree on that subject, shall we?"

He pressed his lips together and looked away.

I tried to smile, tried to lighten the mood. "So . . . you like to swim in the ocean. At night. By yourself." I frowned as I looked at the waves behind him. "It seems quite dangerous. Is this a regular habit of yours when you're here?"

A half-smile lifted one side of his mouth. "Not exactly." He took the shirt he held, shook it out, and pulled it over his head. I did not stare at the way his muscles bunched as he did so. At least, I tried very hard not to.

"So why tonight?"

Another half-smile. "I felt the need to do something daring. That is all."

There was something between us. Secrets that we were keeping from each other. I was just as guilty of it as Henry was, and so I had nothing to say in response to his cryptic answer. But I wondered if my idea was feasible at all, considering this new strain between us.

"So, Miss Kate. What did you need from me?" His tone was lighter, more playful. His anger seemed gone—or at least hidden—and my friend Henry was back.

Hope seized me, and quickly, before I could lose my courage, I said, "I need you to propose to me."

CHAPTER 16

Henry looked stunned. He stared at me, completely still, and I felt like the biggest dolt alive.

"That didn't sound right," I hurried to say, my face hot with embarrassment. "I made a bargain with Mama before I left. She said that if I receive and reject three proposals, she will give up hope of ever marrying me off and allow me to go to India. I don't need you to tell me how mad this scheme was, but I was desperate when I agreed to it. I don't know what I was thinking." I drew in a shaky breath. "But Sylvia told me last night—she told me how stupid I was to think that three men here would propose to me."

Something like anger flashed across Henry's face, and he opened his mouth to speak, but I held up a hand, stopping him. "Let me finish. Last night you told me that there had to be more than one option. And then this morning I found my other option! I remembered that Mama and I had agreed to three *proposals* rather than three gentlemen, and you told me that if I ever needed saving, that you would . . ." I swallowed and said softly, "that you would save me."

Henry's expression erased my newfound hope. It was stern and bleak, and there was that anger again. "You want me to propose. Three times."

I nodded.

"You do understand the position I am in, do you not? I am here to court Miss St. Claire. To propose to her. I cannot appear to be courting you as well."

I blushed in spite of myself. My embarrassment was almost too great to allow me to press forward. It was a mark of how much I yearned for this trip to India that I continued. "I am not asking you to *court* me, Henry."

He moved closer and looked down into my eyes. "Then what are you asking?"

I took a quick breath and spoke past my embarrassment. "I just need three proposals. And I promise I will reject you. Immediately. Unequivocally."

He flashed a small, sardonic smile. "I never supposed otherwise."

"So you will do it?"

He took a deep breath, and now he looked away. There was such a struggle evident in his expression that I almost felt sorry for him. But whatever his struggle was, I could not believe it tormented him as fiercely as mine did me. I could not believe that his reluctance for me to go to India could feel to him as fierce and unyielding as my desire to go felt to me.

Finally he said, "This is a difficult thing you ask of me." He turned back to me. "But if this is the desire of your heart . . ."

"It is. It truly is, Henry." I clasped my hands together, in front of me, and felt so impatient and hopeful and fearful at the same time that I hurt all over. "Please. Please do this for me." His look was tortured. Impulsively, I reached out and grabbed his arm. "I will pay you."

His head reared back with surprise. "What?"

Here I stood, desperate, clinging to his sleeve, offering to pay him for a proposal. Three of them, to be exact. And if there had been a witness to this scene, it surely would have seemed that I was doing precisely what I had sworn never to do—to beg and barter and steal in the name of marriage.

But there was an essential difference here—it would not end in an engagement. And this was Henry. If I could ask this of anyone in the world, it was he. He would not misjudge my intentions. But a pang of doubt struck me, as I thought of Eleanor and what Henry knew of her.

"Henry." I tugged on his sleeve, as if I could pull on his will by doing so. "I promise you that there is no trick at play here. I will refuse you, and no one will learn of this. There will be no repercussions for you. I swear it. I will not entrap you. You will suffer nothing from this. You may be sure of that."

A sound escaped his lips—a soft, mirthless laugh. "You promise to reject me. You promise that I will suffer nothing. That is your assurance."

"Yes." My voice came out low and rough, reflecting the desperation I felt.

He moved even closer. "And what will you pay me?" His voice was suddenly different, and there was something about the way he moved closer, as if he was taking charge now.

It made my pulse quicken. I let go of his sleeve. What would I pay him? I had spoken impulsively. I had no money—nothing that I could think of that he would want. But I had to answer him before he changed his mind. At a loss, I finally blurted out, "Whatever you want."

I immediately wished I could recall the words. But before I could speak again, Henry said, "Then I accept."

His words surprised me, and I wavered for a moment between feelings of relief that he would help me and unease about what he would ask for payment. But then I reminded myself that this was Henry, who was as good a man as one could find in all of England. He would ask nothing of me that I didn't want to give. I was sure of it.

I reached out my right hand toward him. Henry looked down at it with a look of bemusement. "This is how it is done in business," I told him. "We shake hands on our bargain. That makes it binding."

Henry took my hand in his, holding it as if it was a new thing, when in reality he had had many reasons over the years to take hold of my hand.

But now he looked down at my hand in his, and he lightly brushed his thumb over the back of it. He might as well have stroked my heart for the way it plummeted at his touch. I had to steel myself not to pull my hand away, not to let on how fast my heart pounded. I was terrified that he would feel my racing pulse for himself.

His thumb traced over the scratch near my wrist. "This is new," he said in a soft voice. "What did this?"

"The, uh, rose bushes. Outside the window that I climbed through."

His eyes lifted to mine, full of soft amusement. "I should have guessed." Then, taking a firm hold on my hand, he shook it once. "There. The bargain is sealed."

He was just looking at me, smiling indulgently, but there was a twinge to his smile at the same time—as if something in this moment made him sad.

"Well?" I said, gesturing to the empty space in front of me. "Are you going to do it?"

His eyes widened. "What? Right now?"

"Well, yes. Of course."

He shook his head. "It's late. Come. Let's go back inside."

I followed him reluctantly as he walked up the beach toward the steps I had used. "But it would be easy. And fast. Just say the words."

He stopped and turned around, walking back to me, his steps quiet in the sand but sure and long. When he reached me he stopped, so close I could feel his warmth, and he looked into my eyes. The moon shone on us both, and the ocean waves lapped against the sand behind me. His gaze stilled my protest, and his voice, when he spoke, was soft but firm. "No. You will not dictate how or where or when I propose. That has to be part of our agreement."

He watched me, his lips a firm line, his jaw a strong angle of shadow and light. I looked up at him, speechless, and wondered where this side of Henry had emerged from—this Henry who swam in the ocean at night and had this strength and this way of looking at me.

I took a deep breath and wondered what had just happened between us, what line we had just crossed. "Very well," I said, and followed him to the stone steps leading up the cliff. He reached a hand back and I grasped it, letting him pull me up when my legs shook, until we reached the top.

CHAPTER 17

Alice was vocal about her displeasure when I rang for her next morning. I couldn't decide which she disapproved of more: my going to the beach at night or my failure to ring for her when I returned. There was a lot of muttering about the sand coating my boots and the hem of my gown. As she pulled the handful of seashells out of the pocket of my cloak, she sent me a dark look and said, "That will be the end of it, though, miss. No more. Especially not when it's a full moon."

I turned from my perch on the windowsill, where I had been listening for birds, and asked, "Why not on a full moon?"

She shook her head, as if completely exasperated with me. Finally she said, "Because smuggling happens on beaches, miss! Especially when the moon is full."

I scrambled down, nearly falling to the floor in my excitement. "Is smuggling really still taking place here?"

Regret filled her eyes. She backed away, my boots in hand, and muttered something about needing to clean off the sand. Then she ran out the door. If only I had not been so curious! She might have told me something of the secrets of Robin Hood's Bay. Hopefully, if I was patient, my chance was not entirely ruined.

But patience did not come naturally to me, and that weakness was never clearer than it was as I waited for a sign from Henry that he was going to propose. I had taken him at his word that I should not push him. But Mrs. Delafield glared at me every time she glanced my way, and Sylvia still had not spoken to me since the night I flirted with her Mr. Brandon. Watching Miss St. Claire hang on Henry's arm was making me physically ill. I had to leave. Soon.

I watched him during breakfast while Miss St. Claire talked to him about the shame of such a grey and drizzly day when she wanted so much to explore Robin Hood's Bay. Mr. Brandon talked to me about the birds he had heard on the moors that morning. But the birds were not something I wanted to share with Mr. Brandon.

Not once did Henry look directly at me during breakfast, and in a moment of panic I wondered if I had imagined it all last night. Or if he had changed his mind and was not going to help me after all. But when I stood to leave the room, excusing myself to Mr. Brandon, I suddenly discovered Henry standing too, and when I walked to the door, he called my name softly. I paused and turned, wondering what he was about.

"You dropped this," he said, handing me a handkerchief I was certain I had not dropped.

I took it, though, and thanked him, and he turned around and walked back to the table. Miss St. Claire shot me a curious look. I slipped the handkerchief into my pocket and hurried from the room. I turned two corners before slipping into the first empty room I found. It was the library, and at this hour of the morning, it was completely empty. Turning my back to the door, I carefully opened the folded handkerchief. A small piece of paper lay inside, folded as well. When I opened it I recognized Henry's neat handwriting.

Meet me at the entrance to the secret passage at midnight tonight.

I spent the entire day scouring Blackmoore's rooms and corridors for any hint of a secret passageway. It was truly an enormous house. I passed Henry in the hall once in the east wing, that afternoon. He paused long enough to smile and say, "Have you found it yet?"

"No!" I whispered. "Won't you just tell me?"

He shook his head, stubborn as always, and smiling with mischief. "You have bothered me about this for so many years, Kate. You will have to find it yourself."

As he started to walk away, I said, "Just give me a clue, then."

He looked back, and although I was sure he was not going to help, at the last moment before he turned the corner he said, "It is behind a painting."

There were hundreds of paintings at Blackmoore. I searched every room and corridor in the top two floors of the east and west wings. The other rooms in the west wing had clearly not been used for some time. The furniture was covered in sheets, and dust motes hung in the air. I was not so bold as to enter any of the rooms in the east wing. Surely Henry would not have sent me on a quest to intrude on others' privacy that way. After hours of exploration I concluded that the upper floors of the house did not hide any secret passageways.

Then it was time for dinner, and I had to hurry to change and have Alice do my hair so that I was presentable. Dinner lasted much too long, and I sat by nobody interesting, thanks to Mrs. Delafield's seating arrangements. As the ladies left the dining room, I stayed toward the back of the group, and when everyone else turned right toward the drawing room, I turned left and hid just inside the door of the library. There were plenty of paintings there, and I had not had a chance to look in all the rooms of the ground floor yet.

The library, though, proved to be a disappointment, as did the large entry hall and the corridors leading off it on both sides. Finally there was only one room left: the second music room. The bird room.

I stopped in front of a painting hanging on a wall covered in dark wood paneling. I stared at it, amazed that I had not noticed it before. It must have been the bird and the pianoforte that had caught my attention before to make me overlook this work of art.

It was Icarus. I knew it immediately. His father was tying on the wings he had created for him and pointing toward the sky with a look of disapproval, as though warning Icarus not to fly too high. It was a beautiful rendering—an original, it appeared, by Anthony Van Dyck, according to the signature in the corner.

I touched the frame and felt still for the first time all day. And then the frame moved, and the wall swung out toward me, revealing the secret passageway.

CHAPTER 18

I stole out of my room at ten minutes before midnight, using a candle to light my way down the back stairs to the bird room. It was dark and empty, the bird quiet in its cage. I sat on the bench in front of the pianoforte and nervously waited, straining to hear footsteps. Finally, when my heart had begun to race with nervousness that he was not coming, the door silently swung open and Henry walked into the room.

"You found it," he said in a low voice, quiet for this quiet, dark night.

"Of course." I could not keep the pride from my voice. I stood and looked up at Henry, taking in what I could see of him in the candlelight. It was enough to see his dark hair and the flash of his smile and a hint of excitement in his eyes.

He held up a shuttered lantern. "We won't need the candle." I followed him to the Icarus painting and watched as he slid his hand behind the frame and pressed the switch I had accidentally triggered earlier.

The wall swung open, revealing a dark emptiness. Henry lifted the lantern and moved a shutter so that a ray of light shone, and with another grin and a gleam of excitement in his eyes, he led the way into the darkness.

I had not explored the passageway at all earlier, afraid I would get dirty and have to explain my appearance to another guest or—heaven

forbid—to Mrs. Delafield. Now, though, I followed Henry and the light
he carried, ducking when he warned me to, easing around a tight corner,
feeling the walls change from stone to earth as we climbed down a tight
spiral staircase for what felt like a long time. I forgot to count the steps, but
I thought it was not quite so far as the climb down to the beach had been.

The passageway had taken us through the house, and now we were
in an underground tunnel that was shored up by wooden support beams,
the walls and floor earthen, the walls occasionally holding a bracket for
a torch. I touched a few of the torches, thinking of Alice and smuggling.
But the torches all felt as cold as the walls around us. Unused, then, at
least recently.

We must have walked half a mile underground when we came to another stairway. Henry took me up the stone stairs. I followed the light he
carried low so that it illuminated the steps for me to see. The stairs carried
us up and up. He turned his head and whispered, "We're almost there." I
was panting, feeling the burn in my leg muscles from the climb. And then
he paused, boots still on the steps before me, and I heard a dusty, protesting creak. A breeze chilled me, and then Henry's boots moved again, until
they disappeared into a square of starlight.

I paused, my head at the opening of what must have been a trapdoor.
Above me stretched the night sky streaked with starlight. I grasped at
the sides of the opening and was surprised to feel grass beneath my fingers. Surely we had climbed higher than mere ground level. Then Henry
reached down to me. I put my hand in his, and he pulled me up the
remaining steps. I emerged, wide-eyed. It was certainly grass beneath
my feet. But we were encircled by a crumbling stone wall, and there was
nothing but the sky to see beyond it. No trees. No ocean. No moors. I
looked at Henry in confusion and saw the strangest expression on his face,
which was half-lit by the lantern he held aloft. He seemed both excited
and nervous. I had seldom seen Henry nervous. His lips were closed tight,
and his eyes were too darkened by the flickering shadows of the lantern
for me to see them clearly.

"What is this place?" I asked him, walking cautiously forward, not sure if the ground would hold me, for this place seemed to defy the rules of nature.

"Come see," he said, walking toward the stone wall. I followed him. The wall came to a crumbling stop at my chest level. I peered down and quickly gripped the stones in front of me as my head swam. We were very high. I knew those trees. I knew how tall they grew. And now I could see their tops below us. I turned, looking to my right—a sea of trees swaying in the breeze below us. To my left—the crashing of distant waves, frothy white in the moonlight. The ocean.

I looked up and saw again the stretch of sky without a tree to block my view. And then, suddenly, there was a raucous cry and dark shadows fluttered, filling the air. The haunting cry of the rooks pierced the darkness. The birds were loud, and their cries scratched at my soul like an etching on glass.

"It's the ruined abbey," I breathed.

"It is the highest tower of the ruined abbey, to be exact." I heard the smile in his voice. "Do you like it?"

"I do," I whispered. "I like it very much."

Now Henry's smile broke free, and he rested his elbows on the wall and faced the ocean. "I have come here nearly every night of every visit, ever since I discovered the secret passageway when I was ten. When I was twelve I decided I wanted a comfortable place to sit and look at the stars. So I lugged up buckets full of dirt every night. It took an entire month to carry enough dirt up here to cover the floor. Then I begged some grass seed from the gardener, and I spread it the night before we were to leave. I had to wait an entire year to find out if the grass had grown."

I bent down and ran my hand over the soft blades of grass. It was strange to think of twelve-year-old Henry planting something that I would see and feel all these years later.

"Have you ever brought anyone else here?" I asked, thinking of Sylvia and trying not to think of Miss St. Claire.

Henry drew in a breath and leaned back against the wall, looking at me quietly for a moment. "No." The word rested in the silence between us for a long moment, filling me with such gladness I could not keep myself from smiling. "I must confess something, Kate."

He had my full attention. A confession from Henry was a rare and highly valuable thing.

"What?" I breathed, moving closer.

"I didn't love Blackmoore when I was young. Not for years."

I looked at him with surprise. "I don't remember that."

"No. I didn't tell anyone. I was supposed to love this place, you know. I was meant to inherit it. But it seemed so strange and so far away from what was home to me. I didn't love it. Once I found the secret passageway, I used it to escape the house every night. But when you were so intrigued by the idea of Blackmoore, when I saw how much you wanted to come here, and how you peppered me with questions upon my return, I began to feel differently about it. I began to treasure it, because you did." He moved closer, and I could see the faint smile in his grey eyes. "I always knew I would bring you here some day and tell you that. To thank you."

I was so surprised I did not know how to respond but only stood there as something soft and sweet grew within me. Somebody appreciated me. Not just somebody—Henry. I smiled and whispered, "You're welcome."

"I thought this would be a good place for fulfilling our bargain," he went on. "The three proposals. And what you will pay me."

My smile slipped. I had momentarily forgotten about the question of payment.

"Yes, the payment. Have you decided what you want?"

"I have."

He leaned down, resting his hand on the wall behind my back. I had to tilt my head back to look at him. My heart quickened with nervousness. "Your heart's desire is to leave all of us and fly away to India. And my heart's desire is to unravel the mystery of Kate Worthington."

I laughed nervously, trying to find room to back away from him. But the stones at my back offered no escape, and I felt much too vulnerable so close to Henry in this dark night with the stars like jewels overhead and the dark rooks our only chaperones. "I am no mystery, Henry. How you exaggerate."

He leaned down so that I could see the intent look in his eyes in the moonlight. And when he spoke, his voice was low and strong and unwavering. "Two years ago something happened to you. The Kitty I knew suddenly became Kate." There was no trace of amusement in him. "The Kate who refused to dance with me. The Kate who declared to all the world that she would never marry. The Kate who gave her heart to her cat and no one else." He paused, and I felt the weight of his words as if they were a confession. "I lost something then. And for two years I have wanted it back. Or at least to understand why I lost it."

My thoughts were reeling, and I gripped the stones behind me as if the world was turning and they alone could keep me from falling off the edge.

"So that is what I will trade you, Kate. Three proposals for three of your secrets. The answers to the mystery that you became two years ago."

I could not believe he had just said those things. I could not believe he would ask this of me. We had gone so long without talking of these things—so long that I had been confident my secrets would remain mine forever. I tried to draw a steady breath, to process what he was saying, to wrap my mind around the idea of Henry in the moonlight.

But he was too close. I could do none of those things with him standing so close to me, leaning into me so that I felt his warmth. I could easily picture exactly where I would touch him, and how I would pull him to me, and I could count the breaths I would steal from him if I could kiss him.

My breath came quicker and quicker, and the tension between us became a palpable thing that quivered and stretched and made my skin burn with wanting. And finally, I could take it no more. I twisted out of the corner he had backed me into, ducking under his arm and slipping away quickly. Then, several steps away from him, I turned back and said, "I will agree to your terms. Three secrets in exchange for three proposals. So let's have it. Say 'Will you marry me?' three times, and I will answer no three times, and then you may ask your questions, and we'll be done."

He shook his head. "No. Not in a hurry. Not to get it done. I will give you one proposal a night."

I was panicking with the vulnerability I felt. "Why not just do it all at once?"

"Because," he said, his voice tinged with sadness, "I am in no hurry to throw you to the wind and watch you fly away."

It was the sadness in his voice that took me off guard. I swallowed my surprise and then said, faintly, "Fine. I agree to your terms."

Henry stepped close to me, reached out, and gently took one of my hands in his. My heart was pounding with nervousness, and I felt on the verge of either laughter or tears—I couldn't tell which. I was afraid my hand was sweating. I bit my lip and shifted from one foot to another. My sweaty hand was limp in his. There was so much that was wrong about this scene.

"Katherine Worthington."

I raised an eyebrow. "Katherine?"

"Shush. I am being formal. It's fitting."

He knelt on one knee before me.

"Oh, no," I muttered. "Please don't. Get up. Please."

He glared at me. "No complaining allowed." He took a breath and looked at my hand in his and said, "Katherine, you have stolen my heart."

A strange urge to laugh took hold of me.

"I cannot bear the thought of living without you."

My hand was so sweaty it slipped in his. Another urge to laugh bubbled up. But I should not laugh. My lips twitched; my shoulders started to shake. I clapped my free hand over my mouth to cover my smile.

"And I beg you to—"

I choked back a giggle.

Henry frowned up at me. "Are you laughing?"

I shook my head, biting back another laugh.

"Yes, you are." He stood, dropping the hand he had been holding. "Let me see your mouth."

Another almost-laugh burst from me. I covered my mouth with both hands, shaking my head.

"Kate," he said in a warning voice, stepping closer. He grasped my wrists and pulled my hands away from my mouth. I bit my lip, but I could not bite back the giggle that erupted. Henry dropped my wrists with a look of disgust and backed away.

"This was a mistake. You will never grow up, will you, Kitty?"

I gasped. "Kitty? How could you?"

"You laughed at me!"

"You were acting ridiculous!"

He threw a hand out. "I was *trying* to be serious!"

"Well, I wish you wouldn't."

"And why should I not? It was my first proposal. I wanted it to be good."

I stared at him as realization dawned on me. "Your first proposal." I reached out and put a hand on his arm. "Oh, Henry. Are you . . . do you feel . . . compromised?"

His head jerked back, and then he laughed a short and mirthless laugh. "Yes," he said in a sardonic voice. "I feel compromised, Kitty." I could tell he was rolling his eyes. "No! I don't feel compromised! What do you think of me? That I'm some sort of pansy?"

I pulled my hand off his arm. "Don't bark at me, Henry Delafield. I was *trying* to be sensitive."

"Well, don't. It doesn't suit you at all."

I lifted my chin. "Then I won't."

"Good."

We looked at each other for a long moment, the air charged with hurt and anger and misunderstandings. After a moment, I turned away and walked back to the stone wall. I rested my folded arms on the top of the wall, my chin on top of them. "What a disaster this was," I muttered. "We have not fought like this in *years.*"

After a long moment I felt Henry come to stand behind me. "True. We have not." His voice was quieter now.

"And now you are back to calling me *Kitty.*" A sigh broke from me, and I felt inexpressibly forlorn and dejected and so hopeless I wanted to cry. Henry had been my last hope. Without his help, I would not realize my dream of going to India. But I would not accept help from him at the cost of our friendship. If only I had not wanted to laugh! My nose stung and I rubbed it, thinking it was only fitting that *now* I should cry, rather than earlier, when it might have helped my case.

Henry sighed. "Don't go rubbing your nose. Please. I have such a weakness for that."

"I can't help it." I rubbed it again, blinking back tears.

He sighed again. "I am sorry. *Kate.*" Well, at least that was back to the way it should be. "I find myself very . . . out of sorts lately."

I sniffed and blinked hard and cursed my wayward emotions. "I am sorry too. I don't know what came over me."

"Shall we try again?" he asked in a quiet voice.

I rubbed my nose one last time, wiped my eyes, and turned back toward him. "If it's going to be like this, Henry, then it's not worth it. I'll find another way to India. I don't want us to fight with each other."

"Just . . . give me another chance," he said, smiling.

I nodded.

This time he did not take my hand or kneel down or call me Katherine. He just stood in front of me and said, "Kate, you are stubborn and silly and horribly unromantic, except when you are dreaming of foreign lands. For these and many other reasons, I would love to marry you."

I chuckled, wiped my nose on my sleeve, and said, "That is more like it. No, thank you, Henry."

He looked at me for a long moment before drawing a breath and saying, "Now for my payment."

My heart thumped hard.

"Do you remember the day I gave you your heart's desire?"

I shook my head. "You did not give her to me."

"I still want to hear you call me that, by the way."

I laughed softly. "Never."

"Perhaps we should change the terms of our agreement. You share with me three secrets *and* you call me The Giver of My Heart's Desire."

Smiling, I shook my head. "It will never happen, Henry."

I knew he was smiling too. He leaned on the stone wall, resting his elbows there and looking out across the trees. "The day I gave you your cat was the day you asked me not to call you Kitty."

I nodded, solemn now.

"What happened that day?"

Taking a deep breath, I leaned on the wall next to him and let the realization of what he was asking sink into me. How did he know the questions that would pierce me so dearly? How did he guess what I most wanted to hide? I had to ask myself again whether this was worth the price.

CHAPTER 19

THREE YEARS BEFORE

Eleanor stood beside me and pointed at the bonnet through the glass window of the shop. "That one. With the broad lace trim. In the middle."

I inspected the bonnet in question from every available angle. "It is too dear. You would have to save up your pin money for months to afford it."

"Mama will buy it for me." She spoke with her characteristic, unfailing confidence. I wondered if such assurance came from being the eldest or if it came from being Eleanor.

"She will not," I said, but my voice carried a hint of doubt. Where Eleanor and Mama were concerned, I had been surprised more than once.

Eleanor smiled as if she were a cat with a canary between her claws. Leaning toward me, she lowered her voice and said, "She will when I tell her that Henry Delafield will not be able to keep his eyes off me when I wear that bonnet to the picnic next week."

I scowled at her mention of Henry, a fierce, protective urge blazing to life within me. "Leave him be, Eleanor."

Her smile stretched. "Do you think you're the only one with eyes around here?" She tilted her head to the side, studying me. "Or do you have eyes, little Kitty? Hmm? Have you noticed how handsome he has grown?"

My face burned. I pressed my lips together, refusing to answer her question, because it did not deserve an answer. Just as she did not deserve Henry's attention.

She laughed and, reaching out, pinched my cheek. "You are too serious for your own good."

I pulled my head back and swatted her hand away. "You cannot have Henry, Eleanor," I said in a fierce whisper. "I will not allow you to make him into a plaything."

Her smile fell, and her eyes grew hard, a challenging glint in them. "You will not allow me?"

I knew in that instant that I had made a terrible mistake. I tried to undo my error: I shrugged and said in a voice I forced to sound casual, "Or do play with him. Do whatever you like."

Her smile curled back into place. "I plan to." Her gaze shifted to something beyond my right shoulder. "Oh, look. There's Mama now. I am going to ask her for the bonnet." She waved, calling out "Mama," but I did not look. I stared at the cobblestone street and fought the resentment that threatened to consume me.

"What is it, Eleanor?" Mama was annoyed. It was apparent in her voice. But before Eleanor could say more than "Do you not think this bonnet will—" a new voice joined the conversation.

"Mrs. Worthington." It was a man's voice, and it was rich with secrets.

I looked up sharply and moved closer to Eleanor, who had pulled away from Mama and shut her mouth quickly. He was tall and young and wore a red officer's coat. And Mama was looking at him in the same way she looked at the gentlemen who came to dinner.

"Who is he?" I whispered to Eleanor.

She lifted one shoulder and whispered back, "Her latest flirt. She hasn't told me his name."

The man did not look at either me or Eleanor. In fact, he appeared to have eyes only for Mama as he stood close to her and smiled. "It has been too long since we last saw each other. How have you been?"

I glanced around quickly to see if anyone else was watching them. Eleanor shifted so that between the two of us, Eleanor's parasol, and the wall of the store, Mama could hardly be seen by any passerby. I waved my fan furiously and nodded, wearing a broad smile, pretending the man was addressing all of us.

Mama laughed and murmured something too quiet for me to hear. Then the man said, loudly enough that my face burned, "You are much too coy, my kitten."

I fanned all the harder and grinned like a fool, but inside I had to fight the urge to retch. Eleanor leaned closer to me and murmured, "He must be half her age." I looked at her sharply, sure I must have imagined the admiration I heard in her voice. But no—it gleamed in her eyes as well, and in that moment it became clear to me that Eleanor saw in this spectacle not something to be disgusted by but something to aspire to.

The man was leaving, thank heavens. He whispered something too low for me to hear, and with a wicked grin he walked away. I dropped my fan and my stupid grin, and without a word to either Mama or Eleanor, I walked away in the opposite direction. Working hard to keep my face expressionless, I left the village by the shortest route possible, ending up close to the river. I walked with measured steps until I reached the broad shade of a tree by the river.

I threw off my bonnet and knelt at the water's edge, thrusting my hands into the cold water and then splashing it on my burning cheeks. The shame would not leave me; the water would not cool the burning of it. And it would not wash away the memory of that man's wicked grin and what he had said to my mother. My stomach heaved at the thought.

I had seen hints of such behavior in my own home with the gentlemen who came to dinner. I had witnessed my father's growing disdain across the table. But this was the first time I had seen her behave indiscreetly in public. In our own village, where anyone might have seen them. It was enough to ruin us—all of us, if she continued down this path. It was enough to ruin any chance at a respectable marriage for Eleanor or me or Maria or Lily. Oliver would not be hurt by her, but we would. We would be hurt in ways we would never be able to recover from.

I sat back on my heels, pulled my dripping hands out of the water, and *stared at the reflection of sunlight on the water as despair and shame threatened to overwhelm me. I was ashamed of my mother, and soon I would be ashamed of my older sister as well. For it was more apparent each day that Eleanor was following in Mama's footsteps. The thought of her flirting with Henry—of toying with his feelings—hit me with a fresh onslaught of shame. And then, in the midst of that shame, the words came to me:* I am not like them. I will never be like them. *The words formed themselves, and I caught onto them like a lifeline. "I will never be like them," I repeated over and over, first with desperation, then with a growing conviction. I would do something different. I would be something different.*

A sound broke into my reverie—harsh and grating. It was a group of boys, standing upstream from me, yelling and laughing and fighting over something. Then, as I watched, one of them swung something dark, back and forth, and with a cheer from all of them, let it sail into the air. I was on my feet as it arced over the river. I was running when it struck the water. And I was diving headfirst into the river when it began to sink.

The cold water made me gasp and I coughed, choking on water, stroking through the current to reach the sinking dark object. I dived under, keeping my eyes open, stretching and kicking and flailing until my fingers brushed the burlap sack. I grasped it, turned toward the surface, and kicked hard. My boots and dress weighed me down. The sack, though, was worse. It was like an anchor, and it became heavier with every passing second. I kicked harder, my lungs begging for air. But the surface retreated, the sunlight moved away from me, and my legs burned and the sack was too heavy and I had to breathe.

Suddenly an arm was around my waist, legs were kicking next to mine, and I was pulled up, out of the water. I sucked in air and coughed and struggled to hold onto the heavy sack.

"Calm down. I have you." It was Henry's arm around me, and it was Henry's voice in my ear, and I relaxed at once, knowing I was safe. He was three years older than I. He was strong. He was dependable. I was safe.

It felt like an eternity before we were able to fight clear of the current and reach the bank of the river. I heaved the wet sack out of the water and fell onto the grass, panting, still coughing up the water I had sucked in. Henry sat on the grass beside me, out of breath, and shook his wet hair out of his eyes.

"What were you doing out there?"

I knelt and turned the sack around, looking for the tied opening. "I had to rescue them." There was the twine, but I could not make my fingers unravel the knots. I shook too much with the cold, and water dripped from my hair into my eyes, making it impossible to see clearly. But Henry was quicker than I was, and in seconds he had pulled off the twine and spread open the mouth of the burlap sack.

Six grey-and-white kittens lay motionless within the sack. I picked them up one by one, rubbed their wet bodies, and lifted them to my face, trying to feel their breath or their hearts beat. Henry did the same, both of us moving quickly, silently, until Henry said, "Here!"

The grey-and-white kitten cupped in his hands moved weakly and meowed plaintively. He handed it to me, and I cradled it to my chest, my hands shaking, and suddenly I was crying. I sobbed and shook from the cold, and Henry stayed very still beside me.

"Do you think it will live?" I asked through my tears.

"Hold it close to you for warmth," he said. "And let's get it dry as soon as possible."

Wiping my streaming nose, I sniffed and looked up at him. "Thank you," I said, as tears continued to pour down my cheeks. He nodded. His cheeks were red with the cold, and his hair was plastered to his head. But his eyes were so kind, so full of compassion, that he had never looked more handsome to me. I do have eyes, Eleanor, I thought. And at the thought of my sister, the same protective surge I felt for Henry earlier rose in me again, even more fiercely this time.

"Are you hurt, Kitty?" he asked.

I shook my head. I could not explain to him why I was crying so and why this kitten's life was worth risking my own. I could not tell him about Mama and Eleanor. But I lifted my chin and said to him with a quivering voice, "I don't want to be called Kitty anymore."

A slow smile lifted his lips. "Very well. What do you want to be called instead?"

"Kate."

His smile widened. "Kate it is, then."

The kitten meowed, a small, weak sound, and I felt it tremble from the cold. Henry stood and grasped my elbow, pulling me to my feet. "Come. Let's get you two home." He walked me to his horse, which was standing near the bank of the river. He must have been riding into the village when he saw me jump into the river.

Stepping in front of me, he put his hands at my waist, ready to lift me onto the horse. But I stopped him. With a hand on his shoulder, I said, "Henry, wait. I must tell you something. It's important."

He paused.

"You must stay away from Eleanor."

He studied my face for a moment before nodding and saying just as seriously, "I will." It sounded like a promise, and I breathed a sigh of relief.

He helped me up, then climbed on behind me, reaching his arms around me to hold the reins. His chest was broad and warm, and I leaned against him as he took me home.

CHAPTER 20

PRESENT DAY

The birds flew high, crying and wheeling, drawing me back from my reverie. I watched their shapes until they settled back into their roost at the top of the next tower, and I thought of how to answer Henry's question.

"Those are rooks, you know," I finally said, nodding up at the top of the tower. "Rooks claim a place as their own, and they stay there for centuries. Generations ago, rooks were here, haunting this tower. The offspring follow the habits of the parents." I watched the birds settle, then fly again, then settle with another round of cries. "They do not question, do they?" I took a deep breath. "But I do."

I looked at Henry now and found his gaze on me. "That day you rescued me from the river . . ." He nodded. "I was running away from my mother that day. She was in town, with a . . . captain . . . of the militia." I blushed and looked away. Even in the dark, I could not look at Henry and tell this story. "She was . . . indiscreet. I saw her. I heard what they said to each other. He called her a kitten." I spit out the word with distaste. "*His* kitten."

My hands trembled. I folded my arms tightly across my chest. "It was the first time I had witnessed such a thing. I daresay I had been blind before, or too naïve. But I saw it that day." Henry was still and quiet beside me. "I am not like her, Henry," I whispered fiercely, clenching my hands into fists. "I am *not*."

"I know," he said, his voice quiet.

Something calmed within me at his words. He knew. He *knew*. I breathed. My limbs stopped their trembling. We stood in silence for a long time, until the wind blew a chill through me.

"Is that all?" I asked. "Is that the secret you wanted to know tonight?"

"Yes. That is all." Henry picked up the lantern and I followed him to the trapdoor. But before he began the climb down, he turned to me and said quietly, "Thank you."

CHAPTER 21

"Oh! A letter from my dear friend Miss Louisa Wyndham!" Miss St. Claire's cheerful voice brought me sharply awake. I had fallen into a brown study while sitting in the morning room with her and Sylvia after breakfast. Most of Mrs. Delafield's guests were older, married women who took their breakfast in bed and did not come downstairs until hours after we had eaten. So only the three of us occupied the morning room, and I had quickly slipped into my own thoughts while Sylvia and Miss St. Claire chatted. Sleep had not come easily to me last night after sneaking back into my room. I lay awake and thought of Henry taking my hand, of him kneeling before me, of him declaring his love for me.

And to look at Miss St. Claire and imagine him doing those things with her, but to have them be real, sickened me.

"You remember I introduced you to her in Town," Miss St. Claire continued. "Now *that* is a well-connected family. Too bad they do not have any more unmarried sons. For your sake."

I glanced sharply at Sylvia, and she shot me a look of warning in return. Had she not told Miss St. Claire of her attachment to the elder Mr. Brandon?

"Yes, that is too bad," Sylvia said, giving me another meaningful look.

I smiled at her, letting her know she had nothing to worry about from me. And she smiled back, tremulously, with a hint of relief.

"I shall have to read her letter to you, Sylvia. You will be most interested in what she writes about some of our acquaintances from Town." She cast a glance at me. "Although I don't know how interesting this correspondence would be to someone who had never been to Town . . ." She folded the letter. "How rude of me, Miss Worthington, to speak in front of you about things you cannot be a part of. I am so sorry. How you must long for a Season! And I understand your mother is not likely to give you one. Well," she smiled brightly, "never mind. We shall speak of other things while you are here."

I stood up. "You are too kind, Miss St. Claire. Indeed, you are the epitome of thoughtfulness. But I think I will do something else and let you two have your chat."

"Where are you going, Kitty?" Sylvia asked.

"I think I'll explore the house again, since it is too rainy for the moors."

Miss St. Claire frowned at the window. "It is most unsatisfactory that it has rained two of our three days here. But we shall entertain ourselves. Perhaps later we can play some charades. Or whist. Or we could organize a ball! Oh, let's do organize a ball. It will be such fun for the other guests. We are responsible for their entertainment, you know, and I would so hate it if any of our guests were to feel bored here."

I walked across the room, ready to be rid of Miss St. Claire's exhausting thoughtfulness.

"If it clears up this afternoon, Miss Worthington," Miss St. Claire called to me before I closed the door, "we should all walk to Robin Hood's Bay."

She was so unbelievably kind. She made it most difficult for me to dislike her. I smiled. "I would like that very much."

But instead of exploring the house immediately, I went to the bird room. Touching the painting of Icarus, I thought again of the tower and

Henry's confession last night. I thought of the secret he had asked for; the memories that had awakened stayed with me all day. I was, for a short time, transported back in time, to three years before, to the days immediately after Henry saved me from the river.

CHAPTER 22

THREE YEARS BEFORE

The weather had turned unpredictable, and grey skies became the backdrop upon which the stifling boredom of my time played out. Finally, on the fourth day of rain, I took my kitten, bundled her up in an old shawl, and tucked her inside my coat. Then I tied on my bonnet, picked up a parasol, and marched through the woods to Sylvia's house. I saw Sylvia through the French windows and ran up to knock at them. She hurried to let me, dripping, into the morning room. Luckily her mother was nowhere to be seen.

"I could not stay away any longer," I announced as she helped me take off my dripping wet coat. "Eleanor has been talking ceaselessly about her latest interest, and I cannot listen to one more syllable about his many fine qualities." I held up my scarf-wrapped bundle. "So I have brought my kitten for us to play with." Sylvia cooed and pulled away the scarf until we could see the kitten's grey-and-white face, eyes closed in sleep.

"I am so glad you have come," Sylvia said, taking the kitten from me and cradling it like a baby in her arms. "I have been dying of boredom. Henry too. He has been in the most impatient, short-tempered mood these past few days. Always complaining about the rain and watching out the window."

My heart quickened, as it had every time I had thought of Henry since he had rescued me from the river. But I said nothing to Sylvia about it. I had told her I found the kitten but not about Henry jumping into the river to save me. It was the first secret I had ever kept from her.

"So what have you decided to name her?" Sylvia asked.

"I haven't chosen a name yet. I was hoping you could help me think of it."

Sylvia looked into the kitten's face. "I think she looks like a Mimi."

I wrinkled my nose. "Mimi?"

"Yes. Or perhaps Dorothy, and you could call her Dot for short."

I shook my head.

"Why not? Those are good names."

"Let's keep thinking," I said. Sylvia rattled off more ideas, all of which sounded too silly to me. But I was not paying real attention to her. The impatience that had plagued me for the last four days was as strong as ever. I realized that I was impatient to see Henry. In fact, the longer I sat here in his house without seeing him or hearing his voice, the more restless I became.

Finally I stood and said, "Let's ask Henry. He always has good ideas."

Sylvia followed with the kitten, muttering something about having better ideas for a cat's name than a boy would have.

I knew where Henry would be. He spent most of his afternoons studying at the large round table in the library after spending the morning with his tutor. He took his education very seriously. The window was usually open, bringing a bracing chill into the room, fluttering pages of his books and notes. Today, though, it was closed against the rain, and candles were lit all around to combat the gloom of the overcast day.

"Henry, we need your help," Sylvia said as we walked into the library.

Henry lifted his head and looked directly at me. I froze where I stood, feeling as if he had just told me a secret with that look. It was new. It was a question and a statement and a quick, hidden secret all at once, and then he glanced back at his work, set down his pen, pushed back his books and papers, and turned to us again. And that dark, secret look was gone. There was only Henry, with a little lift of the corner of his mouth.

"What do you need my help with?" he asked.

She held up my kitten. "We cannot think of a suitable name."

"Let me see it," he said, standing and crossing the room toward us. Sylvia handed the kitten to him, and he walked over to the seats in front of the fireplace, where the light was brightest. A rug cushioned the floor, and chairs encircled the warmer space. Sylvia and I followed. Henry sprawled out on the rug, leaning against the settee, and held up the kitten, inspecting her from all angles.

"Whatever you do," he said, "do not give in to feminine temptation and name it something silly, like Mimi or Dot."

Sylvia made an outraged sound. I smiled to myself and sat on the floor near Henry.

"There is nothing silly about Mimi or Dot," Sylvia said, sitting beside me and reaching out for the kitten. As she took the cat from him, Henry glanced at me sideways. He leaned toward me, quickly, while Sylvia was distracted, and whispered in my ear, "Are you well?"

His whispered breath sent a shiver across my neck and down my spine. I nodded. "Are you?" A quick glance at Sylvia. She had her face buried in the kitten's fur and was saying, "I think Mimi is a fine name. Do you not agree?"

"You have not caught a cold, have you?" I murmured. I did not know why this was a secret between us. I did not know why I didn't tell Sylvia how Henry had jumped into the river to rescue me. I only knew that I wanted this secret between us. I also knew, with a surge of relief, that Henry felt the same way. My heart lifted, over and over, at the thought.

His mouth quirked up, a sardonic smile, and he shook his head. "I have been swimming in much colder water than that." I looked down, seeing how close his hand rested next to mine on the rug. "But thank you for your concern, Kate," he whispered.

A smile sprang to my lips, a quick burst of happiness in my heart, and I threw him a quick glance out of the corner of my eyes, to let him know I had heard him—and there again was that new look, that look that was part question, part secret, part statement. But what he was stating, I could not say. And what he was asking, I had no idea. And the secret, I feared, I would never know.

"Well, if we cannot use Mimi or Dot," Sylvia said, "you must help us think of another name."

"It is Kate's kitten, you know," Henry said. "Perhaps she should think of her own name."

"Kate?" Sylvia looked from Henry to me with an expression of confusion. "What is this?"

I reached out and took my kitten from Sylvia, feigning a casual expression as I placed her on the floor and took the piece of yarn from my pocket that I had brought for her to play with. Once she was batting it around with her paws, I lifted my gaze to Sylvia and said, matter-of-factly, "I have decided I wish to be called Kate from now on."

Sylvia blanched and shook her head. "I could never call you that. You have always been Kitty to me and you always will be."

That was that, her voice said. My heart sank. Perhaps everyone would feel the same way as Sylvia. If my best friend would not allow me to change, then what hope had I of anyone else giving me that freedom?

I glanced down, watching my kitten, feeling my heart lift and fall. I had felt for quite a while that I had no proper place for my heart. There was no one I could entrust it to. There was too much buying and selling and stealing and ignoring of hearts among the Worthington women. I wanted a safe place for mine. Perhaps this kitten would be a safe keeper of my heart—this gentle creature who did not coerce or bargain or demand anything.

"What is the Latin word for heart?" I asked Henry in a whisper.

"Cor," he whispered back, leaning toward me as he did. I met his gaze, and his dark grey eyes were looking into mine as if there was another secret—a secret only Henry knew.

"You could name her Cora," he whispered, a little smile tugging half his mouth upward. "Then nobody would guess."

He saw me. He saw so much of me, just in that look, and those words told me that he understood. He somehow knew that this cat was a place for my heart to belong and that I would not want anyone to know something so personal. Except for him. For some reason, I did not mind that he knew this secret about me. I leaned away from him just a little and cleared my throat. "Cora. I shall name her Cora."

Sylvia frowned. "Cora? For a cat?"

I shot her a dark look, my brows furrowed. She might refuse to call me by the name I had chosen for myself, but I would not let her bully me about my cat's name. After a start of surprise, she said meekly, "I like it."

When I glanced at Henry, he was watching me with a thoughtful expression, as if I was a new thing he was trying to puzzle out. I liked his watchfulness. I liked his grey, thoughtful eyes. And when he stood and walked back to the table and his books, I watched him go, and I felt, for the first time, the knowledge that I would choose him for a friend over Sylvia.

He slid a book toward an empty chair at the large round table and said, "If you're interested, either of you, here is a new book from a bookstore in London. About birds."

Sylvia acted as if she hadn't heard him speak. She lay sprawled on the rug in front of the fire and dragged her finger over the kitten's back. I looked from her to the table and back, and then I stood and walked across the library.

"I am interested," I said, taking the empty chair and pulling the large book toward me. It was an old, beautifully illustrated collection of drawings of birds, with their names written underneath. I glanced up just as Henry looked down at his book, but I did not miss the small smile that he tucked away, creasing a line in his cheek. I stared at that line for a moment, feeling something shift within me. And then I began my study of birds.

CHAPTER 23

PRESENT DAY

I shook myself awake from my daydream when I heard the bird fluttering about in its cage. Surely I had something better to do than sit in this quiet room and reminisce about things that had happened years before. Taking myself to task for the weakness of my heart, I set about actually accomplishing something.

My wanderings the day before had been focused on finding the painting that hid the entrance to the secret passageway. Today I wanted to see the house as I had wanted to see it as a child—as an endless treasure trove, a place to which Henry and Sylvia went away and came back happy.

I found a part of the house I had not discovered the day before. It was easy to overlook, as the house had been added onto so many times over the centuries that there was no real pattern or logic to its structure. A doorway took me into a wing I had not seen before. It must have been on the back of the house, facing the moors. I walked down the hall but paused at an open door. I heard the soft murmur of a low voice. I eased closer, treading carefully on the old wood floor that I was sure would squeak in places.

The door to the bedchamber stood wide open. I paused outside the doorframe, not hiding but not announcing myself either. It was Henry's voice I had heard—it was Henry's voice I knew, even at a distance, even when it was just a murmur. Resting my hand on the doorframe, I watched him quietly as he sat before the large window that overlooked the moors. Two high-backed chairs were drawn before the window, facing each other. Henry's attention was fixed on the old gentleman sitting in the other chair. The old gentleman's gaze was fixed on the scene beyond the window.

"The moors are as beautiful as ever," Henry said. "Aren't they?" He paused, but his grandfather—it had to be his grandfather—said nothing. "You should have heard what Kate said about them. She called them ugly—so very ugly." I heard the smile in his voice. "You would have something to say about that, wouldn't you? You would convince her that they are beautiful, even at this time of year." He paused again, but still no sound came from his companion. "Do you remember how you always told me to come before the heather was in bloom? You always told me that anyone could find beauty here in the fall, when the heather was bright and the moors were brilliant with color. But it took a real eye to appreciate the beauty in this land the rest of the year. You told me . . ." Henry's voice softened. "You told me that if I was going to be the master of Blackmoore, that I would have to love the land the same way you do."

A clicking sound reached my ears, and I tilted my head, wondering what caused the new noise. Then I saw that his grandfather held seashells in his old hands. Now he moved his hands, and the shells clacked together, but still he said nothing, and did not move his gaze from the window.

"Yes, Kate is here," Henry said, as if his grandfather had spoken. "I have finally brought her. You remember her, of course. She is the one I made the model for. That was one of the most enjoyable visits I've ever had here, Grandfather. The hours we spent working together on that . . . the splinters you had to pull out of my fingers . . ." A wistful tone had crept into Henry's voice.

His grandfather turned his head and looked at Henry. My heart quickened with anticipation. And I forgot that I had not been invited to this scene. I leaned forward, waiting to hear his words.

"Who?" he said, in a voice that sounded frail and rough from disuse.

"Kate. Kate is here. At last." A note of pride and relief colored Henry's voice.

The old man shook his head. The shells clacked more loudly in his fumbling hands. "Who are you?"

My heart fell. After a brief pause, Henry said, "I am Henry, Grandfather."

"Henry. Which Henry?"

"Your grandson." His voice was hardly more than a whisper.

The shells clacked more furiously, and several fell to the floor with a clatter. Henry leaned over and picked them up, setting them gently in his grandfather's lap, and covered his old hands with his.

"Never mind," he said in a quiet voice. But I saw, in his profile, a broken look on his face. "I have rambled on too long. Shall I read to you instead?"

Grandfather pointed a trembling finger at the stack of books on the low table in front of them. Henry picked up the top book, looked at it, then set it aside. He did the same with two more books. The fourth book brought a smile to his face, and he asked, "Would Shakespeare suit you?"

The old man nodded briefly. His gaze turned back to the window, and as Henry cracked the cover of the book, the clicking of the shells quieted.

Henry's voice reached me like a lullaby. I closed my eyes and listened to him read the words I had heard him read before, years ago.

Let me not to the marriage of true minds
Admit impediments. Love is not love
Which alters when it alteration finds,
Or bends with the remover to remove:
O, no! it is an ever-fixed mark,
That looks on tempests, and is never shaken,

It is the star to every wandering bark,
Whose worth's unknown, although his height be taken.
Love's not Time's fool, though rosy lips and cheeks
Within his bending sickle's compass come;

Henry's voice cracked. He cleared his throat, and a tear fell on my cheek. I leaned against the doorframe, weak with sorrow, my hand pressed over my breaking heart. I heard his roughly drawn breath, and then he went on:

Love alters not with his brief hours and weeks,
But bears it out even to the edge of doom.
If this be error, and upon me proved,
I never writ, nor no man ever loved.

I kept my eyes closed as his voice faded, feeling the full measure of devotion of this young man for the grandfather who had forgotten him.

"Again, please," his grandfather said.

I opened my eyes in time to see Henry reach out and place another fallen shell in his grandfather's hands. He started reading again, and I backed up carefully, knowing I had stayed too long. I had seen and heard many things in my life that I had not been invited to. I had regretted eavesdropping more times than I could count. It was always too hard on my heart.

I walked away with soft footsteps and tried to shut my heart to what I had witnessed. But my heart protested the closing, and stayed open, tender and raw, and it whispered to me, *There is nothing more beautiful in the natural world than what you have just seen. There is nothing more moving than that devotion, that steadfast love.*

But I shushed my heart. I did not want to be told such things, and I certainly did not want to feel. I did not want beauty to move me. I did not want to be won over by my heart. This was my path. This was how I would change the course of my life: by rejecting everything that Worthington women did naturally.

CHAPTER 24

TWO AND A HALF YEARS BEFORE

I was spending more and more time in the library at Delafield Manor. I now had a stack of my own books on one side of the table, and when I was not reading, I was debating with Henry. He had a tutor all morning, and so he had plenty of time to learn more than I did. It took most of my afternoons to feel even halfway caught up with the progress he was making. My own mother cared little for my education, just as she cared little that I spent most of my day away from home.

Sylvia was content to lie in front of the fire and dangle a piece of yarn for the kitten to play with. When I needed a break from my more rigorous studies of philosophy and science, I always turned back to the illustrated book on birds. My greatest frustration, though, was being unable to hear their calls for myself. Surely I had heard them—everyone hears birdsong. But I wanted to know them individually, to be able to identify them and connect each bird with its song.

"Have you ever heard the call of a woodlark?" I asked Henry.

He looked up from his notes. He was writing a paper comparing the Greek myths of Icarus and Phaeton, a subject we had discussed at length the previous afternoon. "I can't say that I have," he said, casting his gaze on my open book.

I sighed.

"What?"

I shrugged. "I would just like to be able to hear some of these calls."

"Our gamekeeper is a great birder. I could ask him about it."

"Would you?" I looked up, finding Henry's eyes right on me. He looked at me in silence for a moment, and I remembered, just as if it was happening again, how he had pulled me to safety—how strong he was when he had lifted me onto his horse—how he had called me Kate when I asked him to.

"Yes," he said quietly, a little smile curving up one side of his mouth. "I would do that for you, Kate."

He looked down then, with a smile tugging at his lips. He pressed it away, and a line creased his cheek, near his mouth. I stared at that crease, feeling something melt inside of me.

It was full dark when the pebble hit my window. I jerked awake, then immediately cursed myself for oversleeping. I was not even dressed yet. Scrambling out of bed, I lurched toward the window and threw it open.

Leaning my head and shoulders out, I looked down and spied Henry standing near the rose bushes beneath my window. "I need to dress," I whisper-called. "Wait just a moment."

"Be quick about it. Carson said this is the perfect time."

I had my clothes already stuffed under my pillow. And not for the first time, I was grateful I did not share a room with any of my sisters. I hurried to pull on my dress, two pairs of my thickest stockings, and my boots. The laces were tricky in the dark, but I wasn't going to risk lighting a candle and being caught. I was ready in record time. Henry was pacing impatiently under the window, and when I was halfway out he softly called out, "Just jump and I'll catch you."

"I can do this," I hissed, searching for my customary footholds in the lattice. I felt clumsy. After a few fumbling steps down the lattice, I felt Henry grip my ankle.

"*I have you,*" *he said, and knowing he could catch me if I needed him, I hurried down the rest of the way until he grabbed me by my waist and pulled me away from the wall, setting me down on my feet. He gave me not a second to catch my breath but grabbed my hand and started running for the woods.*

I ran too, looking over my shoulder to check for any lights in the house—for any sign that I had been heard and was about to be discovered. But the windows stayed black, and the full moon lit our way. I grinned and faced the woods, and the clearing, and the birds that awaited.

Carson was an old man. As old as the land, it seemed. He waited in the clearing, and when we crashed through the last of the trees, panting and laughing with the thrill of our adventure, he shushed us as if we were naughty children.

I had known him as long as I had known all the servants at Delafield Manor. It had been a second home to me, and the people there were like a second family. Carson, a man of very few words, always tipped his hat to me and always had a shy smile for me.

I sidled up next to him and said, "Thank you for doing this."

He nodded briefly, a curt acknowledgment of my words.

"Your arthritis is not bothering you this morning, is it?"

"No, Miss Katherine." His voice was low and gruff.

Henry moved closer to us, his warmth blanketing that side of my body from the chill of the morning. "Have you heard them yet, Carson?"

"How can a soul hear a thing a'tall, with you two blathering on the way you are?" he muttered.

I covered my mouth to stifle a laugh and felt Henry's shoulders shaking silently beside me.

"This way." Carson nodded his head toward the woods on the other side of the clearing—the Delafield side. When he finally stopped his slow creeping through the trees, the sky was beginning to change, imperceptibly, from

night to morning. A lightening was taking place all around us, and when we crouched down and sat, surrounded by bushes, the ground was wet with dew. I sat between Henry and Carson and close to them both, letting them warm me as the wet grass seeped through both layers of my skirts. Carson lifted one finger, warning us with a look to keep quiet, and then cupped his hand to his ear.

Henry flashed me a smile full of excitement and anticipation. I gripped my hands together tightly and leaned toward the clearing. We were just on the edge of the clearing, where we could see and hear the birds both in the woods and in the clearing. Here was our best chance, according to Carson, of hearing a woodlark.

Birdsong started softly, but as the sky lightened, and the birds emerged from their roosts to forage for breakfast, it was all around us. Every time we heard a different song, Carson would whisper, "Blackbird," or "Swallow," or "Thrush." And still we waited, until the sky was golden and peach and the lightest of blues all at once, and I held my breath and hoped. I hoped for a woodlark, more than anything.

And then, a new sound, and I felt Carson go still beside me. I looked at Henry, with wide eyes, as the air was filled with a high, haunting song. A piercing, downward spiral of notes that ended in melancholy before beginning again and again.

"There he is," Carson whispered. "Woodlark."

I closed my eyes and breathed in deeply and let the birdsong fill my soul with melancholy and heartache and beauty. And when it ended, I pressed a hand to my chest, making sure my heart was still in one piece, before opening my eyes. I had to blink away tears, and I turned my head to see Henry, to make sure he had heard it too.

Henry was watching me, and I saw in his eyes the same thing I felt in my own heart. I saw the heartache and the beauty.

He leaned toward me, and his breath brushed my neck, sending a shiver down my spine as he whispered in my ear, "What do you think of your birdsong?"

I paused, feeling my heart swell with so much emotion I wondered how I would be able to contain it all. "It was . . ." I shook my head. "It was the most hauntingly beautiful thing I have ever heard."

His gaze swept over my face, his eyes looking like a reflection of my heart, all dammed emotion threatening to overflow. "Yes," he said, his voice low, only for my ears. "Hauntingly beautiful." He reached up and brushed away the hair that had fallen over my eyes, with a gentle touch and a familiarity that awakened me and startled me. "That is exactly what I was thinking."

My breath came brokenly, and my heart was beating much too fast. In fact, in that still moment, with the sun pouring gold into the air and Henry's hair still rumpled from sleep, his freckles still showing in that dusting across his cheeks, his eyes that charcoal grey, and his gaze settling on me with an unexplained weight—with the stubble on his jaw and the curve of his mouth and the breadth of his shoulders—I caught my breath, realizing that there was just as much poignant beauty in the face before me as there had been in the birdsong.

In an instant, everything changed. I felt more than just the melting I had felt with Henry before. I felt a sudden flame—a burning—and I was immediately consumed by it. My face turned hot, and I looked away from him, but not before I saw a little smile twitch Henry's lips. I found Carson watching me.

"Well, Miss Katherine?"

I cleared my throat. "It was beautiful. Thank you," I added, moving to stand. My legs had gone numb, and I wobbled on my feet until Henry stood beside me and gripped my elbow. "Stamp your feet. It will help."

Blushing, I kept my face down, as if I needed to focus all of my attention on my tingling feet. "I should be getting home. Before I am missed."

"I'll walk you there," Henry said, but I moved away from him and flashed him a bright smile, covering up my pounding heart and my shaking legs.

"No!" The word came out sharper than I intended. I did not feel quite myself. In fact, I did not feel at all myself. My heart was on fire, and I was

terrified that it showed in my face. "No, thank you. I'll be fine. Thank you again, Carson. Thank you, Henry." And then I hurried away, as fast as my trembling legs could carry me, but I did not go home. I hid behind a tree just outside the rim of my garden, and I pressed a hand to my chest and wondered what had happened to my heart.

CHAPTER 25

Miss St. Claire kept her promise, finding me that afternoon when the sky cleared to tell me we would all three of us take a walk to Robin Hood's Bay. When I met her and Sylvia in the entry hall, Miss St. Claire carried a basket of food. "For the poor," she told me, gesturing to it with one graceful hand. "It is the duty of every lady blessed enough to be in my position to be mindful of those less fortunate."

"Indeed," I muttered.

As we walked down the hill to the town and I watched Miss St. Claire carry that basket with a sunny smile on her face, it struck me how perfectly suited she was for her station in life. I could see why Mrs. Delafield had chosen her for Henry. I could easily envision her as the mistress of Blackmoore. She had been trained for this position. She had prepared all her life to take her rightful place at Henry's side. And the truth I could not deny was that she would make him proud. She would be proper and lovely and thoughtful and generous and absolutely predictable in every way. For all of these reasons, I heartily disliked her.

The street into Robin Hood's Bay was steep and cobbled, following the path of a ravine to the sea. The red-roofed cottages tumbled down the slope, all angles and tenacious grasping to land that looked anxious to tumble into the sea as well. I could guess that a hard living was earned here by fishermen with hands that were cracked and brown, weathered faces that looked like the wind itself had etched the lines in them the same way it pushed the waves and marked the sand. I admired these families, pitting their will to survive against the will of the sea to devour them and their houses and their town as well.

Miss St. Claire drew closer to me, her basket bumping against my side.

"Surely such a quaint village should not smell so strongly of fish," she said, pressing a gloved hand to her nose and looking at the ground. The cobblestones were wet, and the smell of fish was very strong. But what did she expect from a fishing village?

"One would think these fishermen's wives could keep their streets a little cleaner," she said as she stepped around a woman hanging her wash on a line. I saw the dark look the woman cast Miss St. Claire, but the elfin queen did not seem to notice. "I believe I shall do something kind for them. Perhaps I shall teach them how to keep their streets and homes clean so it does not smell quite so bad here."

She fanned at her face with one white-gloved hand. "Thank heavens it doesn't smell like this at Blackmoore."

Then, as if suddenly remembering her basket, she paused, drew out a bundle of food, and held it out to the woman hanging her wash.

The woman wiped her wet hands on her apron, her look still dark with suspicion as she took the bundle from Miss St. Claire.

"Here is some food, courtesy of Mr. Henry Delafield of Blackmoore."

The woman bobbed a small curtsy and muttered a gruff thank-you before thrusting the food at a child by her side. She went back to her washing, and Miss St. Claire turned her sunny smile on the street and the people in front of her.

"Did you see that, Miss Worthington?" Her smile stretched wide, her eyes shining with goodness. "Did you see her face? It is such a joy to help others. The faces of the people I help are all the reward I will ever need. It is what motivates me in everything I do. And Henry will be so pleased to know I am already fulfilling my duty, won't he, Sylvia?"

Sylvia mumbled something in reply. Judging by the look of exhaustion on her face, I thought she was probably just looking forward to finding somewhere to sit after her taxing walk from Blackmoore.

"Oh, is that a bakery? How quaint! I didn't remember a bakery here before. Come, let's get something to eat. Perhaps it will smell a little better inside." Miss St. Claire picked her way across the cobblestones to the small, narrow stone building with the bread in its front window.

Sylvia followed her, and the two of them stopped twice for Miss St. Claire to hand a bundle of food to a passing villager. I hung back and tried to talk myself into liking Miss St. Claire. She was the epitome of thoughtfulness and generosity, and yet everything she said and did irritated me to no end.

"Come on! Mother said we have to hurry!" The child's voice drew my attention to the two small girls walking past me. One looked to be about seven. Oliver's age. She had a firm grip on the arm of a small girl, who was pulling back and crying. As the older sister tugged, the younger one slipped on the wet cobblestones and fell, hitting her head on the ground.

I swiftly crouched next to her. "Oh, dear. Let me help you." I reached for the little girl, who couldn't have been more than four. Her dirty cheeks were streaked with tears, her long brown hair falling in her eyes. Her lip quivered, and she looked at me with large brown eyes as I picked her up and set her back on her feet.

"Mary! What were you doing, falling down like that?" The older sister marched back to her side, but at my glance she fell back a pace. "I'm sorry, miss," she said, dropping a clumsy little curtsy. "I hope my sister didn't bother you."

"No. Not a bit," I said, smiling to reassure her before turning back to little Mary. "Now, let's see if you've hurt yourself, shall we?"

She nodded, then held still as I ran my hand over her head, pausing when I felt the bump on the back.

"Oh, yes. That's a bump. But no blood. I think you will be just fine."

Tears still brimmed in her eyes, and her lower lip quivered in a most pathetically charming way. "Please, miss, can I have a sweet?"

"Mary!" The older girl tugged hard on Mary's hair.

Mary cried out again.

"Oh, no, don't do that," I said, smoothing Mary's hair. "She did nothing wrong, I promise. I don't have any sweets with me right now, but I shall buy some and bring them to you. How does that sound?"

Mary hiccupped a sob. "Y-yes, please."

I smiled at the older girl. "And what is your name?"

"Katherine, miss."

My smile grew. "The same as my name. Well, Katherine, you are being a dutiful little girl, I can see, trying to get your sister where your mother wants you to go. So I shall bring you some sweets as well."

She smiled, and she had the same gap-toothed smile Oliver sported. I suddenly missed him fiercely. I had to stop myself from pulling these two little girls into my arms and hugging them. Instead I stood and said, "How will I find you to give you the sweets?"

Katherine turned and pointed behind us. "That's our house—the blue one."

I told them I would return shortly, and as I turned to join Sylvia and Miss St. Claire in the bakery, I saw more than one of the villagers watching me walk away.

"Where did you go?" Sylvia asked when I found her inside the bakery. Miss St. Claire was daintily devouring a hot cross bun.

"Oh, I was just outside." I pulled my reticule from my pocket and paid for four penny buns, two meat pies, two scones, and a handful of barley candy.

Sylvia looked at my purchase with wide eyes. "Did you not eat breakfast?"

"No, not much."

I took my purchases, looked once more at Miss St. Claire's nibbling, and said, "I have an errand to run. I'll meet you at Blackmoore later."

"What? By yourself? You cannot—"

I turned back and looked at Sylvia, who had been my best friend but was not anymore. I wondered how long and wide this gap between us would stretch. And I felt sad that we had drifted this far apart.

"Are you worried for my safety or my reputation?" I asked.

She drew closer and whispered with narrowed eyes, "Your reputation, of course."

I sighed. "It doesn't matter, Sylvia. I'm leaving soon for India, anyway. A walk home by myself will not make one bit of difference."

It was easy to find the blue house. But once I knocked on the door, I wondered what I would say if the girls were not home. A young man opened the door and stared at me.

"Good day. Are Mary and Katherine home?"

He nodded, looking nervous. "What have they done?"

"Oh, nothing! I have . . . brought them something."

The girls came running, expectant smiles lighting up their faces. I handed them the bundle from the bakery. "Be sure to share with your other siblings."

"Oh, yes. Thank you, miss!" Katherine tried to drop another curtsy as she hugged the bundle to her chest.

Mary turned her brown eyes on me, her face wiped clean of tears. "Yes, thank you very much."

I turned away and wondered for a moment if it really was a good idea for me to walk back to Blackmoore alone. But just then I heard a familiar voice call out, "Miss Worthington! What do you do here?"

I smiled at the sight of Mrs. Pettigrew, my traveling companion. "I was just looking for someone to walk back to Blackmoore with. You are not heading that way, are you, Mrs. Pettigrew?"

"As a matter of fact, I am." She trudged up the hill next to me, and I wondered if I had made the right choice, leaving Sylvia like that. I wondered how much of our separation was due to my choices two years ago. And as I climbed the hill and crossed the moors to the house on the cliff, I thought of that day two years ago—the day Mr. Delafield died—and the choice I had made. I wondered if everything happening now could be traced back to that moment and that choice.

CHAPTER 26

TWO YEARS BEFORE

I ran through the woods that separated our houses. Rain fell on my shoulders in fat drops. I had forgotten my bonnet and my cloak. Leaves covered the ground, a wet and thick blanket of fallen dead things, muffling the sound of my running feet. The sky was dark, the leaves were shades of brown, and there was a large, ancient maple tree ahead. It was halfway between my house and Sylvia's. Its lowest branches started above my head, and it was so tall and substantial, its branches so wide, that it created a canopy—a shelter from the rain. Standing against the trunk was Henry.

I stopped still, my breathing ragged, and stared at him. His head was bowed, his hair dripping wet. His arms were crossed tight over his chest, as if he were trying to hold broken things together inside himself. As I stared, I saw his shoulders shake. Nobody was meant to witness this, and I felt like a thief, standing there, stealing something that was never meant to be mine.

I closed my eyes and breathed and tried to forget what I had just seen, tried to find the courage to do the right thing—to walk away and never, ever let Henry know that I had seen him like this. But a sound reached my ears above the falling rain, the patter of drops hitting fallen leaves. It was a low, muffled sob.

I had known, of course. I had known that morning, when our servant came with the news of Mr. Delafield's passing. He had been on his sickbed for only a few days, and his death was a terrible shock, for he was stout and strong. I had thought only of Sylvia and her grief. I had not thought of Henry until I saw him there, behind the tree, leaning against its trunk as if he were too weak to support his own weight or the weight of his grief.

I made a decision. I opened my eyes and stepped toward him, onto the dry ground, where the leaves were not wet and my footsteps made a sound. His head jerked up, and his eyes flew open. The sight of those eyes would, I knew, haunt me forever. Such sorrow, such emptiness, such aching despair I had never before seen in Henry's eyes. When he looked at me, suddenly, I felt a blow to my chest—as if the force of his grief had struck me, and I could not move or breathe in the wave of this revelation. This Henry—this boy—whom I had known all my life, was, in that raw, grief-stricken moment, so much more than just the boy I had known all my life.

I knew I should not be there, and for a moment I feared he would hate me for seeing him like this. But then he moved. He moved toward me with quick steps, and I dropped all my hesitation and moved toward him. He reached out for me, his arms pulling me to him, holding me tight. The smell of wet leaves clung to him. His hair was wet where it touched my cheek. He buried his face in my shoulder.

"I'm sorry," I whispered, wrapping my arms around him. And then his shoulders shook again.

How long we stayed like that, I never knew. My face was wet from my tears and his, as was my shoulder, where he had buried his face as he cried. Daylight had faded to deepest dusk when his grip on me loosened, and he pulled back. He took a deep breath, then let it out without any sign of a shudder, while looking down at the carpet of leaves. And then he raised his eyes to me. They were red, but calm, and he looked at me as if I was an entirely new person. In that moment, I was sure it was true. I was sure I was a new person, for I had known Henry all of my fifteen years, but I had never really known him until this day.

I felt unaccountably shy in the moment, until Henry bent his head so that he was looking into my eyes. He smiled. It was not a large smile but a peaceful one. It felt like a gift. And then, to my great surprise, he put a hand on my cheek. His hand was cold, and my cheek was wet. He lowered his head and pressed his lips to my brow, where my hair was messy and falling across my forehead. "Thank you," he whispered, his breath brushing my skin as lightly as his lips had.

I felt rooted, as if I were reaching into the earth as deeply as the ancient maple tree we stood beneath. I felt something deep within me—something born of Henry's arms and his eyes and that small, warm smile he had given me like a gift.

"You're welcome," I whispered back. The words came from a place of quiet awe within me.

Then he dropped his hand from my cheek, and his thumb brushed my jaw as he did. He stepped away from me. "I'll walk you back," he said. "It's nearly dark."

I nodded, and we walked together in a silence that was deep and mellow and warm. The silence felt too significant to break, as if everything that might have been said would have trivialized the things that had passed between us without any words at all.

Too soon I spied my house, the glow of candlelight flickering through its windows. I stopped at the edge of the grass, and Henry stopped too. I realized I had forgotten my original aim—to visit Sylvia. To comfort her. To give her my strength, if I could. But I could not go now. I had given what I had to Henry. All of it.

I reached for him without thinking and found my hand grasped by his, easily and naturally. "Tell Sylvia—tell Sylvia I will visit her tomorrow."

"I will," he said, holding my hand as he had held me earlier—as if he needed me. As if he wanted me.

My throat was suddenly too dry for speaking, and so I nodded and slipped my hand from his grasp. Turning, I ran quickly to the house, sure that I felt his gaze on me the entire way.

CHAPTER 27

PRESENT DAY

The evening had never stretched so long as it did on this evening while I waited for midnight to come again, bringing with it another trip to the tower with Henry.

"Where have you been today?" Henry asked, once we had climbed up into the tower.

I loved this place even more than I loved the bird room. I loved being high above everything. I loved seeing the tops of trees and the expanse of the ocean in the moonlight, and I loved hearing the haunting cries of the rooks in the next tower.

"I went into Robin Hood's Bay with Sylvia and Miss St. Claire." Saying her name brought a bitterness to my tone I had not planned.

"But you did not come home with them." He made it sound like a question.

"No. I . . . had something I had to do. But I made it here safe enough, as you see."

He just looked at me, without comment, but I could sense there were things he wanted to say to me.

"Are you going to lecture me about propriety?" I asked, raising an eyebrow at him.

He shook his head. "No. I was just going to say that I would have liked to go with you. I've wanted to show you Robin Hood's Bay for a long time."

I hadn't thought of that at all. "I'm sorry."

He shrugged. "It's not important." Henry seemed aloof tonight. Angry, somehow, deep inside. But I did not know how to fix whatever was wrong.

So I said, "Let us proceed, shall we? You can ask your secret first tonight, if you like."

He folded his arms across his chest, faced me as if confronting an opponent, and said, "I want to know why you are so opposed to marriage."

I took a deep breath. He had asked me this many times before, and I had always refused to answer. But now I was bound to answer him, and the thought of being honest about this frightened me. My chin trembled. I looked away, searching for something within myself to anchor my courage to. India. This was for India, and open cages, and freedom. This was for a land far away, where I would never have to witness the marriage of Henry and Miss St. Claire. I gripped my courage and turned my nervousness to anger and hardness. I thought of my mother and father; I thought of Eleanor and her husband, James. And I said, "Marriage is bondage and misery."

"Bondage and misery?" Surprise turned his voice. He shook his head. "I think of marriage differently. A companionship of like minds. A tie that binds, yes, but in the binding comes strength. A lifetime with your dearest friend as your truest and best companion. That is what it can be. I believe that."

His naïveté infuriated me for a reason I could not explain. "Is that the sort of marriage you expect to have with Miss St. Claire?"

Henry's head jerked back, as if I had slapped him.

He took two breaths before answering. "We are not speaking of my future. We are contemplating yours."

"That is a thoroughly unsatisfactory answer, Henry Delafield."

A smirk lifted one side of his mouth. "You always fall back on addressing me by my full name when you are upset. As if you were my mother."

I scowled at him. "And you always fall back on trying to change the subject when you don't wish to be forthright." I reached out without thinking and grabbed him by the shirt front, pulling him down so that we were on eye level with one another. All I could see in his eyes was surprise and amusement. "Why should I be the only one making myself vulnerable? You have asked me for my secrets; now you should share something with me. It's only fair."

Henry reached both arms around me, resting his hands on the low wall at my back, trapping me. And even though I quickly released my grip on his shirt (what *had* I been thinking?), he continued to lean down, close enough to me that I could see the instant his expression changed from amused to intense. "What would you have me share with you?"

"Something honest. Something you have told nobody else. A secret of your own." I paused, then added, "Something about Miss St. Claire."

He shook his head. "She is not a part of this. This is between you and me."

I felt thwarted and angry because of it. He never spoke of Miss St. Claire. Any information I had about her before this week had come from Sylvia. Through the years, Henry had been consistently reticent about his intended, and I burned with envy. I hated that he had a secret I could not get from him. I hated that he had a month out of every year that he spent here, with her, and I had never been allowed to be a part of it. And I knew from experience that the secrets you never spoke of, to anyone, were the most treasured secrets of all.

I resisted the urge to shove him away, crossing my arms across my chest to rein in the impulse. "You never speak of her. I think it is abominable of you to keep something from me, after everything I have told you."

"I will tell you a secret. I only said it wouldn't be about Juliet."

Juliet. He had called her by her given name, as if there was already an agreement between them. As if he had already proposed to her. As if they were already connected to each other.

"I hate that name, by the way," I muttered.

Henry smiled, as if my hatred of her name gave him great amusement. Joy, even. "Do you? Why is that?"

"It sounds presumptuous."

"Hmm." Henry nodded. "Presumptuous."

"Yes! As if she has something classical about her. As if she could be the star in a Shakespearean tragedy. It is entirely too presumptuous. Did her parents not think how they were setting her up for disappointment? For that is what I felt as soon as I met her—disappointment that she was so very bland."

I stopped, realizing I had gone too far. Henry's eyes narrowed. I was speaking of his intended. Perhaps his affianced. I should not have said what I had.

"Bland? Oh, I see. You object to her because she is not stubborn and willful and outspoken like you. Is that it?"

I pressed my lips together, cursing my loose tongue. But I did not retreat. "Yes. I suppose that is it."

He spoke lightly. "Some men prefer quiet women."

"You do not prefer quiet women, though," I said, lifting my chin. "Do you?" It was pride that made me ask that. Pride asking if he disapproved of me. I had never considered it before—I had never considered that Henry might not approve of me. But now I had to know.

He considered me for a moment in silence, a faint smile lingering on his lips, then he spoke softly. "I think you have misjudged Miss St. Claire. She is intelligent and refined."

I disliked her even more after hearing his praise of her. "Well, if that is all you are looking for in a wife, then I suppose you will be very happy with your intelligent and refined Miss St. Claire." I could not help muttering, "Even though she didn't know the difference between Phaeton and Icarus."

His lip quivered.

"What? What are you smiling about?"

"You are jealous," he said with a laugh.

"I am not," I scoffed.

He smiled, as if everything I had said gave him real pleasure. "Do you want to know my secret or not?" he asked in a low voice.

I took a deep breath. He was standing too close. "Yes."

He shifted his weight, moving even closer to me, so that I felt off balance, as if the world had tilted and if I did not hold onto something, I would fall. My heart quickened its pace, and so did my breathing. I felt his arms on either side of me, anchoring me or trapping me—I could not decide which.

A long moment stretched between us, the silence so taut that I thought something would surely snap. He was looking at me as if contemplating a whole host of secrets he could share, and my curiosity mixed with dread.

"Your eyebrows," he finally said.

My eyes opened wide with surprise. "My eyebrows? What about them?"

"I love them," he stated as if it were a fact. A truth.

I laughed again, breathlessly now, and shook my head. "They are too dark. Too thick."

"No. They give your face character. And there is something so very . . . graceful about them." His voice dropped to almost a whisper. "Perhaps it is their curve. They look like the wing of a bird in flight."

I felt extraordinarily self-conscious, and I was grateful for the darkness hiding my blush. Henry shifted again and lifted his hand to my face. I held perfectly still, trapped with surprise, my heart in my throat. He touched my face as gently and carefully as he had touched the caged bird. His fingertips brushed lightly along the curve of my left eyebrow, tracing the line, his eyes following the path of his fingers. A tremor shook through me and my heart raced. He stroked my cheek with the back of his fingers, lightly, a graze, a burning left in its path before his hand fell off the edge of my jaw.

"I can never look at a bird without thinking of you," he said. "I wonder what you will do with your wings once you have found them. I wonder how far away they will take you. And I fear them, for my sake, at the same time that I hope for them, for yours."

I drew in a breath, feeling the air shudder into my lungs, but could not find any words to speak. He had never touched me like this. He had never looked at me like this. He had never spoken to me like this. My hand crept up my throat, and I felt my burning cheek, sure that some fundamental change had occurred where he had touched it.

"Now," he said, his voice low and husky, and he was gazing into my eyes without flinching, "are we even? Have I made myself vulnerable enough to suit you?"

I could have leaned into him and kissed him. He was that close to me. My heart pounded, and I found myself staring at his mouth. I gripped the stone wall behind me, telling myself not to reach for him, not to lift my lips to touch his, not to hold him tightly and tell him that I did not want to fly away from him.

We were fragile, the two of us, breathing the same air, caught in this taut moment of secrets and half-truths. I could sense how everything could go wrong with one misstep, one misspoken word. So I nodded and did not say a word, terrified to speak and ruin this thing we were trying to balance between ourselves—this fragile and deep and flammable friendship.

"Good," Henry whispered, standing upright and backing up a step. I shivered in the sudden cold without the warmth of his nearness.

"Do you want to go inside?" he asked, noticing my chill.

"No. Let's—let's finish this here." Awkwardness made me feel tongue-tied now. "You want to know why I object to marriage."

"Actually, I've changed my mind. What I really want to know is why you're afraid of love."

My breath came sharply. I tried to laugh but couldn't. He was not supposed to ask me that. He was not supposed to even *know* to ask me that. He crossed his arms and leaned against the wall, as if telling me that he would wait all night if he had to.

I crossed my arms too, wanting to protect myself, and took a deep breath. "My love is as a fever . . ."

"You want to quote Shakespeare?" He shook his head. "You can do better than that."

I glared at him, clenching my hands into fists. Anger was much less complicated than fear; defensiveness was much safer than vulnerability. "It is true, though. Love *is* like a disease. It ravages. It maims. It destroys everything in its wake. I am wise to shun the idea of it, just as wise as if I were to avoid a plague. It is a weakness of the human heart to imagine that something that starts with passion can last. Passion is a fire that burns and leaves nothing standing in its wake. It is illogical and unreasonable. Love is the downfall of men and the entrapment of women. It is a cage that once one enters, one can never escape.

"I have seen it time and time again. With my mother. With my father. With Eleanor. Now with Maria. It is a scourge to all that is tender and good. It is disloyal. It is no respecter of persons. It creates bondage, heartache, betrayal, resentment—" My breath caught unexpectedly, and I had to wait and swallow. I pressed a hand to my chest, where my heart ached so badly I could not breathe. "That is what I have seen of love. That is why I will avoid it. I will be wiser than my parents and my sisters and everyone else who was entrapped by a fleeting feeling and then made to suffer for it for the rest of their lives."

Henry moved toward me, until I could see his face in the moonlight. It was full of aching and compassion and denial. "That is not love you speak of. You have seen the decay of the imitation of love. Your parents never loved. Your sisters never truly loved. I wonder if they're even capable of it. But you, dear Kate . . ." He shook his head. "You are not like them."

But what if I am? I turned the question over in my mind, letting it tear me up with doubt, and then I looked up at the dark sky and sighed.

"I have given you my answer, Henry. Now it is your turn."

I was looking away from him. I was looking at the stars, wishing I could turn back time and not eavesdrop at that ball. I was wishing I could remake our fortunes and change the families we had been born into.

I wasn't prepared for the touch of Henry's hand on mine. A jolt of surprise rushed through me, and my gaze flew to his face. He was watching me with a quiet intensity that made my heart race. He did not merely take my hand in his. He slipped his fingers around the back of my hand, his touch a caress as his fingers encircled my wrist, slid up my palm, then slipped between my fingers. My heart pounded as he lifted our joined hands and bowed his head and pressed a kiss to the back of my hand.

Panic pulsed through me with the racing rhythm of my heart. And something else, too. Some deep, slow melting that made me feel weak all over.

"Kate," he whispered, stepping closer to me, "you are not like your mother. You are a different creature from your sisters. The depths of your soul are fathomless. You are brave and loyal and true. You have such a good heart." He held my hand close to his chest and covered it with his other hand. "It is only afraid. But I would take such good care of it, love, if you would give it to me." He bent his head and pressed his lips to my fingers.

I was all fire and fear and more fear inside. My heart threatened to bound out of my chest. My knees were weak from the melting that was happening within me. I trembled everywhere, and as my thoughts raced, I caught onto the first reasonable one I noticed.

In a shaking voice I said, "Thank you, but no."

I felt him flinch. But when I opened my eyes, his face was turned from me, and he stepped away, letting my hand fall from his grip. I folded my arms into myself, feeling wounded and weak. His back was to me, and with his head tipped back I could see he was looking at the stars.

Or perhaps it was the birds, nesting in the tower next to ours, that he watched.

After a long moment of silence between us, he reached for the lantern on the wall and said, "That's two. Only one more to go."

I nodded and pushed back the weakness that threatened my calm. This was what was supposed to happen. This would give me my dream— my trip to India. This was the right thing to do. We walked back through the secret passageway in silence, and the only words Henry spoke to me when he left me in the west wing were "Good night."

CHAPTER 28

Mr. Brandon found me on the moors. I had been unable to sleep most of the night, and sneaked out of the house before dawn. This morning I could not stop thinking of how quickly my time here was drawing to a close. Just one more proposal from Henry and I would leave this place and probably never see it again. And at that realization, everything became achingly beautiful. The bracken, the peat, the bruised heather, the thorny yellow flowers, the twisted shrubs, and the rock out-croppings. It all became exquisite and dear, and I loved it. I bent and picked some flowers and grass, tore off a branch of heather, and tucked them all into my pocket. I was just straightening when Mr. Brandon called out.

"Miss Worthington! I feel I have hardly had a chance to speak with you lately. You were absent all day yesterday."

The sun was rising behind him as he walked toward me. He was a nice man. He would probably make some other lady adequately happy. But not me.

"Indeed. I took a trip into Robin Hood's Bay."

His eyes looked greener than I had remembered, his hair more golden. He held a hand to his ear. "I have been listening for your birds, Miss

Worthington. But I'm afraid I need someone to help me identify them. I do not know enough about them myself."

I thought of what Henry had said to me—about a man not needing encouragement to lose his heart. I certainly didn't imagine that Mr. Brandon had lost his heart to me, but he was being very particular in his attentions. And it was time for me to do him a kindness.

"I would enjoy that, Mr. Brandon, but I am afraid I am leaving very soon."

Both eyebrows lifted. "Oh? Where will you go?"

"To India. With my aunt."

His face fell. "I was under the impression that was a distant plan. From what Miss Delafield told me, I thought things were not quite certain in that regard."

I clutched the golden flowers. "They are quite certain. I will leave very soon. Perhaps tomorrow."

He stepped toward me, a look of determination on his face. "Then I am happy to have this opportunity to speak with you alone. I have to tell you, Miss Worthington, what must have been already obvious to you. I find you fascinating. And beautiful. And kind. I rarely find a young lady who fascinates me, you know. More often than not, they bore me." He flashed me his infectious grin. "I would like very much to know you better. To have a chance to win your heart. So I would ask you to please—please postpone your trip, and give me a chance."

My heart fell. I had no idea he felt so strongly. I had assumed he was merely at my side every day because I was a convenient companion.

"I am so sorry," I whispered. I cleared my throat. "I should have said something sooner, I suppose. I—I have no intention of marrying. Ever. Please forgive me if I unknowingly encouraged you to feel something for me that I cannot feel in return."

His infectious smile was gone, and disappointment tightened his eyes. "No intention of marrying? You do not have to go that far to refuse me. You could just tell me you are not interested in knowing me better."

"No! It's true." I reached out and grabbed his arm as he backed away from me. "I am not being unkind. You can ask Sylvia. Or Mrs. Delafield. Or Henry. They know. I have been telling them so these past two years."

He pulled away from me. "Well, none of them saw fit to warn me, I am afraid." He bowed his head to me. "Please excuse me, Miss Worthington."

As he walked away, a sharp pain pierced my hand. I looked down and uncurled my fingers. The limp, thorny flowers I held were mixed with my blood.

I lingered outside the open door, chewing on my lip uncertainly. I had come this far. I had my pockets full of seashells and flowers I had picked on the moors. I had watched the routine of the servants and waited long enough to make sure the maid on duty was fully engaged in her afternoon nap by the fire. I could see Henry's grandfather sitting in his chair by the window.

Taking a deep breath, I pushed open the door and with soft steps walked inside. I did not want to startle him. The maid snored softly in front of the fire. The chair next to Grandfather's was empty. Waiting. I touched the back of it and tilted my head to look at Grandfather. His gaze was vacant, his face turned toward the window. His hands rested idly in his lap, covered by a blanket.

"Hello," I said softly.

He stirred, moving his shoulders, shifting his legs. But he didn't look toward me. I edged around the chair and slid onto its cushioned seat, careful not to bump his chair or the low table in front of him in the process.

"Do you mind if I sit here?" I asked, watching his face carefully. His eyes moved, shifting in little jerks back and forth, but still looking out the window.

I waited a moment, but he made no further movement. Reaching into one pocket, I grasped a handful of shells and drew them forth. I leaned forward and carefully set them out on the low table, one at a time, some curved down, some up, with their translucent bellies showing. I did not look up until I was finished with my task.

When I did, his eyes had moved from the window to the table.

"I know you like shells, so I found these on the beach and brought them to you." I reached into my pocket again and pulled out the remaining shell. "This one is different than all the others." I showed him the strange, bullet-shaped, dark shell I had found. It did not look like a shell, but it clearly belonged on the beach. "I wondered if you knew what it was."

He pulled a hand out from under the blanket that covered his lap and held it, trembling, toward me. I set the shell in his hand, and he twisted it between his heavy-knuckled fingers. "It's a—" His voice came out as a hoarse whisper. He cleared his throat and spoke again. "It's a fossil. A very old fossil."

I bit back the smile that threatened to burst through my careful control. He had spoken to me.

I slipped my hand into my other pocket, pulling out the golden flowers I had gathered on the moors. I laid them on the table next to the shells. I had pried loose a sprig of dark, purple-brown heather, and a few blades of the hardy, laurel-green grass that grew on the moors. These too I set down, then sat back and waited.

He picked up the yellow flowers, and I reached to warn him, to remind him of the thorn, but before I could, I saw him wince, then look with surprise at the drop of blood on his thumb. He turned his gaze to me for the first time. His eyes were a familiar grey. His eyebrows were thick and white and wiry. His face was sunken in. But the eyes were clear, and I suddenly realized why they looked familiar. They were Henry's eyes. Or, rather, Henry's eyes were from his grandfather.

"Who are you?" he asked, just as he had asked Henry the other day.

"I am Kate. Kate Worthington."

His craggy eyebrows lifted. "Henry's Kate?"

My heart stuttered. I felt my cheeks grow hot. "Henry's Kate? I am his friend. We grew up together." He was still waiting. "Um . . . I suppose . . . I am."

"You finally came, then." His eyes were clear, his gaze direct. He was seeing me. His thoughts were organized. I had heard before, from Henry, that he had occasional moments like these. But I was surprised to have stumbled upon such a happy incident on my first try.

"Yes." My smile felt wide enough to split my cheeks. "Yes, I finally came."

His gaze touched my face, and he sat back with a pleased smile lifting his features. "You are lovely. So very lovely. Just as he said."

I clenched my hands together in my lap, hardly daring to breathe, my face on fire. "Just as Henry said?"

But his gaze had drifted to the window, and a softness replaced the sharp clarity I had seen in his eyes a moment before. His fingers twitched in his lap, restlessly, as if they were missing something. I leaned toward him and gently placed a shell in his hands. His fingers turned the shell over and over, tracing its grooves and curves.

I watched him expectantly but knowing all the while that he had slipped away again.

Taking a cue from Henry's visit, I asked, "Shall I read to you?"

He nodded, with his gaze out the window, and as I reached for the stack of books, he said something softly. So softly I could not hear him clearly. I leaned toward him.

"What did you say?"

"The Woodlark," he murmured, turning his shell over and over.

I looked from his face to the window he was gazing at. But I could see no sign of a bird within its frame.

"Pardon me?"

"The Woodlark. Henry's woodlark. The Woodlark." He pointed a trembling finger at the table. I picked up the first book on the stack in front of me, showing it to him with raised eyebrows. He pointed again. "The Woodlark." I lifted another book, and another, and then I found a piece of paper wedged between two books. It was a poem, it seemed. Handwritten. And at the top of the page were the words "The Woodlark by Robert Burns."

I picked it up and showed it to him. "This? You would like me to read this to you?"

He sat back, a look of contentment on his face, and nodded.

He had called this Henry's woodlark. I cleared my throat, and with a quickened heart I read,

> *O stay, sweet warbling woodlark, stay*
> *Nor quit for me the trembling spray,*
> *A hapless lover courts thy lay,*
> *Thy soothing, fond complaining.*
> *Again, again that tender part,*
> *That I may catch thy melting art;*
> *For surely that wad touch her heart*
> *Wha' kills me wi' disdaining.*
> *Thou tells o' never-ending care;*
> *O' speechless grief, and dark despair:*
> *For pity's sake, sweet bird, nae mair!*
> *Or my poor heart is broken.*

I held the paper gently after I had finished reading. "That is so beautiful," I murmured.

"His heart is broken," Grandfather said, looking out the window. "That is why he loves the woodlark."

I stared at him. "Who? Whose heart is broken?" I asked in a whisper.

He turned his face to me, and I saw the clarity in his grey eyes. He was present. He was sure of what he was saying. He opened his mouth to speak.

"What are you doing here?"

I jumped at the sound and whirled around to face the door. Mrs. Delafield came striding into the room, ready for battle.

I stood quickly and edged away from the chair I had occupied. She looked from me to her father. I saw her gaze take in the seashells and the flowers.

"I was just . . . reading to him," I said, knowing it was not an adequate excuse. I knew I was not supposed to be here. The sleeping guard attested to that fact.

She gestured for me to come to her, which I did with a pounding heart and dread pouring through my veins. She backed into the hall and closed the door soundly before facing me. I stepped back a pace.

"What did you say to my father? Did you talk about his will?"

My mouth fell open. "No!"

"It can't be changed, Kitty. I don't care what he said to you or what you said to him. The will can't be changed. So if that was your design in visiting him—"

"No!" I was appalled. "I never said a word about his will!" I stared at her as realization dawned on me. My heart pounded. I thought back to that evening eighteen months before, at the Delafield ball. I thought back to that dark room and the drapes that hid me from view as I listened to a conversation I had not been invited to. "Why would you think that?" I asked, my voice quiet. Scared. The smell of peonies was so strong in my mind I almost looked around to see if they were nearby. "Why would you suspect me of talking to him about his will?"

Her eyes were all cold blue suspicion. "My father is unwell. Whatever he said to you cannot be believed. And no usurper is going to come here and change my plans for my son."

"Mama!" It was Sylvia. Her call sounded urgent. She came walking around the corner of the hall, moving faster than I had ever seen her move. When she saw me standing by her mother, she stopped suddenly, a look of dread on her face.

"What is it?" Mrs. Delafield went to her. "What's wrong?"

Sylvia looked at me when she answered. "It's your mother, Kitty. She is here. She has brought Maria."

CHAPTER 29

"No. No no no no no," I muttered to myself as I hurried through the halls and down the stairs. When I reached the entry hall, the butler was standing alone with several traveling trunks piled around him.

"My mother?" I asked.

He bowed. "In the drawing room, miss."

I ran to the drawing room, my feet sliding on the marble floor, and entered the room breathless.

Her laugh rang through the room—husky and sultry. She sat right next to the younger Mr. Brandon on the settee. She was sitting so close to him her leg was pressed up against him and her bosom rested on his arm. My gaze darted around the room, finding Miss St. Claire with her mouth open in surprise, and Mr. Pritchard with a scathing look of reproach, and Herr and Frau Spohr, and that older couple whose name I kept forgetting, and the Delafield cousins, and more. At least half the guests were here. At least half the company was witnessing my mother practically sitting on Mr. Brandon's lap.

"Mama!" I hurried to her. "I was not expecting you. At all."

She looked up at me, but for a startled moment I had the strange sensation that she didn't recognize me. Her gaze went right through me.

Then she said, "Kitty! My dearest girl! I missed you too much to stay away."

Her hand wrapped around Mr. Brandon's arm and squeezed. He was not looking at me.

I tried to calm my racing heart. "Oh, did you? How silly. But where is Maria?"

She waved a hand. "Upstairs getting changed. But I could not spare a moment away from this marvelous company, and now I see how right my instincts were." She looked at Mr. Brandon, and their faces were so close together they appeared to be breathing the same air. She licked her lips.

"Mama." The panic in my voice made it louder than I intended. "I must speak with you. Immediately."

She turned her gaze on me slowly, and there, in her eyes, was that dull gleam of determination that I had seen countless times before. "Don't be silly, Kitty."

"Kate," I said, clenching my fists.

She laughed lightly. "Don't be silly, Kitty. I am going to sit here with Mr. Brandon." She turned her gaze back to him. "You were telling me about your estate. Do go on."

Mr. Brandon flicked a glance at me. It was full of pity. My stomach turned at the sight. He was probably, right at this moment, thanking his good fortune that he had not connected himself to me.

He edged over slightly, moving his arm away from Mama, and said politely, "My father's estate is in Surrey, Mrs. Worthington."

"Surrey! I must hear all about it."

He smiled politely at her but looked at me as he said, "I am happy to oblige."

Mama followed his gaze and seemed surprised to see me. Her brow creased in a frown. "What are you doing still standing there, Kitty? Go and see to your sister."

Frustration and fear and helplessness filled me, and I looked about the drawing room, and back to Mama. Finally I turned and hurried from the room.

"What are you and Mama doing here?" I yelled as I entered my room, which was where the butler told me Maria had been deposited.

Her boots and stockings and bonnet were strewn all over my lovely plum-colored bed, which she was lounging on.

She looked up and scowled at me. "Why should we not be here? You were the one who thought to invite me in the first place."

"Yes, but then you were ill! And you were not going to come!"

She propped her chin in her hand, and her gaze slid over me with a vague curiosity. "I was not ill. What gave you that idea?"

I stared at her. "Mama said you were ill with a fever the morning I left for Blackmoore."

She snorted. "I was not ill."

"Then why did Mama say you were?"

She waved a hand. "I don't know! She told me that we were invited here but that we had to wait a few days before we could join you." She laughed. "Did she really tell you I was ill? And this is all a great surprise for you? Oh, that's rich. Mama is so clever."

"Maria!" Panic had me in its grip. I grabbed everything of hers that was on my bed and threw it to the floor. "This is no laughing matter! Mrs. Delafield does not even want *me* here. How do you think she feels about *Mama* being here?"

"I'd wager she's ready to spit nails."

"Exactly!" I grabbed Maria's arm and pulled on it.

"Ow! What are you doing that for?"

"You have to leave. Immediately. Put your shoes back on."

She pushed me away, and when I did not let go, she used her foot to send me sprawling backwards across the room. "I am not going anywhere, Kitty. Why should you be the only one to have any fun?"

I caught myself against the wall and advanced on her again, grabbing a foot this time and pulling. "This. Is. Not. Fun!"

She scrabbled for something to hold onto and ended up pulling all the bedclothes off the bed with her as she landed in a heap on the floor. Panting, I ran around the bed and looked for her shoes and stockings. Where did that other shoe go? I got down on all fours and reached under the bed, saying, "We will just send you right back in the carriage you came in, and it will be as if this never happened, and I will win my trip to India, and—"

"No! I shan't go! You may be older than me, Kitty, but you are not in charge!"

I stood, holding one shoe and her stockings, as an overwhelming frustration took hold of me. I shook her shoe at her and yelled, "Kate! I wish to be called Kate!"

She crossed her arms and glared at me. And something in me broke. I threw everything to the floor and walked out of the room, slamming the door shut behind me.

I ran across the moors until I reached the large outcropping of rock. I climbed it without thinking about being careful. And then I sat at the top of the rock and looked across the moors and let the wildness and the solitude of the place seep into every broken crack of me. Birdsong reached me—the cry of the birds of the coast and the moors—and I regretted that I had never come out here with Henry. He would have known some of the birds here. He could have told me the name of the one that sounded like wind across water.

With the unexpected arrival of Mama and Maria, I knew my time here was over. I knew, as certainly as I knew my name was Kate

Worthington, that they would ruin everything. Mama might already have ruined everything. I might return to the house and find Mrs. Delafield in an uproar and ready to throw us all out before we could cause a scandal that would taint her precious family name.

The sky was grey today, the wind cold. I felt the hint of rain in the air, the occasional chill of an errant raindrop landing on my arm. I breathed in deeply and thought I smelled the ocean. It was a tantalizing scent—a beckoning of freedom and adventure and escape.

This trip to Blackmoore had not been the dream I had nurtured for the past ten years. I had imagined an idyllic holiday with my two best friends, Henry and Sylvia. It had turned out so vastly different from my imaginings that I felt deeply disappointed, both in the reality and in myself. I had never thought I would regret something I had longed for. I had never imagined feeling this heavy emptiness here. And it saddened me deeply.

It frightened me, too. For if Blackmoore could disappoint like this, what guarantee did I have that India would not disappoint as well? I climbed down from the rock and wandered the moors until the worry about what my mother might be doing overcame my desire for this uninterrupted solitude. Finally I turned back toward the house and the trouble that awaited me.

I had crossed the entry hall and was approaching the drawing room when I heard Mrs. Delafield.

"Katherine!" I froze. Mrs. Delafield was coming in my direction at a fierce pace. "May I speak to you a moment, please?"

Mrs. Delafield's smile was all cold fury and controlled rage. I glanced at the butler standing nearby and felt an almost overwhelming desire to throw myself at his feet and beg him to protect me.

Her hand closed around my arm. She gestured toward the arch that led out of the domed entry hall. "In the library, if you please."

My heart quickened with dread and nervousness. But in the wake of that icy politeness and that cutting, threatening smile, I didn't know what else to do but go with her.

I followed her with a pounding heart as she led me to the library and closed the door behind us. She stepped away from me and took two long, deep breaths, before turning around to face me.

"I allowed my children to convince me that your company might be acceptable here. But now you have brought that *woman* into my childhood home and brought scandal to me, to my father, and to the Delafield family name. I am certain all of my guests are looking for somewhere else to be for the rest of the summer."

My face was hot, my clenched hands trembling. "I promise I had nothing to do with my mother's presence here."

Her eyes narrowed in disbelief. "She told me that you invited her and that sister of yours."

I shook my head. "No. I only invited Maria. Not her."

She lifted her chin, looking down at me, and her voice shook with umbrage. "And who authorized you to do such a thing?"

"Henry."

It was a mistake to name him. I could see it at once and wished I could snatch his name back from the air to undo the damage I saw in her. Bright spots of red dotted her cheeks. Her head began to shake, back and forth, back and forth, and I could see the fury building in her eyes.

"I will speak to my son. But let us be clear on this point: you will never become mistress of Blackmoore. You will never bear the name of Delafield. You do not deserve the honor of being connected to the Delafield family—not you, nor any of your sisters, and especially not your mother." Her trembling finger pointed at me again. "Do you understand?"

Shame coursed through me. "Perfectly," I whispered.

"Now." She drew her shoulders back and smoothed her hair. "See if you can rein in that woman before she ruins everything. If not, the three of you will be leaving at first light tomorrow."

She stalked out of the room. I sagged against the nearest wall and dropped my head in my hands. It would do no good to cry, especially now when I still had work to do. As soon as I reached the drawing room,

I was grabbed by the arm and pulled to one side. It was Sylvia, and she looked fearsome.

"This is a disaster, Kitty!" she whispered. "My mother is ready to strangle your mother. She's been flirting with every man here, and *my* Mr. Brandon just told me his plans have changed and that they might very well leave tomorrow! You have to do something before things get completely out of control!"

"I know. I'm going to fix this. I promise." I tried to smile. I tried to look confident, so she would believe me. But in truth, I had no idea how to fix my mother.

Mama had made the same mistake I had made and was talking to the abominably rude Mr. Pritchard, who was looking at her with unfiltered contempt. My cheeks were hot with embarrassment as I approached them.

"Mama," I said in a quiet voice. "Maria is not feeling well. I think you should check on her. Come. I will take you to her right now."

She laughed. "Nonsense. Maria is in perfect health."

I glared at her, feeling Mr. Pritchard's gaze on me. "In truth, Mama, she is most unwell."

Mama leaned close to me and said in a loud whisper, "Stop trying to ruin my fun, Kitty!"

"Mrs. Worthington." I started at the sound of Henry's voice behind me and whirled around to see him walking toward us, a wide smile on his face.

"Henry!" Mama turned from Mr. Pritchard and held out her hand for Henry to take. He bowed his head and pressed a kiss to her hand. She giggled. "Oh my! You are ever so gallant!"

Henry took her hand and pulled it through the bend of his arm, holding it there with his other hand. "I heard you were here and came immediately to beg the honor of taking you on a tour of Blackmoore."

"My own personal tour! How you dote on me." She squeezed his arm.

His smile stayed perfectly in place. His glance moved to me. "Kate? Would you care to join us?"

"Oh, no!" Mama answered before I had a chance to speak. "She must take care of Maria, who became very ill in the carriage ride here. In fact, I am surprised she has left her alone for this long. What are you thinking, Kitty? Abandoning your sick sister like this? Hurry away now, or else you will have everyone thinking you are completely unfeeling."

I wanted to scream at her.

Henry touched my shoulder. "You should go, Kate," he murmured, and I realized he was trying to save me from myself.

I nodded, turned, and walked silently through the door and up the stairs to the west wing. I sank against the wall of the corridor outside my bedroom and couldn't find the strength to enter it.

CHAPTER 30

A YEAR AND A HALF BEFORE

"I was hoping I would find you here." Henry emerged from the woods and crossed the clearing to where I sat in the shade of a tree with my sketchbook. I looked up with a smile as he sat on the grass next to me, sprawling out with a sigh.

"What's wrong?"

"My aunt Agnes has arrived." Cora immediately rose from her feline lounging position on the grass and slunk over to Henry, rubbing her head against his chest until he scratched her behind her ears.

Henry's aunt Agnes was his father's oldest sister. Since Mr. Delafield's death, she had made it a point to visit every year and in general make life at Delafield Manor completely unbearable for everyone there with her nosiness and her prying and her rearrangement of things.

I smiled, thinking it wasn't such a bad thing for the Delafields to be miserable once a year. Henry had life entirely too easy, what with inheriting his grandfather's estate and being so handsome and smart and likable as well.

"I am glad she's here," I said. *"Somebody needs to keep you humble."*

He smirked. *"I don't know what you're talking about. Humility is my finest quality, Kate."*

I rolled my eyes, then watched with disgust as Cora stretched and purred and nuzzled his hand with her nose. "She acts more like a dog than a proper cat whenever you come around."

Henry chuckled. "You sound jealous."

"Of you?" I scoffed. "I understand, as you obviously do not, that nobody can really own a cat, and that cats give their affections without logic. I simply don't understand why she behaves that way with you."

His smile flashed, a glint of mischief in his grey eyes. "I meant that you are jealous of the cat."

I lifted both eyebrows. "Of the cat?"

He nodded, his smile ripe with mischief, as Cora rubbed herself against his chest.

"Don't be absurd. I have never felt the least desire for you to scratch me behind my ears."

Henry laughed, a full-throated, hearty laugh.

"What is so funny?" I asked him.

He shook his head.

I frowned. "Tell me."

He looked down, a smile teasing his lips. "Not funny," he murmured. "Just delightful. The way you take everything literally."

I frowned and watched him with misgiving, trusting neither his words nor the smile that did not fade from his mouth or his eyes.

"And as for why Cora acts like this around me, I think you know the answer to that as well as I," he said, his voice quieter now. He leaned closer, as if to whisper a secret. I saw that even now he still had a faint trail of freckles across the top of his tanned cheeks. I saw that his eyelashes were still black as coal. I saw that the grey in his eyes still had that ring of charcoal around the edge. My heart quickened at his nearness, as surely as it had every time he drew close like this. Ever since the day he rescued me from the river. My heart was predictable that way.

"Why is that?"

"Because Cora is your heart, and your heart loves me."

My face turned hot. Cora further embarrassed me by stepping on Henry's chest and rubbing her head against his chin.

"Look at this, Kate. Look at how your heart loves me. Your heart adores me. It worships me, even."

"It does not, Henry Delafield." I threw a handful of leaves at his head.

He ducked, came up grinning, and said, "Your heart would like to curl up next to mine and never leave—"

"Hush! It's not true! Someone will hear you!" I threw another handful of leaves, as he ducked and yelled out, "Kate's heart loves—"

Without a thought in my head I lunged at him and covered his mouth with my hands. He fell backward, laughing, and I grabbed more leaves and threw them at him and he was saying all sorts of nonsense about my heart, and the leaves were flying in the air between us, and one got stuck on my mouth, and I laughed and threw it at Henry's head, and suddenly he grabbed my wrists, and I fell back, off balance. "Admit it," he said. "Admit your heart adores me."

"I will never surrender," I said, laughing, and wrenched my wrists free, pushing him over and finding the spot under his arms where he had been ticklish as a boy. I grabbed him around the ribs, tickling. He laughed, surprise in the sound, and squirmed. But I was relentless.

"You rob me of my dignity, Kate," he said, chuckling, and grabbing at my hands, pulling them away from his ribs, pulling me over, rolling over so that I was pinned beneath him.

He had my wrists pinned to the ground, by my head, and he leaned over me, his eyes crinkled with smiles, his grin as bright as I had ever seen it. My cheeks ached from smiling. I felt his chest rise and fall against my own, felt the weight of his legs across mine. My heart picked up speed. The sun cast its golden glow over the clearing, over us.

"I remember you saying you had outgrown being ticklish," I said, breathless.

"I thought I had outgrown it." His cheeks were red, and leaves were caught in his hair. His dark grey eyes smiled into mine. "I suppose there are *some things I will never outgrow." His smile softened, lifting up higher on one corner than the other, his eyes full of something like regret and affection mixed together. "Like you." His voice was nearly a whisper now, husky and threaded with remnants of his laugh. "I doubt I will ever outgrow you, Kate."*

And in that moment I knew. I knew that he was right—my heart did adore him. I adored him. I loved him. My heart was pounding, my breath coming fast. Something was happening. Something was shifting, changing. We were approaching a line we would never be able to uncross. His gaze moved from my eyes to my mouth, and I saw, with a leap of my heart, a look of longing in his eyes.

"Will you dance with me tonight?" he asked in a low voice. Tonight was the ball at Delafield Manor. I swallowed hard, my heart galloping so furiously I was sure he could feel it. Yes, I wanted to dance with him. Of course. I opened my mouth to answer, but before I could, a voice cried out in surprise.

"Henry? Kate?"

Henry jerked, and I did too, at the sound of Sylvia's voice. He rolled away, and I sat up quickly, appalled at how we must have looked.

"What . . . what is . . ." Sylvia stopped, her face shocked, as if she was too stunned to find a question for us. "What is going on?" she finally asked.

"Oh, that?" Henry said. He was lounging back on one elbow, looking as if nothing could disturb him. "Kate was just stripping me."

I nearly choked. "I was not!" I cried, throwing him a furious look.

"Stripping me of my dignity, I mean." His expression was all merriment and mischief. "She was tickling me. Quite an undignified moment for a strong young man like myself, to be bested by a little girl." He levered himself to his feet, stood, and held out a hand to me. I slapped it away and lurched to my feet.

"I am not a little girl," I muttered, and looked ashamedly at Sylvia, my face on fire. "Your brother is an atrocious tease, and I was simply trying to hold my own. Which is practically impossible."

Sylvia's gaze moved from me to Henry and back. She did not look anywhere near as amused as Henry. My heart fell. This was not good. I could tell it by the closed, distant expression on her face.

"I was just coming to find Henry because Mama is looking for him. Ball preparations, I assume." She bit her lip.

"Yes!" I pushed my hair back. "Yes, I am sure you both need to get back. I will . . . see you there. At the ball." Henry was watching me with that mischievous look and something else too—something that made me blush and made my heart pound. It made me wonder if he knew the truth—if he knew that I did love him. Sylvia looked stern and uncomfortable. I wondered if she knew the truth as well. I wondered what she thought about it if she did know.

It was too awkward for words. I backed away, gesturing over my shoulder. "I should . . . go."

I ran home with fear and hope battling for dominance within my pounding heart.

CHAPTER 31

PRESENT DAY

I had debated whether or not I had the strength to endure dinner at Blackmoore with Mama and Maria. As it turned out, I had barely enough self-control left to me. Mrs. Delafield had placed them as far away from her as she could without displacing Miss St. Claire in the place of honor on Henry's right hand. They were both too loud, and I cringed every time one of them spoke. In my embarrassment I avoided looking at Henry or Sylvia. I caught Mr. Brandon's eye once—the younger Mr. Brandon—and it continued to hold that pity I had seen in him earlier. After that I kept my eyes on my plate and thought of the ocean and India and a long voyage away from my shameful family.

Herr and Frau Spohr performed for the company again, which I was quietly relieved about, as that made it difficult for Mama or Maria to make a spectacle of themselves. As soon as the recital concluded, Mrs. Delafield approached Mama and said, with a cold smile, "You have had a long day of traveling and must surely want to retire early. Come. I will show you to your room."

Mama looked around, as if searching for someone to rescue her. "But I have not yet been introduced to all of your friends."

Mrs. Delafield gestured toward the door. "There will be plenty of time for introductions tomorrow." The two women stared at one another, both wearing their cruel, cold smiles. I could not guess who would win. Mrs. Delafield had the advantage of standing in her ancestral home; Mama had the advantage of not caring one whit if she made a scene.

I did not wait to see what would happen next. I grabbed Maria by the arm and pulled her toward Mama, saying, "It is time for all of us to retire. Come, Mama. I will show you the west wing." I touched my mother's elbow, begging her with a look to come quietly. After a long moment of staring at Mrs. Delafield, Mama finally drew a deep breath, lifted her chin, and said, "I would like nothing better, Kitty."

I breathed a sigh of relief as I dragged a protesting Maria and an audaciously offended Mama from the drawing room and up the stairs. I stopped at my bedroom door and surveyed the two additional trunks in the room. It seemed Mama and Maria were not to be given their own rooms. I looked at the bed and sighed again, this time with nothing short of misery. Perhaps I would find somewhere else to sleep. Anywhere would be better than here, with these two.

It was almost midnight when Mama and Maria finally stopped talking, which consisted mainly of complaining about their reception from Mrs. Delafield, and fell asleep. I had let them take the bed, insisting I would be comfortable on the chair in front of the fire. Alice had helped them undress, had watched and listened to us with wide eyes, but had said nothing. Finally, after all their talking and moving about and complaining about every little thing, the two of them were asleep. I quietly stole out of the room, then practically ran to the bird room, afraid I would be too late and that Henry would leave. But when I burst into the room, there he stood with the lantern and a smile meant just for me.

"This is awful," I declared as soon as I saw him.

"I know." He stepped toward me, held out a hand, and said, "Come. Let's escape together."

I slipped my hand into his and felt his fingers curl around mine. My heart thumped hard in my chest. I would hold onto him for tonight.

When he tugged on my hand, I followed him into the darkness of the secret passageway.

The sky was dark with clouds, only an occasional cluster of stars stealing through to light the night. Henry set the lantern on the grass of the tower and lifted all of its shutters to illuminate the space. The dark sky and the birds cawing in the towers made this place feel like another world. And I felt almost as if I had stolen back in time. As if Henry and I had found a secret passageway to the way we were two years ago, before the ball at Delafield Manor that had changed everything.

We sat on the grass and I leaned back on my hands, content to stay up here for a very long time. Content to sleep up here, if need be, just to forget about Mama and Maria and Mrs. Delafield all waiting for me in the house with their anger.

Henry leaned closer, nudging me with his shoulder. "Kate."

"Hmm?"

"What are you most afraid of?"

I glanced at him, but his head was tipped back, like mine, and his gaze was focused on the dark night sky.

"Is this for our bargain?"

He sent me a sharp look, his brow furrowed. "Does everything between us have to be about that bargain?"

"No," I said, smiling at his response, glad that he cared still.

I thought about his question, and then I stood and walked around the tower, listening to the haunting cries of the rooks, feeling the wind, and smelling the ocean. This was a wild place. All of my careful constraints had come undone here in just a matter of days. I felt untethered and unraveled and wild as the gale blowing my hair into dark tangles. This night signaled the end of our bargain, and therefore the beginning of my escape, and in this moment of things coming undone, I wanted to confide in Henry. I wanted to confide everything.

"I am afraid of India," I finally confessed.

Henry stood and came toward me. He looked confused. "I thought India was your dream. Your ideal."

"Yes. I have thought that. But what if it's not? What if I feel just as . . . restless . . . and—and caged and unhappy there as I do here? What if it doesn't fix anything? What if I have gone to all of this trouble for something awful?" I crossed my arms over my chest, trying to stop the trembling that had overtaken me. Hearing myself speak this truth shook me. "Truly, it frightens me to think that all of my dreaming will end in disappointment. And the thought of being disappointed in India makes me feel completely helpless. As if I am incapable of truly being happy. As if my ambition will be my curse. My dreams will turn into my condemnation."

I ran my fingers through my loose hair. And more words tumbled out, as if once I started talking about my fears, I could not stop myself. "And what will I do after I have seen India? I am not yet twenty years old, Henry! What will I live for? What if life does not hold anything significant for me, and I waste my days with this restlessness plaguing me, and it's all for . . . nothing?"

Henry's gaze on me was dark and troubled, and he thought about my words for a long moment before sighing and saying, "Truthfully, I would spend all my breath trying to convince you that you have made the wrong choice, if I could. I hate the thought of that journey—the danger of the voyage, the unknown threats of that country. But I would not rob you of your dreams." He shrugged. "So, if India is not your heart's desire, at least you will know. At least you will never have the regret, the wonder of what would have happened had you simply dared . . ." His gaze locked on mine.

Dared. The word snagged on my thoughts. I remembered what Henry had told me the other night, about why he had gone swimming in the ocean. That he wanted to do something daring. And suddenly, I very much wanted to do something daring. I wanted to face something truly fearsome and walk away from it alive. The dark birds rose from the tower next to ours. I tipped my head back and watched them soar. And then I knew what I wanted to do.

I reached for the wall with one hand and held the other one out to Henry. "Give me your hand."

He raised an eyebrow.

"I am in earnest. Give me your hand."

He held it out to me, as if it were a gift. I grasped it and tried to climb up on top of the stone wall while holding onto him. He tugged me back to the ground. "Wait. What are you doing?"

"Something daring. Like you. Only I am going to fly."

I smiled at him, my heart quick with nervousness, and he looked as if he would refuse me. But finally he said, shaking his head, "This is madness."

He released my hand and moved closer. His hands slid around my waist. I gripped the folds of his jacket. His grip tightened, and then I was in the air, with Henry lifting me high, and suddenly there was stone beneath my feet. I wavered in the air, bent over, trying to hold onto his jacket.

"Let go, Kate," he said, a laugh and a warning in his voice. "You have to let go of me."

I did as he said and stood upright, and he moved his hands, one at a time, from my waist to my left arm. My right arm was outstretched, over the open air. I stood upon the wall of the tower, the stones beneath my feet, Henry's hand wrapped tightly around my wrist, while I gripped his wrist.

"Are you ready?"

I nodded. The rooks called in the tower next to ours.

"Don't let go of me," he warned.

"I won't." My heart pumped with fear.

"Watch your skirts and look straight ahead. Not down at your feet."

I gripped Henry's wrist even tighter.

He took a step forward.

I stepped forward too, and then Henry took another step, and another step, until I was walking on the wall, high above the trees and the ocean and right next to the starlight.

A laugh burst from me. I felt light-headed with both exhilaration and fear.

"Faster?" Henry asked.

"Yes." He walked faster, never lessening his grip, and we went around the circular tower once, twice, faster and faster, until he was running, and so was I, and it was the most frightening and the most exhilarating thing I could imagine, running like that, around and around, with the wind in my hair and the birds all around and Henry—strong, secure Henry— holding me tight. Then he yelled, "Now jump!"

And I did not pause. I did not hesitate. Not even a second. I leapt, with my eyes closed, and felt nothing but wind and freedom and Henry's grip on my arm, and then he pulled me hard, to the side, and his arm caught me around the waist, and my arms stretched wide and I flew. I flew in the night like the blackbirds and the rooks and the woodlarks. I turned and turned, and I laughed, and the birds cried. And then we slowed, and I dropped my arms and opened my eyes and looked down into Henry's grinning face. My arms fell around his shoulders as he stopped turning and slowly let me slip down, until my toes touched the grass.

I was dizzy. I leaned against him, closing my eyes as I buried my face in his chest, feeling his quickened breath and his arms around my waist, holding me, keeping me close. Finally, feeling the world settle in its proper order again, I tipped my head back and smiled up at him.

He was shaking his head, smiling at me as if he couldn't believe I was real.

"I think," he said, his voice just a husky whisper, "that you have nothing to fear in life, Kate. I think the world needs to watch out for you, not the other way around."

I felt breathless and buoyant and torn up inside, as if everything within me had been rattled around by my brief flight, and now I could not remember how to stand still on the earth beneath me. I wanted to keep flying, or I wanted to find an excuse to stay this close to Henry for a long time. Both were dangerous desires.

So I stepped away from him and bit back the sigh that would have betrayed my disappointment when his hands fell away from me and we stood separate and alone. I shivered in the sudden chill, turning to look up at the dark shadows of the birds crying out in the tower above us. Awkwardness filled the spaces where we no longer touched. I had to say something.

"Now it is your turn," I said, forcing myself to smile.

"To do something daring?"

"No. It is your turn to confess. What are you most afraid of, Henry Delafield?"

He looked at me for a long moment, and I felt sure he would deny my request. But after several heartbeats of waiting, he said, "All my life I have known what my future holds. I knew where I would live, how I would live. I have even known, for years, who my parents would make me marry."

He drew in a breath, and his voice sounded hoarse and vulnerable and soft when he said, "You were the only surprise in my life, Kate. And I am afraid—I am very afraid—that once you leave, I will never be surprised again."

I did not expect the tears that stung my eyes. These were words of parting that Henry had just uttered. I felt like my heart had been cleft in two. Blinking back the tears, I wrapped my arms around myself, trying to keep myself from shaking, and took in a steadying breath. I had not asked him for something about me. I had not expected a confession that would tear at my resolve like this. I moved farther away from him, needing distance and clarity.

Two steps away, then five, and I paced the circle of the tower wall before I returned to him and said in a brusque voice, "Shall we move on to our bargain?"

He cleared his throat. "If you want."

"Go ahead, then. Ask me your last secret. Your payment."

"Payment first again?"

I nodded. I could not make it through another proposal right now, with the wild strings of my heart unfettered as they were. I moved toward the wall, putting my back against it, needing its support. But Henry moved with me, and stopped just a pace away from me, keeping my heart racing. He stood too close. I could grab him too easily.

"I want to know what happened at the ball a year and a half ago. The ball at my house. The one you left early, without dancing with me. I want to know exactly what happened that night, Kate. What made you leave early. What made you run away from me when I called after you. What made you tell me and Sylvia the next day that you planned never to marry."

We were here, at the brink. I had not thought this bargain would bring us here. My heart fell with a sickening drop.

CHAPTER 32

A YEAR AND A HALF BEFORE

Maria saw me in the hall and whispered, with a look of unholy amusement, "Mama has Mr. Cooper by the arm and is looking for you."

I shuddered with repulsion. "I cannot dance with him. I cannot. I'm afraid of catching whatever disease he has."

Maria smirked. "You had better hide, then."

The sound of Mama's voice drifted down the hall. Maria's eyes grew wide, and she giggled. I shot her a dark look and hurried down the hall, looking for a way to escape or a place to hide. The door to the morning room was cracked open. I slipped into the dim room and held my breath, waiting for them to pass by. But after a long moment, the door eased itself open, and I hastened to hide. Two options presented themselves: behind the sofa or behind the drapes. I chose the drapes, pressing myself against the wall behind their thick folds. The sweet scent of peonies wafted toward me. There, in front of the window whose draperies I hid behind, stood a tall table with a vase full of my favorite flowers. They had been all over the house tonight. The Delafields must have secured every peony in the county for their decorations.

I held perfectly still in the drapes, for I would do anything to avoid touching the diseased Mr. Cooper and smelling his fetid breath. I waited to hear Mama's voice, but the door closed again with only the sound of footsteps. Then a creaking of the settee.

"Oh, it feels good to sit." I stiffened. It was Mrs. Delafield.

"Indeed it does. My feet are not so used to dancing as they once were." This voice was vaguely familiar. I peeked around the edge of the drapes. Henry's aunt Agnes sat next to his mother on the sofa. I eased further into the shadows, grateful for the dim lighting. As long as I did not make a sound, they would never guess I was here. Emerging from behind the drapes now would only make me look foolish. I would wait until they left before going back to the ballroom.

"I am glad we have this chance to talk privately," the aunt said, "for I feel a bit concerned about you, sister, since my brother died."

"Oh? Concerned? About what?" Mrs. Delafield's voice was guarded, defensive.

"A subject of the gravest importance, I am afraid."

I should not be listening to this. But I could not leave without being seen. I cursed my bad luck and hoped that their conversation would not be too personal nor too long.

"I am concerned that you are not doing your duty to protect the Delafield family name from scandal."

My eyes opened wide. I wondered that she would dare to say such a thing. And by the affronted, frosty tone of Mrs. Delafield's voice, I gathered she agreed with me. "What do you mean?"

"I saw the Worthingtons here. I cannot believe you would invite them, after the scandal at Brighton—"

"Eleanor is not here, you will notice. And the scandal has not yet been confirmed. It has not even reached this part of the country yet. Excluding them would create more gossip locally. You know how I detest gossip. Putting up with their company is a small price to pay to keep our name unconnected with theirs."

"Yes, but still! The Delafield name, sister!"

Mrs. Delafield's voice hardened. "I am very well aware of the Delafield family name and what it is worth. I was aware of it when I married your brother, and I am even more aware of it now. I have done nothing to disgrace it. In fact, with George's match, I believe I have helped to elevate it."

"Yes, George's match was well done, but there is still no title. We need a title in the family."

I rolled my eyes. This all went back to their distant relative receiving a title from the Emperor of the Holy Roman Empire. Now that they had a count in their family lineage, they were puffed up in their own opinion of their family and what they thought was their due.

"I know we need a title in the family, and I have planned accordingly. The St. Claires have a title in their family. And Henry's match with Miss St. Claire is secure."

"But that title will mean nothing if Henry falls for one of those Worthington girls instead!"

My face burned hot.

"There is nothing to worry about on that score," Mrs. Delafield said, her voice dismissive and final.

"Are you certain of that? Because from what Sylvia told me . . ."

"I am certain." A pause, and then she asked, with a note of curiosity but no worry, "But what did Sylvia tell you?"

"She told me that she believes Henry and her friend . . . the one with the eyebrows . . ."

"Kitty."

"Yes, Kitty. She has grown beautiful, hasn't she? Despite the eyebrows?"

"Oh, yes, quite. Very striking. But do go on. What did Sylvia say?"

"She believes they may be forming an attachment."

To have Sylvia and her aunt and mother talking about Henry and me! I thought of what Sylvia had seen in the clearing and burned inside with embarrassment.

Mrs. Delafield spoke briskly. "You are worrying for nothing. If they have formed an attachment, I will sever it. Immediately. In fact, if there is even a hint that Kitty has set her sights on Henry, I will separate all three of them. I will send Henry to Blackmoore and Sylvia to live with you until I have *convinced the girl that she will rue the day she ever thought of loving Henry. I have thought of all of this. I will tear them apart without hesitation and without compunction."*

"Why allow her to associate with them at all? Why not separate them now?"

"Because it will cause gossip! Conjecture! And that one little girl is not worth the risk. Besides, I do not mind Kitty for Sylvia's sake. Without her friendship, Sylvia would grow even more slothful than she is naturally, and it would be difficult to arrange a good marriage for her. No, it is fine for her to be friends with them at this point—as long as it goes no further."

"Do you think you can really control such a thing?" Doubt tinged the older woman's voice.

"Of course I can." Derision rang in her voice. "Besides, I have something Henry wants very much—something he can have only if he does what I want in this matter."

"What is that?"

"Blackmoore."

My heart fell. A long pause. "Have you done it legally?"

The settee creaked again. "I am no simpleton. I had the solicitor up there last summer. My father's condition was already deteriorating, and the solicitor agreed with me that it was in the best interest of everyone involved to make any final changes at that point, before more of his memory was lost. My father was easily persuaded to sign the new will. And the best part is he does not even remember anything about it!" Mrs. Delafield laughed lightly. My stomach churned. "Now it is done, and if Henry tries to marry one of those Worthington girls, or anyone else I do not approve of, he will lose Blackmoore—the house, the estate, and the living that goes with it. It will all go to George."

I felt sick. The smell of the peonies near me was suddenly so revolting that I wanted to retch. I leaned against the wall, needing the support I found there.

"I can see that I have underestimated you," the aunt said.

"Quite." Mrs. Delafield sounded so pleased with herself, so smug. I felt I was suffocating in the folds of these drapes.

"I have told you this in the strictest of confidences," Mrs. Delafield said. "I have not told Henry yet. I do not want to unless it's necessary."

"Of course! There is not a young man alive who takes to the idea of being kept on a short leash."

"True." She paused. "I know how to spot the enemy at the gates, sister. And I know how to guard against it. You should not have doubted me."

"As long as you have things under control, I will be content."

"Believe me, I always have things under control."

I could not remember, later, how long I hid behind those heavy drapes, waiting for the women to leave. They talked of other things while I tried to breathe without smelling the flowers that made me want to retch. Sweat was dripping from my forehead when they finally left the room. I waited a few moments before slipping from the room, sick with shame and devastation. I saw Henry down the hall, but there were many guests all trying to escape the heat of the ballroom through the french windows. He called my name and tried to reach me, but I turned from him and fled through the crowd.

Nobody noticed when I walked to the edge of the lawn and just kept walking. I walked home through the woods with only the full moon for company, and I shivered in the cool air. Nobody noticed when I opened the back door of our house and walked up the stairs to my room. And there, in my room, sat the model of Blackmoore. A gift. A dream. A future that I would never have, no matter how much I wanted it.

I sat on the floor and slowly unlaced my boots, taking them off one at a time. I stood and stared at the model. I had not cried during that whole walk home. But now I was suddenly furious. I threw my boot at the model, and it sailed over the top of it. I threw the next one, harder, and it crashed through the roof, splintering the wood. I felt better for two seconds.

And then my anger returned, hot and implacable. I threw open the door of my room and marched down the hall to Eleanor's. I opened her door without knocking. She looked up from the stool in front of her dressing table, where she sat brushing her hair.

"Good heavens! Whatever is the matter, Kitty?"

She had come home one week earlier, and there had been hours of hushed conversations between her and Mama, which I had not been able to listen in on. But now I wanted the truth. I deserved the truth.

"I want to know exactly what happened at Brighton."

She carefully set down the brush and smoothed her hair, pushing it back behind her shoulders before answering me.

"I tried to secure a marriage proposal, and I failed. That is all."

I moved closer, leaning down to look into her eyes so that she could see exactly how furious I was.

"How did you try? How did you fail? What precisely was the scandal?"

She pursed her lips, regarding me for a long moment, until I wanted to scream with impatience. Finally she said, "I will tell you this only because you may want to try it for yourself some day. I stole into Lord Rule's bedchamber one night and waited for him."

I staggered back a step. "No," I whispered.

"It did not work because his valet discovered me and alerted Lady Covington to the situation. She got rid of me before I had a chance to see Lord Rule." She sighed and picked up her brush again. "But it is no matter. I will simply try again, with someone else."

I clutched the bedpost, feeling the need of something steady to keep myself upright.

"You thought to entrap him? So that he would be forced to marry you?"

"Don't look at me like that, Kitty! It is not so bad. Besides, it wasn't even my idea. It was Mama's."

I could not understand her, nor did I want to. But I did want her secrets. "Speaking of Mama, why has Mrs. Delafield had such a hatred toward her these last few years?"

Eleanor went back to brushing her thick, dark hair. "Didn't you know? Mrs. Delafield caught Mama flirting with Mr. Delafield, and she cannot forgive her for it."

My stomach lurched. "She did not . . . do anything more, did she? More than flirt?"

"No. He wouldn't have her."

I looked at our reflections in the mirror. We looked so similar, and yet I felt when I looked at Eleanor as if I were seeing a stranger. So I left her, feeling numb inside, and walked back to my room. As soon as my gaze caught the destroyed model of Blackmoore, the numbness left me, and I possessed only the dark, searing pain of loss. I sat at the foot of the ruin I had caused and wept with despair.

CHAPTER 33

PRESENT DAY

Henry waited for my answer. The rooks were quiet. I could smell the hint of rain in the night air. Misery consumed me. I couldn't answer him. I could not reveal the secrets of that night to him, no matter what the cost. I shook my head. "No."

"No?"

"No."

He leaned down, looking into my face, his grey eyes tight with some strong emotion I couldn't name. "I need to know."

I bit my lip and tried to banish the smell of peonies from my mind. "I'm sorry," I whispered.

He moved away from me suddenly and walked across the tower, pausing at the opposite wall before turning around. "Even if it means losing out on your trip to India?"

My refusal to answer might cost me my trip to India. But more importantly—more importantly? Yes, I really did just think that—it might cost me what I now had with Henry—this closeness, this transparency, this companionship.

I nodded, swallowing hard. "If it comes to that, yes. Even if it means that, I will not answer that question."

He walked back to me, more slowly this time, and said, "That is the only thing I want to know. Please." His voice was rough. "Please don't fly away to some godforsaken country and leave me wondering for the rest of my life."

I looked away and felt very, very small when I said, "I am sorry, Henry."

We stood there in silence for a long moment, until finally Henry sighed and said, "What are we going to do now?"

"We could . . . renegotiate, I suppose." I had no hope—I deserved no leniency. But I tried anyway. "I could give you something in return for your last proposal. Something you want just as much as that secret."

He looked into my eyes. The light shifted, his gaze dropped, and he was suddenly looking at my mouth. "A kiss," he said in a low voice.

A shiver rippled over my skin. Everywhere. "You are not serious."

"Am I not?" His voice held a note of teasing but something else as well. A husky, tantalizing note that sent shivers through me again.

The wind blew harder, sending another chill through me, and then suddenly, without warning, cold rain fell from the sky. It came all at once, in a sheet of icy needles that made me gasp with surprise.

Henry grabbed my hand, and we ran together across the tower. I took hold of the lantern but dropped it in my haste, extinguishing the flame. The tower was plunged in darkness, and we were suddenly blind. Henry stopped running, and I collided with him. He caught me and pulled me close to him and said in my ear, over the sound of the pounding rain, "Stay close. Let me lead the way. I don't want you falling through the trapdoor."

"All right," I finally breathed.

"Wait a minute while my eyes adjust," he murmured. His arm was strong around my waist, his hand pressed against the small of my back, and I leaned into him while the rain drenched us and my heart pounded and my mind screamed at me to do something—to find a way to fix what was broken between us so that I would never have to leave him. But there was no fixing this. I knew that. So I closed my eyes and breathed in the dusky smell of rain on heather and let my heart break a little more.

All too soon he moved away from me. His hand trailed down my arm until it encircled my wrist. I moved my hand to grasp his, and let him pull me forward until we stood at the edge of the trapdoor. The steps were slick with rain and we moved slowly down the steep, winding staircase.

We paused in the tunnel for a moment, catching our breaths, and I pushed back strands of dripping wet hair. Henry said, "You'll catch cold if we don't hurry. Come on." He kept my hand in his and I followed him through the dark tunnel that led under the moors. And I realized that I would follow him anywhere, if it were possible.

I shivered, my teeth chattering, as the cold increased and my wet clothes clung to me. We exited the secret passageway carefully, with Henry looking to see if anyone was in the bird room or out in the hall before leading me out. He picked up the candle he had left burning and we hurried up the stairs to the west wing, dripping cold rain the whole way. And finally we were in the hall leading to my bedroom. Henry pulled me to a stop outside my bedroom door, his hand warm around mine. He set the candle on the windowsill where we had talked my first night there. He turned to me, his wet hair reminding me of the day he had rescued me from the river. His eyes were as dark as the storm clouds outside, and I could see his chest rise and fall with his breathing, his wet shirt clinging to his shoulders and chest and arms.

I swallowed and stepped away from him, nervousness racing through me, spreading fire through my veins. We were not finished with our bargain. Henry must have had the same thought, because his mouth lifted in something halfway between a smirk and a smile and he said, "About that kiss . . ."

I stepped back until my back was against the wall next to my bedroom. "You were not serious," I said, only half-believing my words. But Henry kept coming, until he stood right in front of me. He rested his hand on the wall above my head. I licked my lips, my heart racing with nervousness. I tried to laugh, but it came out sounding low and husky and not at all the mood I intended.

I could not deny how close we stood—how the water from his hair dripped onto my cheek. But I was terrified. We had never crossed this line. And then his other hand touched my waist. It burned there, through the fabric of my gown. I pressed my palms against the wall at my back, trying to slow my breathing. It was unnaturally fast. So was my pulse. And I worried that Henry would hear it and know that he did this to me. I pressed my hands harder against the wall, fighting the urge to grab him.

"I was very serious," he whispered. His hand tightened on my waist. My hands left the wall and found the lapels of his coat. I did not mean to grab him—not like that—but my hands did not consult me. They bunched the fabric of his coat and dragged him closer. And the time for thinking was gone. We had balanced on this precipice for far too long. And now we were going to fall. I knew it, with a breathless certainty I could not deny.

His hand slid from the wall and curved around my neck, softly, surely, as if he had imagined this a thousand times, and—

A sudden light pierced the darkness of the hall. I started with surprise, and so did Henry. I pushed him away and looked toward the source of the light. Someone was carrying a candle and walking toward us from the other end of the hall. I peered harder at the figure. The flickering candle-light illuminated Maria's face. I swore under my breath.

My position suddenly became shockingly clear to me. I was standing outside my bedchamber in the middle of the night with a man, both of us dripping wet, and I had almost just kissed him. The fact that it was Henry only made it worse. I could have been Eleanor, and this could have been Brighton all over again.

I reached for the door handle and dread fell through me. My bedroom door was wide open. "You should go," I whispered. "Before she sees us."

He hesitated, but I was already hurrying inside my bedroom. I collided with something soft not two paces inside the room.

I heard a muffled *oof* and then I was sprawled on the floor and Mama was whispering for me to get off her. Then Maria was standing there with her candle, looking down at us.

"What is going on?" she asked. She held her candle toward us, and her eyes narrowed with suspicion. "Why are you all wet, Kitty? And why are you on top of Mama?"

I struggled to get up but my wet skirts wrapped around my legs, tripping me and making me fall again. Mama shoved me off her and stood, grabbing the candle from Maria's hand. She stepped over me and lit the other candles in the room, and by the time I was on my feet, there was plenty of light by which to see the happy look of triumph on Mama's face.

"He must marry you. He must!" She cackled with delight and paced in front of me where I sat in acute misery on my bed, getting everything wet but not caring.

"No, he mustn't. Nothing happened between us. He didn't even kiss me."

"It hardly matters, my dear, whether your lips touched or not. I saw you two." She laughed again. My face burned with embarrassment. "You were caught sneaking around with him, alone, at night, and you were seen in an embrace." She laughed again and clapped her hand like a little girl. "Oh, won't his mother throw a fit! But, Kitty, this is wonderful news! Wonderful! Why, you will be better matched than Eleanor, and I can lord it over his mother that you will be mistress of this place."

I groaned. "No, Mama. It will not be like that. He was just—he was just teasing me, saying that I owed him a kiss for the proposal, but nothing happened."

She stopped pacing and looked at me sharply. "What proposal?"

I fell back on her bed and covered my eyes with both hands. "He is the one who proposed to me, Mama. He did it as a favor, so that I could go to India. But nothing inappropriate happened between us. I swear! He was a perfect gentleman every other time."

She narrowed her eyes at me. "You mean to tell me that you have sneaked around with him alone at night more than once since you arrived?"

I shook my head, hating myself for what I had just revealed. "Yes," I muttered miserably.

She grinned and clapped her hands and laughed with raucous triumph. "You are more cunning than Eleanor. I declare, I never expected this from you, Kitty. He will be forced to marry you."

I sat up, panicked, and tears poured from me. "No, Mama. That cannot happen. I cannot force Henry to marry me. I cannot do this!"

She waved away my words with a dismissive motion. "A young lady has to use every advantage at her disposal to secure a good future for herself."

"I won't do it!" I yelled, getting off the bed. She jumped, startled. "I won't entrap him, I won't have him hate me for the rest of my life, I won't watch his respect for me die, and I won't turn my attention to other men! I won't, Mama! I will not become like you and watch Henry become like Papa! I can't stand the thought." I sobbed and then yelled, "I would rather marry that disgusting Mr. Cooper than be forced to marry Henry Delafield!"

My voice rang in the sudden silence. Maria's eyes had gone huge. She stared at something over my shoulder. I turned my head and saw Henry standing outside the open door of my bedroom.

He held my gaze for a long moment before turning and walking away.

"Oh, dear," Maria said. "I think he heard you."

I sat down heavily on the bed. It was done, then. It was finally done. We had fallen off a precipice, and there was no way to climb back up.

"It doesn't matter," Mama said, shutting the door firmly. "We will still force him to marry you."

I shook my head. "It won't work, Mama. He will lose Blackmoore if he marries me. Mrs. Delafield had it written in her father's will. He will be penniless."

She did not so much as pause at my announcement. "Nonsense. Wills can always be changed, and the grandfather is still alive. We'll take care of everything tomorrow. You will go and speak to his grandfather and convince him to change the will."

"No," I whimpered, but the fight had left me when I saw the look on Henry's face.

"Oh, I cannot wait to visit you here once you are mistress of Blackmoore! How she will hate it! To have me here, in her own childhood home, and able to do as I like. And she will not be able to do anything to stop me! Ha ha! I should like to see her try, once you are married. Will she be able to snub me then? No! No one will snub me once you are Mrs. Henry Delafield. Ha ha! This is the ultimate victory, Kitty! I cannot believe you have pulled this off!" She leaned toward me, grasped my face in her hand, and planted a kiss on my wet hair. "How I have misjudged you!"

I shook my head, over and over. "No, Mama. I will not do this. I will not." I said it over and over until she finally stopped laughing and looked at me clearly.

She wiped her mouth with the back of her hand, as if to erase the kiss she had bestowed. "You will not?"

Maria lay back on the pillow. "Don't be a dolt, Kitty. Of course you must see it through. You have gone too far to turn back now."

"No." My voice was weak. "I can undo this. I can . . ."

Mama grabbed my face again, but there was nothing gentle in her touch. She stared into my eyes, her own the color of that rusted trap I had found in the woods with the wounded rabbit caught in its teeth. "Answer me this, Kitty: did you fulfill your part of our bargain? Did you receive three proposals?"

I realized that Henry had not proposed tonight. The rain had kept us from finishing our bargain. "No," I whispered.

"Then, according to the bargain we made, you have to do whatever I want. Do you remember that, my dear?"

I fell back on the bed and covered my streaming eyes with my hands. "I won't. I won't do it, Mama."

"You made the bargain, Kitty. And now you must live with the consequences. Remember—remember what we agreed upon. Remember what you told me. You told me you never changed your mind."

I did remember saying that. I had thought it was true at the time. But now I was convinced that I had never been as wrong about anything as I had been about myself.

"You will speak to his grandfather tomorrow." She planted her fists on her hips and glared at me. She was powerful and manipulative, and I was trapped, trapped, trapped. "What do you think of *that* plan, Kitty?"

"Kate," I whispered. "My name is Kate."

CHAPTER 34

I was sitting on the whispering bench on the south lawn. I had not gone to the clearing, where I might easily have been found. I had not stayed in my room, with the fine splinters of wood trapped in the rug. I had stolen out of the house at dawn and stayed out here despite a little morning rain. Cora was my companion, and I listened for birds in the trees around me. The woodlark's song played over and over—those falling, melting notes of heartache. I wanted to plug my ears and hear it no more. At the same time, I wanted to hear it endlessly. Caught in this battle between mind and heart, I did not hear the footsteps on the grass. Bending down to stroke Cora's soft fur, I did not see Henry approach until his shadow fell over me.

"I've been looking for you." The words were spoken with softness and a hint of accusation.

My heart beat fast. Cora's fur was warm from the sunshine. I could not look up at him. I did not know how to act or what to say.

"Kate?"

I continued to look down. "Hmm?"

Henry crouched down, bringing his face to my level, but I kept my gaze stubbornly fixed on Cora.

"You left the ball early last night," he said, his voice too quiet, too

intimate. "I looked for you . . . I saw you leaving, and I called your name, but you didn't turn back."

I stood abruptly and moved away from him. "Did Sylvia come with you?" I asked, my voice too loud.

"Sylvia?" Henry's voice sounded confused. I saw him move toward me out of the corner of my eye. "What about—"

"Oh, look! There she is now!" I had never been so relieved to see her in my life. She came walking toward us from the house. She carried something in her arms. I still had not really looked at Henry. I could not.

But then he moved in front of me and leaned down, putting his face directly in my line of sight, so that I could not help but see him. His eyes were a dark charcoal today, and his hair looked as if he had spent all morning raking his fingers through it.

"Is something wrong, Kate? What happened last night? Why did you leave so early?" I stepped away from him again, and I saw the surprise in his face when I did.

I chewed on my lip. I knew what I had to do. My heart raced with nervousness. "I have decided something. I want to tell you. You and Sylvia. Both of you." I craned my neck to watch her approach us and wished she walked faster. I could feel Henry's gaze on my face.

"Sylvia!" I called.

She frowned at me.

"I must say something to you!" She kept frowning, and when she reached me I saw that her gaze held a hint of anger.

"What is it, Kitty?"

I did not even bother correcting her, for once. I brushed a trembling hand over my brow, taking a deep breath and trying to drag some courage up into my heart.

"I think I ought to tell you both that . . . that . . ." I stopped, taking in their severe expressions, and my courage almost failed me. It was ridiculous to say it like this. But it had to be said, and the sooner the better.

But before I could force the words through my lips, Sylvia said, "What happened to the model of Blackmoore?"

Henry's head whipped toward me. I stared at Sylvia as dread pooled in my stomach.

"I went to your room looking for you," she said. "What happened to the model?"

I swallowed. "A . . . vase fell on it." I glanced at Henry. "It is only a small . . . a very small . . . hole." I took a deep breath and looked away from him. I could not bear seeing the look in his eyes. "But I have to tell you something I have decided recently. It is this: I do not intend ever to marry. I have no desire for it. I will never desire it. I will stay single, like my aunt Charlotte, and be an adventurer, and I shall never, ever marry."

My neck was hot. I twisted my fingers together.

"Well, that is news." Sylvia sounded happy. I could not look at Henry. "Here. I brought you these flowers from the ball. Peonies. They're your favorite, are they not?"

The scent of the dying flowers filled my head, even sweeter and more cloying than last night when I stood in their shadow. Sylvia was right. I had loved them before last night. But now their smell turned my stomach. They smelled like humiliation. Like rejection. Like crushings and blows and clawings and stranglings. I turned my face away, reaching out a hand toward them, to push away their limp, curling petals, their withered leaves, their shrinking forms, their violent scents.

"Please, take them away."

"What is wrong?"

I took one deep breath through my mouth, trying to clear my head. Only now I could taste the scent of the flowers. It sat heavy on my tongue. I swallowed and felt it slide down my throat. It lodged halfway down, midway from mouth to stomach, and sat there, heavy, despairing, cutting.

"I am unwell. It's why I left the ball early last night. I am unwell." My lips trembled, and I touched my fingertips to them, trying to quiet the shaking within me. "I am sorry. Please excuse me."

I turned then and saw in a blur the white of Henry's shirt, the dark length of his long legs, the bruised and broken flowers at his feet, the hem of Sylvia's light blue dress, and then the grass. Grass, grass, grass, grass, faster, a blur of green, now gravel, stone walkway, and one, two, three steps to the back door. It stuck. Every summer. I pushed hard with my shoulder until it gave way to burgundy curtains brushing my face, blurred paintings, swimming door, looming banister catching me hard in the ribs, and slick wooden stairs. Fourteen steps, then three rooms side by side. The last room was mine. The door stood open. The ruined model of Blackmoore sat, like a dark, deformed thing, on the chest at the end of my bed. The hole in the roof looked like an angry, open mouth.

It had been our daily routine for years. Sylvia and I spent the afternoon in the library with Henry. She usually engaged in some show of reading until our attention was taken by our studies, and then she slipped into her afternoon "doze," as she liked to call it. And nobody interrupted us. Mrs. Delafield did not bother us. George was away on his Grand Tour. And Sylvia had outgrown her governess. We had been in this habit for so many years that I had never had reason to question it.

But today—four days after the ball—I lingered at the threshold of the library and tried to quiet my pounding heart. Henry was already at the large table, his books and papers scattered around him. He glanced up briefly as Sylvia threw herself down on the settee with a sigh.

"Has the day been that hard for you already, Sylvia?" he asked. There was an edge to his voice that I had rarely heard.

"No. I am just that happy to see you, dear brother." Sylvia smiled sunnily at him, but he did not return it. His gaze cut to me, standing in the doorway, and he lifted one eyebrow.

"Are you coming or going?"

The challenge in that raised eyebrow and the curt tone of his voice helped me make my decision. I stepped forward into the room. "Coming."

He slid his books to the side, clearing the space at the table that was usually mine, and I sat down at my usual chair. There was nothing comfortable here, but I was determined to be here anyway. I was determined to reclaim my place. I felt, deep within, that if I did not claim it now, I would lose it forever. Certainly Mrs. Delafield would want me to leave and never give her cause to worry again about her son's future. But Mrs. Delafield was not in this room, and she might be able to stop me from ever marrying Henry, but that did not mean she could stop me from being his friend.

"What are you reading?" I asked as I sat at the table.

He held up a leather-bound book. "Dr. Faustus. By Goethe."

"In German?"

"Naturlich." His curt tone grated on me.

"Oh. Naturlich," I repeated with a sarcastic bite to my voice.

He lowered the book and looked at me. "What is wrong with that?"

"You have everything given to you, Henry. You have your tutor teaching you German and French and Latin, and you can study things I might never be able to. So don't pretend it is 'natural' at all."

Henry held my gaze, his grey eyes reflecting a battle within himself. He seemed about to argue with me. I was sure I could see building in his eyes some fire that he would unleash on me—a fire of indignation, of pent-up arguments, of impassioned feelings. The space between us grew taut with my anger and his, and I saw a muscle leap in his clenched jaw, and his lips pressed together so that a line creased his cheek. I stared at that crease, and in a flare of longing wished that I could simply reach for him and touch his face.

I looked down. I took a deep breath and tamped my feelings down deep, until I no longer felt the ache of longing. And then I said in a quiet voice, "I am sorry. I did not mean to be angry with you, after all your kindnesses toward me."

He reached out and grabbed my wrist. I looked up in surprise. "Don't make me out to be some sort of angelic character," he whispered fiercely. "I have done nothing out of kindness, Kate. Do you understand?"

I stared at him in surprise.

He released me and leaned back, raking his hand through his hair. Then he shook his head and muttered, "I am sorry."

There was so much between us. So much we were not saying to each other. But I could say that. So I did. "I am sorry as well."

And I was. I was sorry for everything. I was sorry for my embarrassment of a mother and my scandalous sister and the fact that I had fallen in love with a boy who could never be mine.

Henry rubbed a hand over his face, then stood and walked to the window and looked outside for a long time—so long that I gave up waiting for him and pulled the top book off my own stack and cracked it open. But I was only two pages into my study of the life of Mozart when Henry returned to the table, sat down, and picked up his book.

"Would you like me to tell you about Faust?" He offered me a smile. "I will translate for you."

I closed my book. "Yes. I would like that very much."

CHAPTER 35

PRESENT DAY

"Good morning."

I cleared my throat and tried again for something louder than the ragged whisper I had just produced.

"Good morning, sir." That was a little bit better. Mama pushed me forward, making me stumble into Henry's grandfather's room. I glared at her over my shoulder. "I told you I would do this. Please stop pushing me."

She waved her hands at me. "Just get on with it. I'll be standing guard out in the hall. That servant will discover he wasn't needed in the kitchens and be back here in under five minutes, unless Maria can distract him." With another shove at my back, she cleared me of the door, which she shut firmly behind me, leaving me in the dim room.

Henry's grandfather was not sitting in his normal chair by the window. He sat up in bed with a tray of food beside him. At the sound of the door closing he looked up, his grey eyes settling on me for a moment.

"Kate Worthington," he said, his gravelly voice quiet in the still room.

My heart pounded out a message that this was all wrong—that I could not go through with this. But I had made a bargain, and bargains had to be fulfilled. I stepped toward him. "Yes. Good morning, sir. I hope you are well today."

At my approach, his gaze shifted from me to the door. His fingers clutched at the blanket covering his lap, twitching at it, and his gaze twitched too, back and forth, between me and the door. His legs moved restlessly, and when I reached his bedside, a panicked look filled his eyes.

"Will you . . ." He licked his lips, his fingers pulling at the threads of his blanket. "Will you go outside and close the door and then come back in again?"

I stopped, looked at him closely, and said, "Of course."

My heart beat fast with the feeling that something was not right. I walked to the door, opened it, and passed through the doorway into the hall. Mama saw me and came toward me, but I shook my head at her as I closed the door, waited a moment, and then opened it again. He was waiting for me to come back in. His look was alert and suspicious and worried. As I stood again inside his room he said to me, "Now . . . which Kate are you?"

Dread and fear pooled in my stomach. I looked around, as if I could find an answer to his madness here in the room. "I am Kate, sir. Kate Worthington."

"*Whose* Kate Worthington?"

I swallowed hard. I was certainly not Henry's Kate. And I was not my mother's or my father's. I was, in fact . . .

"Nobody's. I am nobody's Kate."

His gaze pierced me for a moment before he closed his eyes and began to move his head back and forth, back and forth, while muttering, "Nobody's Kate. Nobody's Kate. Nobody's Kate."

It made my heart quicken with fear. Dismay filled me. I should not have come here. I should never have seen this. Backing up slowly, I reached for the door handle and quietly eased the heavy door open.

Mama stood right outside the door, leaning toward it eagerly. "Well? What did he say?"

I shook my head. "Come away from here, Mama. He is not well today. We must leave." My hands were shaking.

"Nonsense." She brushed past me. "Every man can be persuaded. Even the mad ones."

I watched with dread as she entered his room. Upon seeing her, his eyes grew wide, fear and alarm etched in his wrinkled face. He dived under his blankets, lifting the covers so roughly that the tray of food clattered to the floor, and pulled the blanket over his head. She reached for the blanket, as if she would pull it off him, like forcing a turtle from its shell.

"No!" I yelled, suddenly terrified for him. I rushed forward and grabbed her arm. She looked at me with eyes wide with shock. "You mustn't do this. Leave him be!" I pulled her even when she tried to push me away, and I did not stop pulling her until I had wrestled her toward the door.

"What's this?" The butler appeared in the open doorway. "What are you two doing in here?"

Mama yanked her arm free of my grip and quickly smoothed her hair, shooting me a dark look before turning to the butler with a smile.

"My silly daughter was trying to give me a tour of the house, and she became completely turned around, I'm afraid. Perhaps you could tell us how to reach the main staircase."

The butler looked from us to the bed, where Henry's grandfather hid under his blanket, to the food scattered all over the rug. My cheeks burned with embarrassment when he turned his accusing glance my way.

"I shouldn't leave my master at the moment," he said, his tone clipped, his expression bordering on hostile. "However, I am sure you can find your way out of this area well enough on your own."

Mama lifted her chin and squared her shoulders. Her face was red, her hair escaping its pins from our struggle a moment before. She looked wild and fierce, and she said in a haughty tone, "No matter. I shouldn't like your assistance even if you were to offer it."

"Come, Mama," I murmured. "We should go."

She spun on her heel and strode to the door. But at the door she paused and said to me in a loud voice, "Take heed, Kitty, and remember this lesson: An ill-trained servant is the mark of a weak and sloppy master."

Shame burned through me. Putting a hand on her back, I pushed her through the doorway and did not stop pushing until she was in the corridor and I had shut the door behind us. As soon as I dropped my hand, she whirled around and faced me. Her steel-trap eyes were blazing with anger and indignation.

"How dare you push me from a room?" she hissed. "How dare you set a hand on me to turn me away from what I want?"

I said nothing. I couldn't speak past the shame that choked me.

"You have made a grave error today, Kitty." She pointed a finger at me. Her voice trembled. "A very grave error, indeed."

I thought of the mistle thrush singing against a storm. I thought of perching myself high on a tower and singing into a gale and never stopping. Power and resolve surged through me. I turned around, and I walked away from her. It was what I should have done last night or this morning.

"In fact," she called, "I no longer think you deserve Henry. I think I shall have Maria trap him instead. You shall have Mr. Cooper."

I kept walking.

"What do you think of that, Kitty? What do you think of this end to your bargain? You will not have your precious India after all. You shall have old Mr. Cooper. In fact, I shall write to him immediately and tell him you have accepted his offer."

I reached the staircase and slid my hand onto the smooth wood banister.

Her laughter rang out louder than my steps. "So you see, child. You see? I have won in the end. Just as I always knew I would."

CHAPTER 36

Something was different about the small music room. I sensed it as soon as I crossed its threshold. The pianoforte stood in its proper place. The drapes were pulled back, letting in the weak light of an overcast morning. The painting of Icarus hung in its accustomed spot, guarding the entrance to the secret tunnel.

I looked around, trying to pinpoint what had changed in the room. I closed my eyes and stood very still and listened. And then I realized what was missing. There was no sense of stirring here. My eyes flew open, and I crossed the room with quick strides, worrying that Miss St. Claire had already done something—that she had already taken my dark bird away.

The cage stood where it always had. I breathed a sigh of relief at the sight of its curved bars. But two steps away from it, I faltered, then stopped and stared at the empty perches. My hand crept to my throat. My dark bird lay still, on its side, on the floor of its cage.

I sank onto a chair as sadness threatened to overwhelm me. I felt in my bones that I was responsible for this tragedy. That lifeless body was somehow my fault. Touching the bars of the gilded cage, I wondered what had caused its death. Was it injured when it beat itself against the bars? Was it the night of freedom it had enjoyed? Or was it returning to its cage after experiencing that freedom?

I sat there in silence for a very long time. And after a long time of feeling only sadness and grief over the loss of this bird without a song, I felt something else. I felt some truth rise up within myself. And the truth was that I was just a broken thing who never should have dreamed of having wings. The truth was that nobody was going to open my cage for me and that I was a fool ever to believe I could escape.

Closing my eyes, I considered my options for my future. I could give in to Mama's demands and speak with Henry's grandfather. I could ask him to change his will. Or I could continue to fight her and return home with her, where she would wield her persuasive force to make me marry Mr. Cooper. Or I could go home meekly and do . . . what? At every possibility I faced another cage. I could be caged by my own betrayal of my feelings, or I could be caged by an unwanted marriage, or I could be caged by going nowhere and realizing none of my dreams.

Everywhere I turned in my mind's eye I saw cages. And considering my future, I thought, *This, too, is death.*

"Miss Worthington?"

I lifted my head.

"You are just the person I was looking for."

Herr Spohr crossed the room to me, gripping a bundle of papers, his hair even wilder than usual. "I hoped you might be here." He looked at me, then looked harder. "Is something wrong, Fräulein? You are not well?"

I shook my head. "I was just thinking, Herr Spohr."

"Oh? Of what?"

I could not look away from the limp body and the dark feathers spilled across the bottom of the cage. "I never learned what kind of bird this was. I never heard its song," I murmured.

"Fräulein?"

I pulled my gaze from the birdcage. "I was thinking of Faust, actually."

He sat in the chair next to mine and leaned toward me. "What is it you were considering?"

I gestured at the birdcage. "I was wondering if he could have been content, before his bargain with the devil. Do you think it was his restlessness that led to his doom? Could he have bridled his passions? Subdued his restlessness? Could he have been happy in a cage?"

Herr Spohr's eyes lit up with interest. He sat back in his chair and rubbed his hand over his head, further disturbing his already untidy hair. "Hmm. You pose an interesting question, Miss Worthington." He peered into the birdcage. "A very interesting question. Was Faust's restlessness the cause of his fall? Perhaps. His yearning for more? Definitely. Could he have changed his nature, fundamentally, so that he no longer yearned for more? So that he was not, fundamentally, restless?" He lifted one shoulder. "That is a difficult question to answer. A pointless one, as well, I think, in Faust's case. A better question is what he might have done differently with his restless nature. He did not have to make a bargain with the devil, for instance. He might have had just as much success in life by using his own knowledge and wit and talent."

I thought about his words. This was not the answer I was looking for. I had already made my bargain. I had to live with the consequences. I could not go back in time and remake that decision.

"Well, then, let us say he has made his bargain," I said. "Do you think it was worth it to him?"

"Is anything worth being damned in hell?" Herr Spohr shrugged. "I doubt it very much."

I rubbed my nose. This was not helpful at all.

"But I have come with something for you, Miss Worthington." Herr Spohr handed me the bundle of papers he carried. "I believe this might suit you very well. It might suit your Faustian struggle. That was what I was trying to tell you the other night, at dinner. That your playing reminded me greatly of Faust's great struggle. I heard that restlessness in your fight with the music. And I think this might be better for you."

I looked at the sheet music, my gaze catching on the name at the top of the composition. "This is an original? One of yours?"

"Yes." Herr Spohr stood. "One of my Romantic pieces. Try it. See how it fits with your demon."

"But I do not know how to play Romantic music."

He waved a hand, a casual gesture. "Let your demon decide how to play it. There are no rules."

He began to walk away but then stopped at the door and turned back to me. "I forgot to mention: there is more than one version of Faust's story. In my opera, he is damned for eternity to pay for his mistakes. He must fulfill the terms of his bargain. But there are other versions—versions that end well for him. He is saved by the innocent and lovely Gertrude, who pleads his case in heaven." He gestured at the birdcage and smiled kindly. "Something worth remembering. There may be more than one option to what some would consider a foregone conclusion. And perhaps it was not its restlessness that killed the bird, but the cage itself."

His words burrowed into my mind, finding room to take root among the miseries there. I stared at the cage for a long time before walking to the pianoforte. I sat on the stool and spread out the papers. I took a deep breath, set my fingers to the keys, and began to play Herr Spohr's "Meine Kleine Vogel."

It was not Mozart. It was not like Mozart at all. These notes were not obedient little soldiers marching in their proper ranks. These notes were wild things that flew like rooks above a crumbling tower. My inner demon recognized this music as the dark, unleashed thing it was. And after an hour of playing, my inner demon had whipped itself into a fury. It flew into the banished corners of my soul and swept up the accumulated grief and frustration and anger of years. It whipped it all into a torrent until tears streamed down my face while my fingers flew across the keys. And my inner demon told me I must fly. It told me I must make a choice now or else I would always feel caged and helpless and powerless and small. I listened to my demon and my heart, until the fury and the torrent had gathered itself into a great surge of courage. Then I stopped playing, picked up the music, and ran from the room.

CHAPTER 37

Alice was surprised to have me ring for her in the middle of the day. I could see it on her face as she rushed into my room. Mama and Maria were with the other guests, no doubt trying to cause another scandal, and I shut the door and locked it behind Alice before turning to her, hope and despair raging within me.

"I need your help, and I am afraid you will not want to help me."

Her brow furrowed. "What do you need, miss?"

"I need to escape from Blackmoore tonight. I need to find a way to get safely to London."

Alice's eyes opened wide. "You're running away?"

Nervousness pounded through me. I swallowed hard. "I am." I crossed the room to where my traveling trunk stood, lifted the lid, and took the ivory-inlaid box from within. "I know it is a lot to ask," I said. "I am sure my aunt will be willing to pay you something for your troubles. But I also want to pay you. Here." I held out the box toward her. "It is very valuable. It's inlaid with real ivory. You can keep it, or you can sell it in London."

She shook her head, pushing out a hand to reject my offering. "No, miss. I won't take that."

My heart fell. "I can pay you something else. I just—"

251

"No. I'm sorry. You misunderstood me." A smile crept across her face. "I will help you. But there are some favors that can't be bought, and some kindnesses that should only be given freely."

"But this is a very large favor you are doing for me." I thought of all the other favors I had bought from others—all the bargains I had made and the mistakes I had paid for. Surely this would cost me as well.

"Aye, but my sisters would not hear of it, miss." Her reserved face broke into a wide smile.

I gave her a questioning look.

"Mary and Katherine. The girls you gave the sweets to. They told me how kind you were—how you came to the house—how you comforted them in the street, even though you didn't know them. So I will do for you what I would do for any friend of mine."

I shook my head and looked down, embarrassed. "It was nothing. Just a few sweets from the bakery."

"It made you one of ours." She said it like a declaration—she was claiming me. The words "nobody's Kate" filled my mind. I banished them. Perhaps they were not entirely true. Tears stung my eyes.

"Thank you," I whispered.

"Will you be returning to India, Mr. Pritchard?" Mama leaned closer to the rude gentleman, whose mustache held the remnants of his dinner.

Mr. Pritchard glanced at her out of the corner of his eye before grunting and nodding his head curtly.

Mama still had not grasped what was obvious to everyone else in the drawing room: the man she had chosen to flirt with had no interest in flirting back.

"Oh, what a shame!" she said. "You really ought to settle down somewhere nearby, so that we can become better acquainted."

Miss St. Claire smiled across her teacup. "But surely, Mr. Pritchard, you will not leave soon. You will want to stay for any . . . momentous occasion that may be happening shortly among your friends. Will you not?"

I looked away so I would not be tempted to look at Henry. I did not want to see his reaction to Miss St. Claire's thinly veiled hint about their upcoming nuptials. Even though Henry and I had occupied the same rooms for more than three hours this evening, I had done a remarkably good job of avoiding him. I had done so well, in fact, that I had not so much as looked at his face once—not during the long dinner, nor afterward, in the drawing room. He had not spoken a word to me. He had not come near me, either. But when I thought of what he had heard me say the night before—those words about preferring Mr. Cooper to him—I did not wonder at his distance. But not wondering about it and not feeling the pain of it, the guilt, and the fresh stab of loss—that was a different thing entirely.

I nearly jumped out of my seat when the clock finally struck ten o'clock. I glanced over at Sylvia, who sat by the fire with her Mr. Brandon. If things continued the way they looked right now, she would probably be engaged by the end of the year. I was glad to see her happy. Maria had attached herself to the younger Mr. Brandon's side. Mama flitted from one man to another like a bee to flowers. Mrs. Delafield gripped her teacup with whitened knuckles and looked as if she would like to throw it at Mama. I looked at all of this, and then I stood and turned to the door.

"Good night, Mama," I said. "I am tired. I'm going to retire early tonight."

She darted a dark glance my way, warning me with a look that she would speak with me later. I had expected as much. "Good night, then, Kitty."

When I reached the door, the temptation to look back was too strong to resist. Looking over my shoulder, I saw Henry watching me steadfastly. My heart hitched in my chest, then began to race at the look in his granite eyes. Fumbling for the door handle, I pulled my gaze from his and hurried from the room.

"Is everything ready, miss?" Alice asked.

I knelt in front of my trunk, looking at my gowns and bonnets and gloves. All of them could be replaced. I picked up the ivory-inlaid box, took my aunt's letter from it, and held the box out to Alice. "Here—take this. Not as payment, but because I want you to have it."

Alice hesitated, then reluctantly accepted the box. "I will keep it for you, miss. You may have it back when you return."

I pressed my lips together, unwilling to reveal my secret: that I would never return. Alice set the box on the mantel next to the letters I had just sealed and set there. She knew what to do with them.

"The other bedroom is ready?" I asked.

Alice nodded. It had been her idea to ready another bedroom in the west wing so that Mama and Maria would not notice my absence until the morning. "I'll tell them you've come down with an illness, and you're not to be disturbed."

"Good."

My aunt's letter and the music from Herr Spohr were tucked inside my traveling cloak, along with Oliver's shells, tied up in a handkerchief inside a pocket. I looked around the room. It was such a beautiful room—as beautiful as the moors had become to me. I would miss it. But it was nearly half past ten, and if I lingered any longer, I ran the risk of encountering Mama or Maria on their way up to bed.

"Yes. I am ready." I handed Alice my gloves, my bonnet, and my cloak. "I will meet you downstairs."

At half past ten precisely I eased open the door to the bird room and slipped inside, then closed it softly behind me. The drapes were open, allowing the light of the full moon to bathe the room with its silver sheen. I moved carefully through the room until I approached the birdcage and knelt in front of it. With a soft creak of metal, I pried open the cage door. I assumed the bird's limp body would be discovered by a maid and disposed of. But I would leave it with its door open, because it's what I would have wanted.

I heard a sound behind me, a soft step. And then Henry's voice. "You're leaving."

My heart jumped. I stood and whirled around to face him, my pulse racing with nervousness.

The door was still closed. He must have been waiting in this room. Waiting for me.

"How did you know?" I asked.

He stood far away from me, on the other side of the room in front of the Icarus painting. The moonlight illuminated only his outline. But I heard the accusation in his voice when he said, "It was written all over your face tonight."

I drew a shaky breath. "You're right. I am leaving."

He stepped toward me. "Because you would rather marry that repulsive Mr. Cooper than be forced to marry me?"

The hard, hurt, accusing tone of his voice struck me like a physical blow. I reeled back from the force of it. My voice came out trembling and quiet. "No."

"Then why?" His voice broke on the last word, and something broke inside me. Something that was keeping me steady in my course broke at the sound of that *why*. I looked down at the birdcage, feeling my heart racing in my chest, feeling my hands trembling. And I spoke the greatest truth I could.

"Because if I don't escape my cage now, I never will."

A long silence followed my words, and then Henry sighed and raked his hand through his hair. He turned away from me and stood looking at the Icarus painting. A great stillness in the room, and in him, reminded me of the bird that no longer stirred. And suddenly I needed to be near him. I needed to be sure that he was not also lifeless. I moved toward him quietly, until I saw the moonlight cast his face half in light, half in shadow.

He had his arms folded across his chest, his gaze fixed on the image of Icarus being granted his wings.

"To be so close to heaven, to fall so far . . ." His voice was quiet, and for a moment I wondered if he was even talking to me. He sighed. "I was a fool to agree to this bargain, Kate. I thought I understood suffering before—those years that you lived a mile away—when I saw you often—when I had your confidences but not your love. Hearing your regular declarations of never wanting to marry . . ."

He rubbed his hand over his face. "That was suffering. But this . . ." He shook his head, and I noticed how tightly he held himself—how a tremor spread through him. "This was madness. This was as mad as Icarus flying too close to the sun. To be so close, to have you in my arms, to whisper the words I have dreamed of saying to you, and to have you reject me, over and over." His voice was low and rough, and the look he shot me sent fire through me, rooting me speechless to the ground. A ragged, shuddering breath shook him. "This is suffering of the most acute kind."

I was afraid to breathe. I stood there with my heart in my throat and my hands clenched into fists and my lips sealed against the words I would not speak to him.

"This is not for the bargain," he said. "And this is the final time I will ask this question, Kate. Never again. I just have to know—apart from that cursed bargain—I have to know. I cannot spend the rest of my life wondering . . ."

Tears ran down my face.

He turned to me, took my hand in his, and rubbed his thumb across my knuckles. He looked into my eyes, the moonlight illuminating his face. "I love you," he said in a hoarse whisper. "I want to be with you always. Marry me. Please."

I had to swallow and could not, and when I finally pushed the word past my lips, it was a choked whisper. "No."

He flinched. I stifled a sob. I could hardly see him at all through my tears. He dropped my hand and turned from me, and I walked to the window and looked at the moon as tears streamed down my face. They came so furiously I could hardly breathe, and my chest shuddered with the attempt.

After a long stretch of time, I felt Henry stand behind me. His warmth at my back was so tempting. He said, in a broken voice, "I have one last question, and then I will let you go."

I wrapped my hand around my throat, trying to stifle the sobs that shook me. I nodded.

He took a breath. I heard it catch. I heard his voice shake as he asked, in a low, husky tone, "If you loved me . . ."

I do.

He was so still. I felt his shock. And then, after a long pause, he breathed, "What?"

I turned around and stared at him with wide eyes, my heart pounding hard.

"What did you just say?" he asked.

I shook my head, my face on fire. Had I really spoken those words aloud? "Nothing. I said nothing." I backed away from him, but he grabbed me by the shoulders and stepped closer and leaned down.

"You said *I do.*"

He pulled me into his arms. And I hardly had time to think before he was kissing me. One hand at my waist, holding me close, the other at the back of my neck, his kisses firm, deliberate, pleading. I stopped thinking. Everything that had been working at unraveling my heart had been too powerful to resist. Now I was nothing but heart, and I was pulling him closer and kissing him, and when I kissed him back, I heard a moan escape him. I pulled away, gasping for breath, and he pulled me back again, as if he needed me more than he needed breath. His hands were pressing me close, and he whispered my name, and suddenly I realized I had to stop this. This was a mistake that should never have happened. It was cruel—too cruel—to do this once when I would never be able to do it again.

I sobbed at the thought and pushed him away. "No, Henry." My voice was a broken cry. I saw the pain in his face before I grabbed him, pulled him close, and buried my face in his chest. I held him tight around his neck, his arms reaching around my waist, holding me close.

"You said you loved me," he whispered.

"I do," I whispered on a sob.

"Then why do you refuse me?" His voice hurt me—the pain in it. The anguish. The sound of broken things.

I pulled away from him. "I know what loving me will cost you. I know, Henry! I heard your mother, that night at the ball. Not quite two years ago."

His brow furrowed in confusion. "What do you mean? What did you hear?"

I shook my head. This was the secret I had never meant to tell. But things had come undone within me, and I found I no longer had the strength to keep this secret. It rose within me as if with a life of its own, intent on escaping its own cage. It burst from me with a fresh wave of sobbing.

"I heard her tell your aunt Agnes that you will l-lose Blackmoore if you connect yourself with anyone in my family. She said she h-had the will changed. That your grandfather signed it. That the solicitor was there. And that sh-she would separate us if I showed any sign of favoring you, if I—"

"*What?* She had the *will* changed?" His voice was raw with shock and disbelief.

I nodded solemnly, wishing I had not been the one to see this look of betrayal on Henry's face.

"Are you sure? I mean, are you completely certain—?"

"Yes." What she had said to me the other day, after catching me speaking with her father, had confirmed it. "I am completely certain." It came out as a whisper, but it fell on the space between us with a finality that felt like a death knell.

Henry raked both hands through his hair, turned from me, and walked four steps away.

"Now you understand," I said, my voice breaking along with my heart. "You understand why I had to tell you—everyone—that I had no intention of marrying. She would have separated all of us. She would have sent you away—"

He turned back and walked toward me with long strides, catching me by the hands, saying, "It doesn't matter, Kate. It makes no difference. I can give up Blackmoore."

I was shaking my head, tears streaming down my cheeks and running off my chin.

"Stop. Stop shaking your head. I can, Kate. I can give it up. I will. For you."

"No. I won't allow you to do that." He was speaking rashly. He hadn't thought it through. He hadn't had countless nights to lie awake thinking about exactly what he would be giving up for me. But I had. And I knew better. "You can't give up Blackmoore for me, Henry. Don't you see what it would cost you? What it would do to us?"

"It's just a house! How could you think a pile of stones could compare to you?"

"It's more than a pile of stones! This is your home. I have seen it in your eyes. This is everything to you. Your future. Your living. The life you have planned for. I have seen how you light up here! I have seen how happy you are here—how fulfilled. How it is where you are meant to be."

He grabbed my hands, holding them in both of his own. He held them tightly, as if trying to keep me from flying away. "No. *You* have done that to me. Not Blackmoore."

A sob shook my voice. "It is too much to give up. Don't you see that?

Don't you see that if I rob you of everything you care about, everything you have ever wanted in life, that you will someday hate me for it?"

"I could never hate you." The words came out soft and hoarse, a whispered declaration.

I pulled my hands from his grip and folded my arms across my chest, trying to hold my breaking heart together. "You could. You don't know. But I do." My voice quivered. "I know what it is to be despised, Henry. I know what it is to be unwanted and unloved and—"

Henry's hands slipped around my face. I caught my breath, biting back my words. He stepped close to me and cradled my face. His hands were gentle, as if I was just as wild and fragile as our dark bird. He bent his head and looked into my eyes, and he was so near to me that I could see his grey eyes, shining even in this dark room. He drew in a breath and he lowered his head and then he kissed me, slowly and gently. His fingers reached into my hair, and his lips tasted of salt and desire. He kissed me until my knees trembled and fire melted through me and I felt thoroughly, achingly wanted.

When at last he lifted his lips from mine, his breath was ragged. He leaned his head close to mine and whispered, "Now you also know what it is to be wanted and loved."

It was too sweet. It was too great a temptation. My heart pounded with wanting what he was offering me.

"I know that you haven't known this kind of love before," he said, his arms slipping around me, pulling me close, cradling me as if he meant to keep me near his heart always. "But I promise you that I can love you forever, no matter what happens to us in this life. I can, and I will."

My resolve had crumbled in the heat of his kiss. I wanted to lean against him and let him continue to make me feel this way. But it was not right, and I knew in my bones that giving in to this temptation would haunt me with questions for the rest of my life. I ignored the yearnings of my heart and pulled away from his embrace. The chill of standing alone and apart from him invaded every bit of me, and I shivered as I stood there and tried to hold myself together. But I could not hold myself together in the same ways that I could before Henry kissed me. Cages had been opened within me, and what poured out of them was just as much anger as fear. I backed away from him as the anger and the hurt I had been hiding for a year and a half unfurled within me. And then I unleashed it.

"Love is not enough!" I cried. "Love turns. Love dies. I have seen the other side of love! I have seen the loathing and the contempt and the resentment. I will not see that from you! I will not live to see a day when you look at me the way my father looks at my mother."

"We are not like them!"

"How do you know?" I drew in a jagged breath. "How do you know what the future will hold? How it will change us? How do you know that you will not wake up one day and hate me for robbing you of your birthright, your future, the life you always meant to live?"

"I know," he said, his voice low and fierce and unwavering. "I know my heart. It has always been yours, Kate. *Always*."

His voice broke, and I saw in the gleam of moonlight a tear on his cheek. It wrenched at my heart.

"I never meant to hurt you." I choked on my words. "I never meant to hurt you with the bargain. I never thought it *could* hurt you."

He rubbed a hand over his face, took a deep breath and then another. He looked so lost and so desperate that I knew I was close to winning this battle. So I delivered another blow.

"How would we even live, Henry?" I asked, my voice dull with hopelessness. "You would be giving up your living if you gave up Blackmoore. What would you do?"

"I am not averse to work! I am quite brilliant, you know. Or maybe you don't know, since I don't like to boast, but I am." I heard the hope in his voice, and I saw the flash of his smile, and it all felt much too cruel. "I'm not afraid of hard work. Just—"

I held up a hand, warding off his words, choking back the sobs. "No. No, Henry. No and no and no."

He stared at me for a long moment. Tears streamed down my cheeks but I did not waver. And finally, all the hope left his face, and in its place was bleak despair. "You will not change your mind."

"No. Never." And even though I trembled in every part of me, my voice was strong with resolve. "I made this decision a year and a half ago, and I have made it again tonight. And I would make this exact same decision again and again and again as long as our circumstances are the same. I will not change my mind, Henry."

He looked away. I saw him press the heels of his hands to his eyes. I walked to the window and looked out at the moonlit sea. And after another long stretch of time, I heard him move behind me. I glanced to my left and saw him standing before the open birdcage. He was so still.

"The bird . . ." He looked at me, a question in his face.

"It died." The words were too blunt, too harsh. Henry flinched and looked back at the cage. When he lifted his eyes to me again there was a new expression in them—a kind of horror that chilled me.

"It doesn't mean anything, Henry. It's not a foretelling of my future. I know that's what you're thinking. But it's just a bird. I will be safe. I will go to my aunt in London, and we'll travel to India together, and I will be safe. I promise."

"Miss Worthington?"

It was Alice, at the door, holding a lantern. Then I knew it was time. It was time to be done with torturing ourselves like this. "I have to go," I whispered.

"Wait." Henry grabbed my wrist as I walked past him and pulled me into his arms. "Wait," he whispered, bending his head to speak softly in my ear. "I still have one last question."

My heart could not tolerate one last question. My heart was hammering at me, insisting that I was making the greatest mistake of my life. But

I could not deny him one final question. So I buried my face in his warm neck and let him hold me one last time. "Go ahead. Ask it."

"If you loved me—" His voice caught, and he cleared his throat and tried again. "If we could be together, which would you choose—me or India?" His breath touched my neck; his lips grazed my ear. I was melting. My resolve was crumbling.

"You," I whispered. His arms tightened around me. And even though I had no right to ask such a thing, I whispered, "If we could be together, which would you choose—me or Miss St. Claire?"

"Oh, Kate." His hand cradled my cheek, and he pulled back enough to look into my eyes. "It was and is and always will be you."

I wrapped my fingers around his wrist, keeping him for just a moment longer, all the while knowing that it was such foolishness in me to do this—it was such a weakness to give in to the unthinking demands of my heart.

And then, finally, I found the strength to let go of him, and I stepped back, and he let me go. His hands fell away from me, and he did not try to pull me back. He would not stop me from leaving my cage, and I loved him all the more for it.

Wiping the tears from my eyes, I walked across the bird room to the door, where escape waited for me. I told myself not to look back. But just as I was passing over the threshold I felt a great tug at my heart—as if Henry were calling it back to him. I could not help myself then. I had to look back. I glanced over my shoulder, to see him one last time, and wished immediately that I could undo it. For there he stood, with his arms folded across his chest, looking exactly as he had the day his father died.

CHAPTER 38

Alice smuggled me out of Blackmoore and onto the moors, where her brother waited with a pony. He handed me a white sheet and directed me to wrap it around myself. "You will be Linger's Ghost tonight, miss." Alice smiled mischievously and admitted that Linger's Ghost was something the smugglers used to keep people off the moors at night.

"You will not forget the letters?" I asked, full of nerves now that I was actually doing this. "The one to Mrs. Delafield, especially."

I could not leave without warning Mrs. Delafield of my mother's plan to entrap Henry using Maria. She was capable of anything, and she was especially motivated when it came to tormenting her one-time friend.

"Don't worry, miss. I'll deliver it to her first thing tomorrow morning. And the letters to your mother and sister and Miss Delafield, as well. It will all be taken care of, just as we planned." She smiled reassuringly, and her brother helped me up onto the pony. I set my face to the north and the road to Whitby.

I traveled the moors with a full moon lighting the way, and I could not stop looking behind me to catch one more glimpse of Blackmoore on the cliff by the sea. My heart tore at me, begging me to go back, but I was free for the first time in my life, and my hope was stronger than ever. And finally, when the pony carried me over the rise of a hill, and Blackmoore disappeared for good, my heart gave way to grief and threatened to drag me back. But I could not go back to that cage of a life. So I left my heart behind with Blackmoore and Henry, and I traveled with only hope as a companion. The birds in the night sang of the sea and distant lands and a freedom I had never known. I cried and smiled at the same time, and the farther we traveled from my mother, the lighter I felt, until I stretched my arms out as if I would fly and felt my soul expand within me. For the first time in my life I felt that I was powerful.

It was late the next night when I arrived in London and knocked on my aunt's door. When I found her in the drawing room, she sat up straight, a hand to her chest in a startled movement.

"Katherine? What on earth are you doing here? At this hour? How did you come here?"

"I ran away. I took the stage from Blackmoore. I am ready to go to India with you."

She stood and walked to me with open arms and a smile. "I am so proud of you, my dear."

I fell into her arms, sobbing.

She patted my back. "My dear child, what are these tears? You should be happy. You are taking charge of your life."

I nodded. She was right. "I am happy. I am." But I could not stop crying, and finally I said the one word I had not been able to banish from my thoughts. "Henry."

She clucked her tongue. "Oh, no. You cannot tell me these tears are for a man?"

I nodded.

"My dear Katherine. No man is worth this magnitude of tears."

I would have said the same thing myself a month ago. I would have said it to Maria, and I would have known it to be true. But it was not true in this case. For if there was ever a man in the world worth grieving over, it was Henry Delafield.

CHAPTER 39

ONE YEAR LATER

I hope you enjoy the little tokens I have sent you. I know they are not much—bird feathers and shells and the sketches I made on my journey. But each little token is sent to you with the hope that you will not forget the sister who has always loved you. Is Cook taking care of your atrocious nails? Are you still watching out for Cora?

I have not seen many cats here, but there are many other strange animals, like monkeys and tigers and birds of every color. Aunt Charlotte and I have moved to a hill station along with many other British subjects to try to find some relief from the summer heat. You have never known heat like this, Ollie. I feel it in my bones. Surprisingly, I find I do not mind it, ~~although I sometimes do think longingly of the cool ocean breeze at Blackmoore.~~

Do you ever hear news of Sylvia? ~~Or Henry?~~ Do be good for Mama and Papa, and I will write to you again soon. Perhaps someone can help you write back to me. I do long to hear of home. I miss you.

Love,

Kate

It was my fifth letter to Oliver. I had not heard back from him yet. But that was not wholly surprising. With the time it took a letter to travel by ship to England and then for an answer to travel back, it was not a surprise that I had yet to receive a letter from England. It did not stop me from watching eagerly, though, every time a ship came to port and mail was delivered.

"Are you ready to go yet, Katherine?" Aunt Charlotte walked toward me, swinging her bonnet by its ribbon, a wide grin on her face. India had been good for her. She had always been an optimistic soul, but here she was utterly, lavishly happy.

"Yes. One moment." I sealed the letter, addressed it, and grabbed my bonnet as I hurried out the door.

Aunt Charlotte leaned close to whisper, "There. In the branch of the third tree to the right."

I focused on the tree she pointed out. We had become quite adept at our little pastime. Aunt Charlotte had keen eyes, but I had better ears for their songs.

"I don't see it," I said, after looking for several moments. "What color?"

"Black. Glossy, iridescent black, with almost a hint of blue. A forked tail. Oh, how lovely."

My eyes caught on a movement—a stirring in the tree—and my heart suddenly leapt within me. It pounded furiously as I kept my gaze trained on the dark bird perched on the branch.

"I know this bird," I whispered. "I saw it at—"

A call suddenly interrupted my words. Low, high high, low low. The bird's tail twitched, and it sang again. Low and high and low again, sweet and clear. I closed my eyes and tried to think of what this bird sounded like, but all I could think of was the music room in Blackmoore and Henry reaching into the cage and watching the bird fly as high as it could.

It sounded like freedom and flight, and at the same time it sounded like death—like broken feathers and a limp body at the bottom of a cage. It sounded like Blackmoore to me—low and high and high and low again. The bird sang again and again, and every time those high notes rang, I knew the song would end in a low note. It would always end in sorrow. It would always die. The fall would always come, no matter how beautiful the high notes of its song.

I brushed my hand across my eyes, then cleared my throat and said, "You know, the heat is a bit overwhelming. I think I'm finished with bird watching for the day."

Aunt Charlotte glanced at me with a sharp look. Her keen eyes missed nothing. I was afraid she would ask me a question I did not want to answer, but today she did not. Today she simply smiled kindly and said, "It is unbearably hot. Let's go find some cool refreshment, shall we?"

Our chilled lemonade was served to us in the shade of a large umbrella on the veranda, where many of our new friends were also enjoying some afternoon refreshment. I sipped on my lemonade and tried not to think of my dark bird or Blackmoore or Henry, but the more I tried not to think of it all, the more I did. This had been my great struggle over the past year. It had not been difficult to be relieved and happy to be free of Mama's influence. It had not been difficult to enjoy my aunt's company and to delight in the foreign land we were discovering. But it had proved immensely difficult to quiet the constant ache of loss.

So pervasively did thoughts of Blackmoore plague me this day that at first I thought I had imagined the mustached gentleman who was walking toward me.

"Miss Worthington. I thought that was you. So you did come to India after all."

I stared at him, shocked beyond words, and found my voice only when Aunt Charlotte nudged me with her elbow.

"M-Mr. Pritchard! What a surprise!"

"Indeed. I didn't think you would actually follow through with your scheme." He looked no more happy than when I had last seen him. He certainly didn't look excited to see me. At his pointed look I recalled my manners and introduced him to my aunt. He gave her a curt nod, then said, "I have something to give you. It's in my quarters. I never thought I would actually see you here, but I promised him that if I did, I would deliver it. I will have a servant bring it to you. Good day," he said abruptly, and walked away before I could collect my wits.

"Well. He is quite lacking in social graces," Aunt Charlotte declared, sipping her lemonade as she watched him walk away.

But all I could think about was what he had to give me and who it might be from. I stood and paced the length of the veranda, in and out of shade, and felt every part of me tremble with nervousness. When a servant finally approached me holding a salver, I nearly tripped over my own feet in my eagerness to take the letter he carried.

I hurriedly thanked him, my heart leaping in my chest at the familiar handwriting declaring that this sealed letter was for Miss Kate Worthington. Aunt Charlotte stood with an indulgent air and said, "I suppose you will want to read your letter in private. Come. I will accompany you back to our rooms."

I was too full of dread and hope and nervousness and fear and pained excitement to do more than nod and hurry ahead of her. Once inside my room with the door shut, I sat at my writing desk and examined the letter. My gaze traced the elegant slope of the letters composing my name. Henry had been the only person to call me by my chosen name. In this moment, holding a sealed letter, everything was possible. And nothing in the entire world looked more beautiful to me than that elegant K-a-t-e.

My hands shook as I broke the wax seal and carefully unfolded the paper. My heart fell with disappointment as my eyes skimmed over the page. It was a very short letter. But it was *something*. I closed my eyes and tried to calm my racing heart and finally I could bear the suspense no longer. I opened my eyes and read:

My dearest Kate,

How long did it take Icarus to fall to his death? I feel I am still falling, and I fear I always will. I will never reach the end of this grief, this longing for you, this suffering. Others may change, but I never shall. I have loved you for as long as I can remember, and I shall keep loving you and wanting you and missing you, forever.

Henry

My heart was lurching about in my chest like a crazed thing. I could hardly see the writing through the tears that welled up. Blinking hard, I looked frantically for a date. October 12, 1820. October! That was nine months ago! That meant he wrote this letter four months after I left. He had loved me for four months, at least. He had loved me even after I left him.

I read the letter over and over and let my tears splash onto my gown without bothering to try to wipe them. Nine months ago he had written this and sent this to me. Oh, to know what he thought and felt this instant!

"Is it good news? Or bad?" Aunt Charlotte stood in the doorway.

I wiped my cheeks. "I hardly know."

I went through the rest of the day and evening in a distracted daze. I couldn't stop repeating the words of Henry's letter to me. I couldn't sit still for more than a few minutes. I couldn't have a conversation with Aunt Charlotte. And when evening came, I lit two candles and placed them on the pianoforte and spread out the music that Herr Spohr had given me. I played it until darkness enveloped the room, and Aunt Charlotte bade me good night, and the moonlight splashed through the tall windows. Then I sat on a chair and looked at the moon, and I thought very hard about choices and freedom and exactly what I had given up to come here.

It had been the right decision for me to run away. I knew that with even greater surety than I had known it one year ago. But, oh, the sacrifice! It was a burden I carried with me always. India had not disappointed me—not in the way I had feared it would. It had granted me the freedom and the power of independence I had longed for so fiercely. Aunt Charlotte had granted me that. But life in this world disappointed me—the life that required giving up my heart for the sake of my soul.

Sleep eluded me all night, and at breakfast Aunt Charlotte peered at me over her cup of tea.

"You look terrible, my dear," she stated.

I grimaced. "I didn't sleep all night."

She set her cup down carefully. "Hmm." Resting her chin on her hand, she gazed at me over the table with a keen look that made me feel very transparent. "It might help to turn your attention to other men. Fill up your heart with someone else."

I shook my head. There was no question of that. If I couldn't have Henry, I didn't want anyone. Besides, I had left my heart with him. It was not that my heart was empty and needed filling up—it was that my heart was absent. It had been thoroughly, irreversibly claimed.

"Well, then, let us think of something else to amuse us," she said. "I have heard a ship has docked recently. I wonder if there will be letters from home. Perhaps Oliver will have written? Or perhaps we may make new friends of the passengers. Somebody might even arrive today!"

I offered a small smile for her sake. "I am not depressed, Aunt Charlotte. Simply . . . contemplative."

Her compassionate smile told me she did not believe me. But she was kind enough to let the subject drop. After breakfast I returned to the pianoforte and played more of Herr Spohr's piece. It did something to the demon within me every time I played it. And this time the demon told me to write. So I abandoned the music for paper and ink. I sat at the writing table in the parlor and wrote a letter of my own.

Dear Henry,

    I have played Herr Spohr's music all night. My heart is as weak as it has ever been, or maybe it is stronger than it has ever been. I hardly know. I only know that my will has weakened with wanting you, my heart longs for you, and if I truly had wings at this moment, I would use them only to fly to wherever you are. I know that I doubted the persistence of love, but I am beginning to doubt my own wisdom. My love for you will not die. It will not falter. It will not leave me alone. If anything, my longing for you grows with each passing day. My emptiness without you grows. And I doubt my experience with love. I wonder if my parents ever knew what it was to love. I wonder if I was wrong about the possibility of becoming them. And for the first time in my life, I—

The sound of a blackbird's whistle pierced my thoughts. I froze, waiting to hear it again. The whistle of homecoming. Had I just imagined it? A soft *meow* pulled my attention away from my letter. I dropped my pen. It rolled off the edge of the desk as a grey cat ran into the room, sliding across the tile floor to rub its head against my leg.

I reached down to stroke its head and saw a flash of white on its chest.

"Cora?" I asked, unbelieving.

A soft rap sounded at the door. I lifted my head and could not comprehend what I was seeing. It was Henry, looking more handsome than ever and more tanned than I had ever seen him, and surely his shoulders had gotten stronger too. He was not moving—just standing there and staring at me as if I were water in a desert. I stared at him, not really believing he was actually standing there. Surely this was a figment of my imagination—a product of too much Romantic music and too little sleep.

"I didn't think it was possible," he said in a quiet voice, as if talking to himself. His voice—good heavens, how had I gone an entire year without hearing his voice? "You're more beautiful than I remembered."

My heart stuttered, then began to race. My hand crept up to my throat. This could not be real. He could not be here, so far from England.

Then Henry stepped into the room. He walked toward me, moving slowly, carefully, as if I were a wild thing he was afraid would fly away if startled. "You said, at Blackmoore . . . You said that you would make the same decision, every time, unless something changed. Well, Kate, I have traveled around the world to tell you that something has changed. I have rejected my mother's plan for my life."

Now I could see the details of his face—his clear grey eyes, the faint streak of freckles across his tanned cheeks. He looked as if he had spent months aboard a ship, in the sun. My gaze took in the rise and fall of his chest, the white of his shirt against the golden tan of his throat and hands, the way his hands clenched into fists. I finally believed he was real. I could not breathe.

"I have told Juliet I will not marry her. I couldn't. Once I knew you loved me—once I had a hope of you, I couldn't marry her. I couldn't have been happy with her." He raked a hand through his hair, leaving it mussed. How many times had I watched him do that very thing? "She understood. She was quite generous, actually. She said she supposed that I had loved you all along, which was absolutely true."

His mouth lifted into a crooked smile. I stared at that smile, remembering how it had felt to kiss those lips, to hold his face in my hands, to bury my fingers in his hair. His hair was much lighter, I realized. It was nearly the gold of his childhood.

He knelt in front of me. My face flushed, and my hands trembled, and my hope lifted again and again, like a million wings beating within me. "I left Blackmoore in the keeping of my brother, George, and I have taken a position with the East India Company. I have traveled halfway around the world to find you . . . to show you that I will never resent you for robbing me of my home, because I have given it up freely. Now I have nothing left for you to rob me of, except my heart, but you have long been guilty of that already." I saw in his grey eyes an ache of hope and dread and fear and love all mixed together with so much light that my heart cracked in two. I covered my face with my hands, overcome.

"Kate," he said in a husky voice, "I am here to ask you one more time if you will spend your life with me. We can be adventurers together. I have followed you this far, my darling girl, and I will follow you wherever you choose to go next. I will love you no matter what happens in the future. You know me. You know I am capable of being just as stubborn as you. I have given up my home to be with you. And so I ask you to give up your fears to be with me, to believe me, to trust me, to . . ." His voice broke. " . . . to love me, as I love you."

My shoulders shook.

"Kate . . . are you laughing? Kate, if you're laughing again, I swear—"

I dropped my hands, showing him my tear-streaked face, and reached for him, and fell into his arms. It felt like home. It felt like the surest home I had ever, or would ever, know. We clung to each other as if we were drowning, and we were the only ones who could save each other. And then he kissed me, all over my tear-streaked face, my lips, my hair, and I hoped he would never, ever stop. And finally, when I had to pull away to catch my breath, I said, "I have to tell you something.

"You—" I started but had to pause to wipe my nose on my sleeve. "You are not The Giver of My Heart's Desire, Henry Delafield."

He threw his head back and laughed.

"No, listen." I held his face in my hands. His eyes were soft and lit up, and his gaze roamed all over my face with such adoration that I felt caressed. He tipped his head toward me and brushed his lips against my cheek.

"I'm listening," he murmured, his arms holding me impossibly close.

"You are not The Giver of My Heart's Desire." I took a deep breath and smiled. "You *are* my heart's desire."

"Oh, Kate," he murmured, bending his head to mine. "You are a Romantic after all."

Chapter 40

FIVE YEARS LATER

"What do you see ahead of us, love?"

Olivia rested her head on her father's shoulder. "Only water, Papa."

"Look again, darling. Do you see the land? Like a shadow in the distance?"

I leaned close, so that her soft, rounded cheek brushed mine, and I pointed to the land rising from the ocean. "Look there. And just wait. It will grow clearer, and then you will see a village full of red-roofed houses, and on a cliff high above the sea, you will see a large house. And do you remember what that is?"

She nodded and blinked her dark-lashed eyes. She had the grey eyes of her father and her great-grandfather. She also had my dark eyebrows, which Henry loved.

"What is it?" Henry asked, smiling down at her and at me, holding us both close.

"It's home."

From far away, across the grey water, I imagined I heard the song of a blackbird.

The End

AUTHOR'S NOTE

I write historical fiction because I love research and I love creating stories. If you're like me and would like to know where fact and fiction meet in a work of historical fiction, read on. If not, you can skip ahead to the acknowledgments. I promise I will not judge you at all.

When I first started dreaming up *Blackmoore*, I knew I wanted it to be set in northern England, surrounded by the moors and looking out over the ocean. But I didn't know if such a place existed. So I flew there, rented a car, and drove all over the north of England, from Manchester to Whitby and back, in search of the perfect location for my story. I found it at Robin Hood's Bay in North Yorkshire.

Yes, this town really does exist. I have tried to describe it accurately, but I don't think words can do justice to the charm and character and windswept beauty of the place. It was a smuggling port for hundreds of years, and over the centuries everyone in the village became involved in that trade. In fact, it was said that a bolt of silk could pass from the beach all the way up to the top of the hill without once seeing the light of day.

How, you ask? All the houses were connected by secret cupboards and passageways. In fact, a villager there told me that someone had recently knocked out a cupboard to do some renovating in her kitchen and found herself staring right into her neighbor's house.

The estate of Blackmoore is set in the same location as the real estate of Ravenscar, which did (and maybe still does) have secret passageways and was involved in the smuggling trade. And there are still elderly villagers who will warn you to stay away from the moors at night or Linger's Ghost will get you.

The ruined abbey is based on Fountains Abbey, which is near Harrogate, North Yorkshire. It had the most lovely feeling of being haunted by very friendly ghosts. Its towers were filled with rooks, and its ruin was both beautiful and tragic.

The interior of Blackmoore is modeled after Castle Howard, also in North Yorkshire.

My characters and their lives are purely fictional. But my research did inspire my story. For example, when trying to choose a surname for Henry, I came across the name Delafield. I liked the sound of it, but I wanted to make sure it was a good historical fit for Henry. When I researched the name, I discovered that the Delafield family name originally came from the family of Count de la Feld, a very old family whose seat was the Chateaux of La Feld in Alsace, France. Hubertus De La Feld emigrated to England in 1066, earned himself some large grants of land, and the family began its rise in stature in England. What really clinched their ambition, though, was when John Delafield became a count of the Holy Roman Empire in 1697 due to his valor at the battle of Zenta. When I read that, I imagined a family that thirsted for another title, an English one, and the Delafield family ambition, which was the crux of the obstacle between Kate and Henry, was born.

Herr Louis Spohr is the one character who is based completely on fact. He was a German musician and composer involved in the shift from Classicism to Romanticism in the early 1800s. He did write an opera based on Faust, and he and his wife, Dorette, did travel to England in 1820 and give musical performances. I don't know if they toured outside of London, however, and I created the name for his piano piece.

I greatly enjoyed researching birds for this story. One site I found very helpful was www.rspb.org.uk/wildlife/birdidentifier. On this site you can view photos of birds, read about their habits, and listen to their calls. Although I did not name Kate's dark bird in the story, I based it on the black drongo, which is indigenous to India.

Much of my research about Robin Hood's Bay, smuggling, and the moors is owed to a book I picked up in a tiny museum in Robin Hood's Bay—*A History of Robin Hood's Bay: The Story of a Yorkshire Community*, by Barrie Farnill.

If there are mistakes or historical inaccuracies, you can blame them on my fallible nature as a human being. Or they could be the product of my being a writer and therefore being willing to bend fact a little for the sake of good fiction.

ACKNOWLEDGMENTS

I could not have written this story without the help of many people in my life. This is my meager attempt to thank them for pushing and pulling and lifting me through a task that felt completely insurmountable at times.

Thank you to everyone at Shadow Mountain for believing in me and this story, even when I was sure it was the worst story ever written and missed my deadlines over and over. Special thanks to Heidi Taylor, for endless pep talks and great lunches; Chris Schoebinger, for his unflappable good humor and optimism; Lisa Mangum, for begging me for a happier ending (and being right about it); Suzanne Brady, for her impeccable editing skills; and Heather Ward, for the drop-dead gorgeous cover and design.

Thank you to my agent, Laurie McLean, who has been a cheerleader, a coach, and a safe harbor in every storm. I would have felt adrift without you.

The Writing Group of Joy and Awesomeness—what can I say? You gave me joy; you gave me awesomeness; you saved me from my demons time and time again. Thank you all for being so wise and compassionate and funny and brave. Here's your shout-out: Erin Summerill, Jessie Humphries, Katie Dodge, Donna Nolan, Ruth Josse, Peggy Eddleman,

Kim Krey, Sandy Ponton, Jeigh Meredith, Julie Maughon, Christine Tyler, and Chantele Sedgwick.

A big thank-you to my dear friend Marla Kucera, for the adventure of our trip to England. You made everything so fun, you didn't scream much from my driving, and the cat following you around the cemetery was just icing on the cake.

Thank you to my beta readers for being friends I can trust with a very rough draft: Jinjer Donaldson, Jaime Richardson, Stacey Ratliff, Pam Anderton, Julie Dixon, my mom, and members of the Writing Group of Joy and Awesomeness.

Thank you to my readers who loved *Edenbrooke* and begged for more. Thank you to all of my online fans for helping me with my brainstorming needs and coming along for this journey. This story is for you!

Thank you to Christine Walter for the beautiful artwork that inspired my story.

Thank you to my dear Fred, Adah, David, Sarah, and Jacob for putting up with me through the stress of missed deadlines, missed family vacations, missed soccer games, and many other missed things. You have my overwhelming love and gratitude. Thank you also to my parents, Frank and Ruth Clawson, for moving closer to me and being a lifeline time and time again. Thank you to my sisters, Kristi, Jenny, and Audrey. I love you lots. And I'm grateful for my in-laws, in all of their numbers: all of the Donaldsons and Hofheins, and Nick, and the Hinmons and Clawsons.

And I once again must acknowledge God's help in my writing. As far as lifelines and safe harbors go, nothing surpasses Him.

DISCUSSION QUESTIONS

1. Repeatedly throughout the story, Kate asks others not to call her Kitty anymore. Have you ever attempted to take on a new identity by asking others to call you by a different name? Do our names play a role in how we are perceived by others or how we feel about ourselves? What significance is there to Henry's being the only one who calls Kate by her chosen name instead of Kitty?

2. Propriety, titles, and reputation play important roles in the lives of the characters. Kate's own reputation is affected by the actions of her sister Eleanor, to the point that Sylvia thinks no man who knows of the scandal would want to marry her. Mrs. Delafield is adamant that there be no scandal at Blackmoore, even chiding Kate for going outdoors in the morning. Did you find the cultural expectations of Kate's society unfair? What cultural expectations of propriety do we see today, if any? To what extent do they affect our lives? Are such cultural constraints unfair or necessary?

3. Kate claims that Henry can't understand her situation because he is a man. What differences did you notice in the novel between what men were allowed to do and what women were allowed to do? How does it compare to the culture you live in? Have you ever felt limited based on your gender? In what ways?

4. After learning of Kate's bargain with her mother, Sylvia accuses Kate of being selfish and manipulative. Do you think Sylvia is right? Do you think Kate was wrong to make such a bargain with her mother or to flirt with men she has no feelings for? Have you ever found yourself manipulating others to get your own way? Is this ever acceptable?

5. What do you think of the friendship between Kate and Henry? Do you think they have a foundation for a strong marriage? If Henry had married Miss St. Claire, do you think theirs could have been a healthy marriage? Why or why not?

6. Were you surprised with Kate's reason for swearing off marriage? Do you agree or disagree with Kate's decisions following the ball at Delafield Manor? Do you think she was right to refuse Henry at Blackmoore, even after he said he was willing to give up his birthright for her? What role does sacrifice play in love and marriage?

7. The character of Kate's father is buried under the oppressive weight of Mrs. Worthington's character. What feelings did you have when Kate briefly mentioned his self-seclusion? How do those feelings differ from those you experienced when Kate met Henry's grandfather for the first time? Do you think it's possible to make a real connection with someone you've never met except through the stories someone tells about them?

8. Kate dreams of escaping by going to Blackmoore and then to India. Have you ever felt trapped or caged? What did you do about it? What do you wish you had done about it? Do you relate to Kate's need to travel? Do you have dreams of traveling to specific places? What do those places mean to you?

9. Kate dreamed all her life about going to Blackmoore, and yet her fantasy trip turned into a mess of mixed feelings, largely disappointment. What dangers are there in projecting your happiness into a "finally" that exists only by fulfilling your hopes and dreams somewhere else? Kate expresses her fear that India also might not hold up to her expectations. What do you believe is the real factor in fulfilling your dreams, in finding your heart's desire? Did you sense that Kate was truly happy in India?

10. When Sylvia, Kate, and Miss St. Claire walk to Robin Hood's Bay, Miss St. Claire has a basket of food on her arm and is intent on giving to the poor. On the same occasion, Kate has a chance to buy treats for two young girls, though she hadn't set out with any intention to be charitable. Does one act seem more charitable than the other? What motives are necessary for displaying true charity? Did Miss St. Claire possess those motives as characteristics or were they a disciplined display of her potential status?

11. When Kate's plan for three proposals turns into a plan to involve only Henry, she believes he will not be harmed by her request, since his future with Miss St. Claire is already decided. How is this concept different from the realization she had the night before that flirting without feeling was something her mother would do? How is it perhaps similar? Even if she believed Henry would not be hurt, why would she put herself through the agony of rejecting three proposals from the man she loved? How do you feel Kate handled her rejection of the younger Mr. Brandon's interest?

12. Many important scenes take place in the second music room in Blackmoore. What similarities do you see between Kate and the bird in that room? What else about that second music room is symbolic of Kate's journey to find her own voice and wings? Toward the end of the novel, when she is in India and is flooded with memories of the bird and the manor, what symbols do you see come full circle? What realizations has she come to about her heart after her dream to visit India is fulfilled?

13. Herr Spohr's words and music have a considerable influence on Kate. He gives her sheet music of an original composition and tells her there are no rules for how to play it. And then of the bird he suggests that it may not have been its restlessness that killed it but the cage itself. How do you think these statements helped Kate choose to leave? How does music influence your life and decisions? Where do you find the openings to release you from what cages you?

14. Ultimately Kate made the excruciating decision to leave Henry so

she wouldn't be the cause of dividing him from his home and inheritance. Do you think Henry could have said anything in that moment of separation that would have made Kate stay? Without her leaving and a drastic change of scenery, would Kate have been able to recognize what her uncaged desires were, where her home really was?

ABOUT THE AUTHOR

JULIANNE DONALDSON is the bestselling author of *Edenbrooke*. Her degree in English has fueled her desire to write. She and her husband live in Salt Lake City, Utah, with their four children, but she takes every opportunity she can to travel the English countryside. You can find her online at www.juliannedonaldson.com.